Phoenix Rising

Copyright

Paperback ISBN: 978-1-961966-62-8

Published by: Carxander Publishing
Minnesota

Opening Quote

When I close my eyes, I'm lying with you. Laughing in my T-shirt that you're gonna lose. You got your head on my chest. Just like you did back then. Might be my mind playing tricks on me. Could be the high from these perfume sheets. But to tell you the truth, if I tell you I'm through, I'd be lying with you.

Lying With You by Chase Wright

Chapter One

☙ Josh ❧

I rub my eyes and lay down on the couch in my office after shutting out the lights. I need to stop working long hours. Or maybe just sleep during the day, and live up to my satanic reputation at night. Take down the bad guys under the cover of darkness. Avoid all the nightmares that hit me when the lights go out.

Who am I fucking kidding? The nightmares are gonna hit me anyway. No matter what I do, they haunt me. Melatonin doesn't work. It just makes me feel more wired. A hot shower to relax me doesn't work. A hot bath with that stupid bubble shit Gavin, my second-in-command, got me doesn't work either. I've even taken up drinking tea, thanks in large part to my British ex-girlfriend. I'm still close to Lyric. We may not have worked as lovers, but that girl will forever be family to me.

There's one thing that keeps the nightmares at bay. As close as I am to Lyric, not even she could chase them away enough for me to get a solid night of sleep. Not that she didn't try.

No.

There's only one thing.

One person.

4

Dallas Cassidy, my best friend's little sister. And I do mean little. She's hardly five-feet and barely eighteen, but she's been around me and my family for the past four years. Ever since we saved her from an ugly fate at the hands of my father, the man who still fucking haunts me.

She's not only my best friend's little sister. She's both of my best friends' little sister. A lot of shit came out of the old man's last escapade, but one of the biggest bombshells is that Alec Cassidy, the leader of the largest and most dangerous motorcycle crew this world has ever seen, is the brother of one of the women I hold closest to my heart.

Jessa Crane.

We found out that not only was she adopted as a young child, but that Alec and Dallas are the only blood family she has left. And if it wasn't for her biological mother giving her up and hiding it all, Jessa would probably be dead. Her story is beyond complicated, and while she's moved on from it and settled into her new life, it's a weight on my shoulders that I can't seem to shake.

After we found all of that out, Alec and I quickly became close friends and allies. And with my relationship with both him and Jessa, I also became close to Dallas.

Only my feelings for her have never been innocent. Hers for me have become increasingly more obvious over the years. Ryan Crane, my cousin and the leader of the Crane Mafia, one of the two most dangerous mafias in the world, mine being the other, keeps telling me that there's nothing wrong with any of this, but I know just how hard his struggle with Ariana, his now wife, actually was.

Just like me, Ryan fell for Ariana before she was of legal age. Nothing happened between the two of them until just before she turned eighteen when he finally gave in. It never went further than kissing, but it's still something he struggled with. All these years later, though, it's still the best decision he has ever made.

I can't say the same for me. I've gone back and forth between letting Dallas in and pushing her away. I've always allowed our friendship, but some days, even that's hard. Having her around me is as soothing as it is dangerous. She's the calm to the chaotic storm always raging inside me. The nights we've fallen asleep on my couch watching a movie are the only nights I've managed to get a restful night of sleep.

And it's the days after that I retreat. I'd never ask her to leave, but I'll hide. I'll take off for missions I don't need to be on. I'll let my mind make a problem bigger than it is just so I can get away. It'd be easy to just tell Alec that if she needs to get away from the Viper's den, then send her anywhere but here. I'm sure Jessa would be happy to see her even more than she already does.

The problem is I like having her around. Even knowing she's in the same house as me is enough. I don't have to talk to her. I can be reading a book in the library while she does her homework, and I'm happy. We're both content. Happy to be together.

I let out a breath. I'd be a complete fool to not admit that we both have incredibly strong feelings for each other that extend into territory I've never been before. We've fucking talked about all of this. I've told her all of the reasons a relationship between us can never happen. I'm not good enough for her being the biggest one.

She deserves a lot better than a man as fucked up and damaged as me. Who the hell knows what I'd do to her in the middle of the night when I wake up from a night terror. I've come to ass naked standing at my front door. No fucking clue how I got there. I've woken up with my pillow in a chokehold.

No.

The nights I've allowed myself to fall asleep with her in my arms have been mistakes. I don't make mistakes. Especially not ones that could cost people their lives. Not anyone I work with, I love, and fuck if I'll make deadly mistakes with her.

I groan and throw an arm over my eyes. I've already made so many. I lost all control one day and kissed her senseless. The only reason I stopped is because she gasped at the feel of my dick against her stomach. Had she moaned or made any other noise at all, I would've fucked her against the wall I had her pinned against. I left for three months after that one and contemplated not coming back at all.

As if she senses the turmoil I'm in, I hear her quietly open the door to my office. It's three in the morning. She has no business being awake, but I'm pretty sure she doesn't sleep well if I'm not near her or safely in my bedroom.

I don't want to, but knowing she's checking on me makes my lips turn up in a faint smile. My heart skips a beat when I sense her coming closer. The physical reaction I have to her is enough, but it's like Fate herself likes to fuck with me. It's more than just physical with Dallas. Her soul calls to mine, and mine fucking gallops to hers like a damn dark knight on a white unicorn.

I hear her sigh and can't miss how melancholy it sounds. If I knew I wasn't the cause of it, all of my protective instincts would be on high alert right now. I'd be taking her in my arms and asking her who hurt my girl.

I really need to stop thinking that. She's not mine. She never will be. I'll cherish being her first kiss for the rest of my life, but that's all it will ever be.

As much as I hate it.

I feel her lean over me and grab the fleece blanket on the back of the couch. Moments later, she's pulling it over me. I grab her wrist when she gets to my waist, near my gun, and open my eyes lazily. I smile just a little more at how beautifully shocked she looks. Her eyes fall to my hand and focus on my thumb softly stroking her wrist.

"Hasn't anyone ever told you to never sneak up on a man as dangerous as I am while he's asleep?"

She blinks slowly as her beautiful, dark eyes meet mine. I don't need light to see them sparkle. I've memorized them. Her dark brown hair cascades down her back, some whispering over her shoulder. I grip my jeans with my other hand to keep from tugging it. Every feature of her is emblazoned in my mind, and I know she's not going to ever be replaced with another. She's carved out her own little nest in my fucking black soul.

She clears her throat softly, but her voice as she speaks is anything but meek. "Every day of my life, Josh. My brother is a powerful man, too."

She jerks her hand away from mine. The movement takes me down a peg. My natural reaction is to tighten my grip, but I don't. She's pissed and has every right to be. I don't even know why she's still here after what I did to her; the things I said.

"Dallas, uh -"

"Don't. Just don't. Please. I can't handle it right now. I just -" She sighs hard and runs her fingers through her silky, dark, auburn locks. I'd give anything to be the one touching her, but I don't deserve to.

I clench my fingers into a fist to keep from doing just that. "Honey -"

She shakes her head and drops her hands to her sides as I slowly sit up. She takes a step back. "I just don't understand. I'm eighteen, Josh. You know how I feel about you."

"I'm still not convinced it's not a trauma bond, sweetheart," I say as softly as I can. I try to keep my voice steady, but that's the last thing I feel.

She barks out a laugh. "Trauma bond? Maybe that's what it was for a little while. I was traumatized by a bomb being strapped to my chest, and then being exposed and so vulnerable to people I've never met. Kidnapped by a crazy asshole who had a vendetta against the Crane and Lucinio name. I understand I've been through a lot. It took time to heal. But over that time, my feelings for you never subsided. They changed. They grew stronger. They went from being comfortable around you because you saved my life, to needing to be near you because I don't *want* to be *anywhere else*."

By the time she's done, I don't need to see her to know tears are streaming from her eyes. I drop my head into my hands and lean back against the couch. I can't watch her cry. It'll break me more than I already am.

"Fuck."

This is all caused by my reckless actions. She came over here a little earlier because things were loud in the clubhouse on Viper's Venom's property. Everything is under construction as they combine with our compound. They have their own entrance but can still get to their homes through our entrance, too.

As the construction resumes, they've already started moving their operations. The clubhouse, or the Viper's den, as they've started to call it, is one of the only places finished. Dallas and Alec stay there. The issue for her is that it's always noisy. She has no reprieve. For a while, she had Alec's actual house to go to, but that was rare because she didn't like to be alone. She felt safer with people, but still needed quiet and solitude. Even staying in her own room, there always seemed to be a party going on.

It was one of the biggest reasons she was allowed here and still is. She trusts me, and so does her brother.

She huffs out a breath. "I know how you feel about me. You've told me. And I've been honest and upfront with you about mine. Yet, here we are. The same place we always are. Me hurting and crying, and you pushing me away because you don't think you're good enough. That I'm some kind of fucking princess that can't be touched by a man like you because if I am, you'll taint me. You'll never be worthy because -"

I stand quickly, having heard enough. Each word out of her mouth slashes me more and more. "You're right, okay? Is that what you want me to say?" I yell.

Once again, she takes a step back. Just watching her do it infuriates me because she knows me better than that. She knows I'd never hurt her. Just when I'm about to lash out at her about the fearful movement, she steps forward and shoves me so hard, I have to take a step back to keep my balance so I don't fall onto the couch.

"No! It's not what I want you to say!" she screams right back at me. She shoves me once more, and I'm so shocked that I nearly lose my balance. But I don't. "I want you to say you love me! That you'll stop all of this ridiculous bullshit and just -"

I grab her arms just as she's getting ready to push me again. My steal-blue eyes flash. I can tell just by her expression dropping from purely angry to completely surprised that she didn't expect that movement. But she should've. She almost falls limp in my arms, but not this girl. Even if she's terrified, she'll stand her fucking ground until it destroys her. It's one of the many things I've fallen in love with, and the one thing that pisses me off the most because it could damn well get her pretty ass hurt. Even killed. She's too stubborn for her own good.

I fight the memories of my father screaming over me. Pushing me. Hitting me. Beating me down until I had no more strength to fight. No one, no matter how fucking small they are, will ever push me again.

I narrow my eyes and look down at her with a warning growl. Just the low rumble coming from my chest has her eyes widening. Her lips form an 'O' shape, and it takes all the strength I have left to not take her lips in a heated kiss. I'm six-feet-two. I'm a big guy. I work out. I'm lean, but muscular. My shoulders are broad. I'm ripped, and I fucking know it. I've worked hard to perfect my body. Turn myself into a goddamn killing machine. I tower over her.

"Scream into a pillow. Go into the gym and punch the fucking punching bag. Kickbox. Do laps in the damn pool. Go for a run. Stand right here and throw a tantrum. Scream at me. But you push me again or hit or kick me, I won't hesitate to put you over my knee and spank your ass until it's red. Understand me?"

She does nothing more than nod, but her eyes fill to the brim with tears once more. Tears of anger this time. I can handle that. I let her arms go and step away from her, deliberately putting space between us as I walk to my desk.

I can feel her eyes burning into my back. I'm vibrating with anger, but the fury is completely directed inwardly.

"I'm sorry," she whispers.

I don't look at her as I sit down and open my laptop. "If you want to stick around, you can. But I can't give you what you want me to, Dallas." I open my emails completely intending to throw myself into work.

"Can't? Or don't want to?"

I glance at her out of the corner of my eye. My heart is beating so fast that my chest feels like it's buzzing. Dallas' eyes have left me. Her head is down, and she's hugging herself. I'm not going to answer her. Not because I don't want to. It's fully because I don't want to lie to her. I'd tell her I don't want to because it's far easier than admitting the truth. I've barely scratched the surface of the hundreds of reason's I'm no good for her. Why I *can't* be with her.

I watch her fists clench around her waist. I see her nod almost imperceptibly. "I can't do this anymore."

Her voice is barely above a whisper. If I wasn't so fucking in tune to her, I'd never have heard the words. I don't have a chance to respond or react before she's running out of my office. Every instinct in me is screaming to go after her. To stop her from walking out of my life.

But as I drop my head in my hands, I realize this is exactly what I wanted to happen. I want her to hate me enough that she leaves. It's the only way either of us are coming out of this alive. I need to keep telling myself that this is for the best. This is my way of protecting her and preserving her innocence.

To keep her from getting burned when I inevitably go down in flames and bring my entire world to hell with me.

Chapter Two

☙ Dallas ☙

I sniffle as I hurry out of Josh's office and head to my room. Only, it's not really mine anymore. It's not like Josh and I haven't had this same fight a lot lately. The closer I got to eighteen, the further away he pushed me. Now that I am, it's worse.

I went to Lance's gala with someone else because it's what Josh told me to do. Forget about him. Enjoy life. So, I did. Then, he glared at me the whole time. The guy I was with is a hockey star. I went to a couple of his games just for fun. He's a nice guy. Well, at least I thought he was.

He asked me if I wanted to go to the gala with him. I was flattered, but I'd hoped that Josh would say something, anything, when I told him. He didn't. He just smiled, and told me to have fun. I don't think he knew I could see the pain in his eyes that he really thought he was hiding. I also don't think he knew I saw it at the gala. It was the one thing that kept me going, knowing he regretted his decision.

The night grew increasingly uncomfortable for me, though. Zack, the guy I was with, became more and more brazen. He would rest his leg against mine, settle his hand on my upper thigh, and try kissing me, even though I turned away. When I got up to go to the bathroom, I tried to catch Josh's eye, but he refused to look at me.

After coming back out, Zack asked me to dance. I told him I didn't want to, but he kept pushing me to dance with him. The only reason I did is because Rosie, my best friend in the whole world, stepped in and said she and her date would dance with us.

I sit down on the edge of the bed when my tears start falling. I don't know if they're caused by Josh and our never ending argument, or the memory of what happened next at the gala. Something I still haven't told a single soul. Not even my brother. I even begged Rosie not to say anything to anyone, especially her dads, Lance and Damon. Both of them work for Josh. They're also as close to him as his own brothers are.

Josh can't know. He'd lose his mind. He might refuse to be anything more than friends with me, even though we both know how we feel about each other, but his protective instincts are second to none. He'll destroy the planet to avenge a wrong committed against someone he's close to. He might not let me close enough to really understand the confusing parts of him, but at least I understand the protection.

I wipe my eyes furiously and stand. I have to get out of here. No matter how much safer I feel around Josh, I can't be near him right now. I have to figure out what I need to do to reach him and make him see he's being stupid. This whole entire thing with us is ridiculous. What we are is hidden in the scars we both have from different aspects of our past. We're made for each other..

That makes me chuckle a little through my tears. Since when did my life become a Miley Cyrus song? I mean, I love her. She's incredible. So many of her songs speak to my soul. I just never thought I'd ever be living the real life version of her song, *Scars*.

I shake my head as I grab a large duffel bag and start throwing things into it. I speak through music a lot. I really should stop that. I know it annoys people. Especially Josh. No one ever says it, but I can feel it.

Well, no one except Zack. I was joking around with Rosie. We were happily quoting songs when Zack got annoyed and said I was acting like a kid and embarrassing him in front of his friend, the other guy with us who was Rosie's date. At least he was nice.

At least he didn't try to cop a feel on Rosie while they were dancing. At least Rosie didn't feel so violated that she couldn't sleep that night. At least he never made her feel like a cheap slut. In hindsight, I'm glad it wasn't Rosie who had to deal with that. I'm glad she didn't have to change her schedule just to avoid all classes with the guy she was with.

I'm glad she doesn't have to deal with the rumors that are going around me and Zack. According to him, we had the time of our lives. We left the gala early and had fun in the back of the limo he rented. He's being praised for being the one to pop my cherry. The princess of Viper's Venom.

If only he knew what would happen to him at just one word from me. A word he's lucky I never uttered.

Help.

That's all I had to say to my brother or Josh or literally anyone around me. I won't because they have bigger issues than some high school drama.

When I finish packing as much stuff as I can fit in the duffel bag, I look around the room. There isn't much left. I could fit it all in a smaller duffel bag. I know I have one. As I look for it, I contemplate calling Lyric. I haven't told her what happened, but I've told her a lot of stuff that's been going on. Specifically with Josh. She's been super supportive and has helped me understand a lot of things, but I can't keep doing this. My heart can't handle being broken so much.

After I get everything together, I give in and sit on the edge of the bed. It's really early, but I know she's up. Her husbands are probably just heading to work. She's also an hour ahead of us. Before I lose my nerve, I call her.

"Hey, sweet girl. Everything okay? It's not like you to call so early," Lyric's soothing tone comes across the line.

I don't know how she does it, but just her voice causes the tension in my shoulders to ease immensely. It's like she has a mother's tone inflected in her voice. The kind that causes warmth to seep through a person's bones.

I let out a deep sigh. "Yes. No. I don't know."

"Uh oh. What did he do?"

"It's just the same stuff. He opens up. I feel like things are going okay. And then he shuts right back down again. I really think it's time I just leave him alone. I've done everything else I can think of to show him how much he means to me. We've talked about our feelings. But nothing has changed. He really feels like he's not good enough for me. I hate being put on that pedestal. I've been treated like some breakable princess for as long as I can remember. And I sound whiny." I groan.

"The issue with Josh, honey, is that he has never really dealt with his past. I know I've helped him, and you've helped him even more, but until he realizes that he, more than anyone, deserves to be loved, he's going to continue this see-sawing crap. I love him to death, but I sometimes want to whack him round the head."

"It's just so frustrating, Lyric," I say softly as I lie back on the bed and close my eyes. "I'm just at a loss. Tell me what to do. I just don't know anymore."

She breathes out a soft sigh. "I think your idea of some distance might just be what he needs to get his head out of his ass. And I think you could do with getting away from all that testosterone. I have an idea. Just a second, love."

I hear a muffled voice in the background before she comes back on the line, but her agreeing with my idea of giving him space is all I really need for my mind to be made up. I open my eyes and sit up with a slight nod.

As she talks to whoever she's talking to, I assume her husbands who are probably about heading out as we talk, I wipe my eyes once more. The tears are drying. If I looked in a mirror, I'm sure I'd look frightening. I haven't slept. I'm still in my pajamas. My hair is tangled. I probably look like I've gone ten rounds in a boxing ring.

"Sorry. How about you come stay with us for a bit? You know we're always happy to have you. I have an event I'm currently planning that could use a younger eye. It's for a Sweet Sixteen party. And you know the boys could use some help with their homework. Lord knows I have no idea what they're being taught." She lets out a soft laugh.

I know she's not talking down on herself. Lyric is British. She was raised in the United Kingdom. Their schooling is different from ours. I can definitely understand why she would say something like that. I'd probably be just as lost if we were in the UK.

"I really wish I could, but I have school Monday. Maybe I could see if Alec can get me down there today, but I'd have to come back tomorrow. I have some tests this coming week."

"Damn. I keep forgetting you still have a couple of months until you graduate."

I giggle a little. "It's okay. If I can't get there, then we'll Skype. I'm going home right now."

"I really hate to say I think it's for the best."

I stand and pick up the larger bag. I put the strap over my shoulder and sigh. "Thank you, Lyric. For always being willing to talk to me."

"You're welcome, honey. I know he's frustrating, but he really is worth it. He just has to see it."

"Maybe one day. I'm trying. I really am. My heart is just too broken right now. I don't know how much longer I can pick up the pieces before I just say it's not meant to be." I take a breath. "Anyway. I'll call you in a bit. I'm just going to walk home. It's not far since the compound is being built behind this one."

"I'm honestly glad about that. Everyone will be even safer." She pauses a moment. "Sometimes, I wish we lived there. We miss our family."

I smile softly as I pick up the smaller bag and put the strap over my shoulder. "I wouldn't be opposed to that. I don't think anyone would." I take a breath. "Okay. I'm gonna let you go."

"Okay. Call me later just so I know you're okay."

"I will. Talk soon." I hang up. I never say goodbye. Alec has always said not to say that. It's too final, and if something happens, 'goodbye' should never be the last thing anyone hears. 'I love you'. 'I'll talk to you soon'. Anything other than 'goodbye'.

Before I lose my nerve or start crying again, I hurry out of the room. The bags are weighing me down, but I don't care. I can't see Josh. I don't know if I'll scream or cry or both, but I know my limits. I know I need to regroup and figure out where I'm going from here because neither of us can live like this anymore. Maybe it's best for me to leave and stay away forever.

I hurry down the stairs, making sure my feet are swift but as light as possible. There's no way Josh doesn't hear me, though. I've learned so much about him over the years. One of them is that he has supernatural hearing. He once heard me crying into a pillow after an argument we had. I was being quiet. He was downstairs. I know that because he told me he'd heard me from his living room. Since then, I've seen him turn at noises I haven't heard only to have someone walk through the door or knock on it moments after.

Josh is truly an amazing man. There's a reason he's so good at his job. He's smart. Diligent. Observant. He's compassionate. I know he has a dark side, but it's a side I've never seen. I don't really need to, though, to know it's there. He's not a feared man with a nickname of Satan, Lucifer, or the Devil Incarnate for nothing.

As soon as I reach the door, I glance over my shoulder. Josh hasn't appeared out of nowhere, thankfully, so I turn the door handle to make my escape. My stomach is in my mouth. My heart is beating so fast, I'm certain it's going to pop out of my chest. I'm sure it'll somehow find a way to stay here. We both know very well that Josh owns it.

I take a breath as I open the door. I barely hold back a scream, or at the very least, a squeak. Standing on the other side is Dane Michaels. He's a Lieutenant with Chicago police. I'm used to seeing him around. I love him as I do my own brother. I'm just not used to seeing him before the sun comes up.

And definitely not with a child holding his hand.

My eyes widen as I look between him and the boy. He looks to be around four. Maybe five. He definitely doesn't look healthy, so he could be older. He looks exhausted. Dane doesn't look like he's faring any better.

Dane clears his throat after his eyes zero in on my bags. He looks back up at me. "I don't know what's going on right now and why you're carrying all of that shit, but stay. Josh is going to need you."

I shake my head vigorously. "No. No, Dane. I can't. I have no idea what's happening, but he and I need space from each other." I try moving past him, but Dane is a big guy. He steps forward just a couple of inches before he's filling almost the entire doorway.

"Dallas," he says, his voice low and gravely. "I called Alex."

I stop in my tracks as my eyes snap to his. "Wh-what?"

He nods almost imperceptibly. "He's on his way." He glances at my bags again. "Please, Dallas. He's going to need you more than he's ever needed anyone in his life. This is a very fucked up situation, and you're the peace he's going to need. I don't know how much Alex is going to be able to restrain him when I tell him what's going on."

I let out a breath and close my eyes, slowly nodding. He doesn't need to explain to me what the significance of him calling Alex is. Alex is the only person in this entire world who can get past his walls. Not even Alec has managed to truly reach the Josh that Alex can. No one has. Without Alex, I don't honestly know if Josh would still be alive.

I open my eyes just as slowly as I closed them. "Okay. I'll stay. Just long enough to make sure he's okay, though, Dane," I whisper as I step back and let him and the boy in. It's cold in the winter in Chicago. I don't want anyone to freeze, especially the little boy.

Dane closes the door once they're inside. He kneels down so he's eye level with the boy. "This is Dallas. She's a really sweet girl. I bet she'd love to read to you. Maybe she can even teach you some fun tricks. What do you think? Want to go see what kind of trouble you two can get into?"

The boy smiles adorably and nods his head furiously. He looks up at me shyly but with a smile that makes me return it with one of my own.

I hold out my hand for his. He takes it and lets me lead him to a small den that Josh uses for a second office. I keep one of my favorite books in here. *Treasure Island* by Robert Louis Stevenson. He looks like a curious boy.

I drop my bags next to the door of the room and turn on a light. I close the door, leaving it open just a little before leading him to a couch. Dane walks down the hall to Josh's office. I take a deep breath and find my book.

"I've read this book so many times," I say gently. The boy watches my every movement with wide eyes. I sit down and open the book to page one. "Want to come sit next to me?"

He tilts his head and looks towards the door. It's open just enough for him to see out, but not enough for anyone beyond it to be disturbed while I'm reading. Instead of crawling on the couch next to me, he sits down on the floor.

I smile again. "Fair enough." I get comfortable, tucking my feet underneath me, and start reading.

Chapter Three

☙ Josh ❧

I look up when Dane pokes his head into my office. "Did she take off?"

"Come out to the living room. We need to talk."

I notice very clearly that he avoids the question completely, but choose to let it go out of pure curiosity. "Why?"

Choosing not to answer again and peaking my curiosity even more, Dane turns and walks down the hall the same way he came. I narrow my eyes and follow him, though cautiously. It's too early for surprises. And if I'm about to face some kind of intervention regarding Dallas, I'll lose my fucking mind. I'm very much not in the mood for anything more than sleep. Not like I can get it at night unless I pass out drunk or take the sleeping pills Dr. Freeman prescribed.

Hell, they're probably expired. I took them once. They knocked my ass out cold. I didn't wake up to anything, not even Gavin coming into my room. I didn't wake up until he started shaking me awake. When I came to, my first instinct should've been to fight and go for my gun. Instead, it was to roll over and put a pillow over my head so I could go back to sleep.

Never fucking again.

When I get to my living room, Dane is letting Alex and Dr. Freeman into the house. My eyes narrow even more. I cross my arms over my chest, watching them.

"Okay, what's going on?" I nearly growl. Seconds later, my heart stops beating. My arms drop to my sides. "Wait. Where's Dallas?" Suddenly, panic rises like a freight train, and I run towards the door.

Alex stops me. "Stop. She's okay. It's not her. No one is hurt. Well, uh. Not anyone you're thinking."

His words do little to ease the intense constriction of my chest. I watch Dane lead Dr. Freeman to the small den that I use as my second office off my living room. The door is mostly closed. My instinct is to follow them, but Alex has a firm grip on my arm. He's the only thing anchoring me right now because I've reached a dangerous level of anxiety and am choking down a full on panic attack.

"Alex, what the fuck is happening?"

"I know you're thinking the worst, Josh, but we need to sit down."

My eyes are trained solely on Dane and Dr. Freeman. Dane gently knocks on the door before opening it. Seeing Dallas sitting on the leather sofa calms me almost instantly. The only reason I haven't fully come down is because I also see the child sitting in front of her looking at Dane and Dr. Freeman curiously. Dallas smiles softly at me. It's all I need for my ruffled edges to relax completely. No one has ever been able to do that with me. At least not in the way she can.

I let Alex guide me to the couch. I sit down next to him while Dane shuts the door to the room and comes to join us. He nearly collapses into the chair near us. He closes his eyes and rubs his temples. Silence fills the room for so long, it feels like I'm suffocating.

"Out with it," I finally manage to say over the lump in my throat. I rub my chest to ease the ache that's subsided but hasn't fully let up. It's almost like indigestion with a dose of a heart attack.

Dane sighs, but doesn't open his eyes or stop rubbing his temples. "I don't even know where to start, Josh."

"The beginning would be nice," I respond, not short on sarcasm of any kind.

Dane's lips quirk into some semblance of a grin before falling once more. "The kid. He's the one Gavin was after. We saved him."

"Okay. That's a good thing. Why the dramatics?"

"Because that's not even the fucking start of it all, man." Dane leans forward, dropping his elbows on his knees. "The story starts five years ago."

I furrow my brows, suddenly uneasy once more. I glance over my shoulder before I focus my attention on Dane once again. "Okay."

"With a miscarriage, missing person's report, and two heartbroken people."

It takes several moments before pieces start falling into place. But none of them makes sense. "What the fuck?"

"You... never stopped looking, Josh," Alex says. "And now he's definitively been found."

I shake my head. "No. It's not possible. I never filed a missing person's report. I just had all agencies notified, nationally and internationally. Nothing was ever filed officially, and I've gotten no hits on any of the leads I did have."

"The call Damon got earlier," Dane begins, "was from a person who came to Lucinio Mafia for help with a little boy on a cargo ship. The guy risked his life to come to us. He's safe right now with guards at one of your safehouses. Gavin is questioning him to get more information, but I did my own investigation to at least get the kid's identity. It wasn't easy, but my team is fucking smart."

Alex lets out a breath that unnerves me even more. "This isn't going to be easy to hear, Josh. You need to stay calm. I know what you're going to want to do, but you need to slip into mafia boss mode right now."

I take a deep breath and do what he says. It's almost like a switch is flipped in my head. I push everything down deep. All of the anxiousness, the panic, the uncertainty, everything is gone. If he says this is the side he needs, then I'll listen because my twin knows me better than anyone.

"Okay. Just spit it out, Dane."

Dane leans back in his chair. "We ran DNA, Josh. You need to hear me on that because I know you. You'll want all the proof you can possibly get. It doesn't get better than that. DNA confirmed the boy's identity. There's only one person he matched with. We ran it against every single source we have. Criminals. Cops. Anyone who has ever given a DNA sample for any reason."

I watch him closely. "Who did he match with?" My heart already knows the answer. It's my head that refuses to catch up.

"Lyric," Dane says after a few moments. "The report was filed by Lyric. I talked to Taylor. He said this report never came across his desk. If it had, you'd have been the first to know. I never saw it either. Cole never saw it." He holds up a hand when I start to talk. "Just... wait. Let me finish. She filed it the day after her miscarriage. The officer who filed the report was Mariah Carter."

Everything is flying through my mind at rapid speed. I probably look like a genius mathematician solving an equation. Like Matt Damon in *Good Will Hunting*.

Only I don't feel like a fucking genius. I can't make sense of any of this shit. "Why the fuck would she file a report? We both thought she miscarried. I'm still not convinced she didn't. I don't even know what the hell is going on."

"You've always felt like something was off, Josh," Alex says. "You told me you didn't feel like it all sat right with you. Obviously, she felt the same."

"But I never told her any of that, Alex." I lean back against the couch and close my eyes. "Why the fuck didn't she tell me?"

"Why didn't you tell her?" Dane asks.

"Because I -" I cut myself off when it all hits me. "Jesus."

"You didn't tell her because you didn't want to get her hopes up," Alex says, echoing my thoughts.

"Because I didn't want her to think I'd lost my fucking mind. We both saw him. He wasn't crying. They worked on him right there in the room. They rushed him off to a room where they had more equipment. He was blue." I look up at Dane and shake my head. "He was fucking blue. There was no cause to believe he was alive. Dr. Freeman looked at him himself."

"But he also said that while he had no cause to believe he was alive, he agreed with you. Something wasn't right. He also said she was further along than you all thought," Alex says, bringing me back a little to all of the reasons I made the decision I did.

I lean forward and scrub my hands down my face. "Fuck. She never fucking gave up, but she thought I did. I never gave her any reason to believe I didn't."

"But she never gave you a reason to believe that she didn't give up either. You both were distraught over all of it. You both hold a memorial every damn year for him."

"We have his ashes." I shake my head. "This makes no fucking sense. You're telling me Jaxon is in this house."

"Yeah. I am," Dane says as he hands me a folder.

I open it to find the paper evidence of everything he just said. DNA results match the voluntary sample Lyric provided. Father is known, but no information is provided. I have to smile a little because I know that's her way of protecting me and my identity.

"Jaxon Austin Lucinio. Age would be five," Dane continues. "Flip to the end. I had one of our sketch artists put that baby picture of him that Dr. Freeman took when he was on the table through a system that ages him. Looks pretty fucking close. If he wasn't malnourished, he'd look identical to that photo."

I drop the folder on the table and do everything I can to keep my temper at bay. "What the fuck did they do to him?"

"He won't talk," Dallas' soft voice says from behind me. We all turn to look at her. "He knows his name, but he won't say what it is. He's mute. Dr. Freeman believes it's completely trauma related. He can hear and see just fine. Everything about him is okay. He's malnourished, but healthy otherwise. He ran some other tests, even an EKG on his heart." Her voice stays soft. Her eyes never leave mine, but mine never stray from the bags over her shoulder.

"That's good to hear," Dane says, breaking the silence.

Dallas nods. "Alec is coming to get me. I'm tired. And... I... think... maybe this isn't my place. This is between you and Lyric and the family." Her eyes drop to the floor after she rushes out the words. She hurries to the door. I'm on my feet before I have time to think, but she still beats me to it.

"Dallas," I say, my voice low. I don't trust it any more than that. I don't know whether I'm going to laugh or cry at all of this, but neither seem appealing to me.

She shakes her head as she sniffles. She hurries out the door, trying to close it behind her, but I catch it in the nick of time and slip out behind her, closing it behind me. I immediately reach for her hand, but as soon as I touch it, she's pulling away.

"Don't. Please don't, Josh. I don't know how much more of any of this I can take." She doesn't turn around, but she does hug herself. "All I know is that there's a little boy in there who's scared. And if all I heard is true, then you and Lyric have a lot to discuss. Maybe even talking about getting back together because -"

"Dallas, stop. Stop right there." This time, I take her arm and spin her towards me. Her bags fall off her shoulder. When she tries to shrug out of my grip again, I pull her into my chest and wrap my arms around her. "First of all, Lyric is happy. And I'm happy for her. We both realized a long time ago that we aren't meant for each other. She's found the people she's destined to be with, and she loves them and their family with all of her heart. This isn't going to change any of that. Not with me. Not with her."

She gives up fighting but her arms stay wedged between the two of us. It breaks my heart because it's the physical version of the symbolic wall I put between us. "She's not going to want to be away from Jaxon, Josh! She's established in Florida. And you're not going to want to be away either. Which means your home is where he goes. I know you." She attempts to push away, but I'm not loosening my grip.

"No. We'll figure it out. You're jumping a hundred steps ahead from the one we're on. We have absolutely no idea what's going to happen." I stay in mafia boss mode because I don't know what else to do. I can't let myself fall apart. Logic. One step at a time. A fucking plan. That's what I need.

I hug her, partially for her and partially for me, because if I let go, I'm going to shatter. It's a selfish move, but I need her to be my lighthouse. My safe harbor. I bury my face in her hair and sway gently with her as Alec pulls in my driveway in his truck. It's a far cry from his Harley, but not even he's crazy enough to ride that thing during a winter in Chicago.

I watch him get out of his truck. The glare tells me everything I need to know. Dallas told him what an asshole I've been. She probably didn't give all the details, but it was enough to piss him off. She's his baby sister and will always come before me and our friendship, no matter how close we are.

He picks up her bags, leveling me with a glare. "Let's go, Dallas."

I feel her breathing deeply. I try to loosen my grip, but I can't. "I'll try, baby," I whisper as I close my eyes. "I'll try, okay? I can't promise it's going to be a fun ride, but I'll try."

She relaxes, but only slightly. "You'll try?" she whispers back. "Or you'll try until you find yourself on stable ground again?"

I let out a breath as I nod. "I deserved that. I deserve it all. I mean I'll really try. I won't give up if it means losing you, and that's how this feels right now. I can't lose you. I don't fucking care how anyone views it. I never have. It's all just been an excuse to push you away."

She relaxes slightly more. "Please stop putting me through the hoops, Josh. I can't take it anymore. And it's never been some stupid trauma bond with you. That's not even the right definition anyway." She looks up at me. "Just promise me all of this is done."

I look down at her with a teasing grin. "I'm pretty sure it's the right definition."

She shakes her head. "It's not. You're thinking white knight syndrome. A trauma bond is when you bond with someone who constantly abuses you. You don't fit the bill."

I raise an eyebrow. "I'm not a hundred percent on that, but I'll concede to the white knight syndrome."

Alec sighs. "Are we leaving this asshole so I can kick his ass? Or are we going to stand here freezing our asses off?"

Dallas looks down as she turns. "I'm sorry, Alec. Things were just... I guess, I felt like we needed to be apart in order to figure out what we wanted and needed."

"Then, I'm going home and back to bed. I'm fucking tired. I had a long night." Alec turns and starts heading for his truck, still carrying Dallas bags.

"Put the bags in the house, Alec. And forget going home. You can sleep on the plane." I finally drop my arms to my sides, but Dallas stays close to me, her back pressed against my chest.

Alec stops and turns. "What the fuck are you talking about? Do I need a team?"

"No. But I figured you might want to see Mariah. We're going to Gainesville. My son is back from the dead."

Alec coughs, choking on his own saliva. "What?" He coughs more, pounding the flat of his hand against his chest.

"Yeah. I'll tell you all about it on the plane."

I turn towards the house, taking Dallas' hand and leading her inside. I don't know how I'm going to break the news to Lyric, but I know it'll be better coming from my lips while I'm standing in front of her than it would be over the phone.

I text her and both her husbands that we need to talk; that I'm on my way there. I know it's going to worry her, but this can't be a phone call.

I know the road ahead is going to be long, but the second I find the person who did this, they're dead on the spot.

Chapter Four

☙ Dallas ☙

"Why are you being so good about this?" I ask Alec on our drive to Lyric's house. I keep my eyes focused out the window as he drives. Josh and Alex are with the little boy, Jaxon, in the vehicle ahead of us, leading us there.

"Being good about what?"

I sigh. "I know you know."

He chuckles. "You're my little sister, Dallas. No one is good enough for you in my eyes. But Josh? He's close."

I lean my head against the window as we pass by the University of Florida. I love Gainesville almost as much as Chicago. It's gorgeous here. There's so much to do because it's a college town. There are tons of different cuisines and so much life. It's like a melting pot of culture. Much like New York, Minneapolis, and Chicago, just not as large.

It's the fact that the population is smaller that I love so much. There's still nearly two-hundred thousand people, but it feels more like a small-town to me. Probably because I grew up in a city with over two-million people. Chicago is one of my favorite places, but it feels stuffy sometimes.

"Dallas, sometimes, a man needs to know when to step back and let his little sister fly. I knew the second I saw Josh walking out of that fucking house with you in his arms and his shirt around you what was happening. I knew right off. I may have been cautious at first, but the more and more I saw you guys with each other, the more I knew. I had that once. It's easy to recognize what's happening when you've been there before. I fucked up and walked away. I let her go. I don't want you going through that same pain that I did."

"I just don't know what to think right now. I'm tired of the constant back and forth with him." I fall silent for a few moments. Alec says nothing. Finally, I sigh. "Maybe it's me."

"Dallas, come on. You know it's not you."

I turn my head enough to look at him while still resting it against the cool glass. "Maybe it is. Maybe when we fall into the same comfortable routine that we have, I push for more. If I were him, I'd be sick of me, too."

It's Alec's turn to sigh. He shakes his head as I focus back on the scenery and buildings passing by. "He's had a lot happen to him. You know that. So much shit that he hasn't dealt with yet because half of it, he doesn't even remember. It's gonna take time with him."

"I know, but I almost feel like maybe it's the best thing for both of us if I just give him time. He's got a whole new life he needs to adjust to right now. I don't even know if I'll get to be a part of that. And my heart is already so broken over him."

"Look, sis. I'm not gonna sit here and say to do one thing or another. That has to come from you and your heart. But I will say that whatever you decide, I'll support you."

I look back at him as he turns into Lyric's driveway. "I still don't understand why you're not trying to drag me away from him. It's not like you. You're overly protective with me. You always have been."

Alec stops and turns the SUV he borrowed from Josh off. He keeps his eyes focused ahead on a silver convertible parked in front of us. "Look. I'm going to level with you. You're old enough to understand. I've always been so protective of you because of our dad. I knew damn well he was planning something, and I was right. He had you specifically to marry you off and expand the crew. That was the purpose of your birth. If I hadn't intervened and killed him, you wouldn't be here." He turns to look at me.

27

His dark eyes look black. "He took away your freedom of choice. I've never stood in the way of your decisions, but I've always guided you towards the right one. You're a smart woman with a good head on your shoulders." He nods towards Josh, who's just getting out of the driver's side of his SUV. "He's a safe bet. He's a good guy, and I know you'll be protected and loved by him."

"You have stood in the way of decisions sometimes."

"Because they've been stupid decisions. You think I'm going to let you go off to Paris with your class without protection? You're not just a regular girl. You're the sister of a very powerful man. You always have a target on your back. Studying abroad and doing all of that other stuff was never on the table for you, as much as I've always hated that. I've never wanted to hold you back, but I can only do so much."

"So, you like him because he can protect me in ways you can't? I don't really believe that."

"You don't need to. All you need to believe is that I'm not going to stand in your way if Josh is the one you want. But I'll also be here in case I need to kick his ass for hurting you." He grins teasingly. "Don't put me in that position, though. I'd be unlikely to survive that fight."

I smile, despite myself. "I just don't know what to do, Alec. I need big brotherly advice on this one."

"Okay. Tread lightly. That's my advice. Follow his lead. And if he backs off, don't let him. You need to be the one to stand up to him. Don't pack your stuff and decide you need time away from each other. That's not what he needs. He needs a woman who can both calm him, like you do, but who will also stand up to him when he's being an asshole. You have that in you. Be yourself with him."

This time, my smile is genuine. I lean over and hug him. "Thank you."

Alec squeezes me tight, then lets me go. "You're welcome. Now, let's get in there. I'm sure Lyric is freaking out. Her hair is probably only half up by now if she hasn't been able to hold back from tugging it. I hope DJ and Matt are here."

"You're probably right. The kids are here. The bikes are on the ground."

We both get out and join Alex and Josh. Jaxon is holding onto Josh's hand like a lifeline and hiding behind his leg, but as soon as he sees me, he steps towards me with his arms raised.

"He feels more comfortable with you around," Josh rumbles. "The ride over here wasn't fun."

"Oh. Um…" I bend and pick him up. "It's okay, sweet boy." He wraps his arms around me and hugs me hard. I hug him back just so he knows he's safe.

Josh smiles and nods towards the house. When I turn, his hand is on the small of my back. I can't help but feel safe and loved by just that one simple gesture. A gesture I've learned so many women today find annoying and misogynistic. This is exactly what I need to feel grounded once more.

Once we reach the door, it opens before Alex has a chance to knock. Two rather tall men, one of them the same height as my six-feet-four brother, stand just inside the threshold with their arms crossed over their broad chests. Both of them are wearing guns, one has a shoulder holster, the taller one has it on his hip. Both wear badges pinned to their pants. The taller one is wearing jeans. The other one, almost as tall, is wearing slacks.

I know them as uncle Matt and uncle DJ. The taller one is Matt. The other one, who is about fifty now and older than Matt by ten years, Lyric by twenty, is DJ. I've never been so happy to see either of them in my life, though I'm not not quite sure they can see me, considering I'm behind both Alec and Alex with Josh behind me. To anyone looking, I'm definitely being engulfed by a lot of large men.

"Before you come in," Matt starts, "tell me just what the hell is going on. Lyric is out of her mind with worry."

"It's best if we tell all of you together," Josh says firmly.

DJ lets out a low growl. "If this is something that's going to send her into a panic, man, you need to give us a heads up."

"DJ, trust me. This needs to be in person. Face to face. All of you together. As a family. End of fucking story. If she goes into a panic, she has me, the both of you, her kids, her brother, and her sister-in-law, judging by the ridiculous flashy car parked out front."

"Stop. Luca worked hard for that," Matt says, glancing over his shoulder. "And they're not married. Yet."

"It doesn't matter how any of us feel about him. He's here for her. That's all that matters. This is a whole family thing."

DJ sighs as Alex pipes in, surely trying to smooth things over. "Speaking of family, how did things play out with Beckett's boyfriend?"

"Layne is good. His parents made the decision to give him to us because they simply couldn't provide for him the way he deserves. They chose drugs and alcohol over him. He's thriving with us. Beckett has been happier since he moved in. We're good," DJ responds. "Come on. In." He turns and walks further into the house. I'm sure he's impatient. I don't blame him.

I cautiously walk in behind Alec as he and Alex follow Matt. Josh sticks close behind me. His hand hasn't left the small of my back. He'll never understand how grateful I am for that. I'm not even really sure I fully understand. All I know is he's my safe place.

It takes us a bit of time to settle. I sit on a couch. Josh settles to the right of me. He's closest to Matt and DJ. DJ has already pulled Lyric into his lap, and for the life of me, I wish Josh had done that with me. Being surrounded by him would calm me immensely. I really feel like all hell is about to break loose.

Jaxon keeps himself as close to me as possible, his face buried snuggly in my neck. Mariah is sitting on a loveseat next to a man I've only met once. Luca. He's Lyric's twin brother. He's nice enough, but I've always found it so odd that something has always come up to prevent him from marrying Mariah. If it's not an injury, it's an unavoidable disaster of some sort. It's like the two of them are sabotaging the wedding, postponing it, and then doing it all over again. Only in their case, it might just be a fateful intervention. It's something I don't understand.

Beckett and Layne are both sitting in an oversized chair. The furniture is in a sort of rectangle, so everyone is facing each other. I've always loved this room. It's organized so the main focal point is family, not television. If they want to watch TV, it's not hard to arrange the furniture so they can. It's just not something they do a lot. They love each other and each other's company.

"Josh, I'm going insane," Lyric says, barely above a whisper. "What's happening?"

Josh glances at me and leans forward. "First of all, I want you to know I never gave up. I never gave up looking for our son. I know I led you to believe I probably had, but I never did."

Lyric's eyes fall on Jaxon. She slowly stands and paces just a little. We all watch her. "I... I knew deep down," she says just as quietly as before. Her arms circle around her waist while her brows furrow. "What are you saying?" Her eyes focus on Josh once more, but they keep flicking to Jaxon. I know this is going to be difficult for her, and I'm not sure what my role here really is.

Josh sighs and runs a hand over his face. He's so tired. He didn't sleep at all last night and definitely didn't on the plane. "You filed a missing person's report." He looks up at Lyric. "Why didn't you tell me that?"

"Wait. What?" Matt asks, shocked. "I thought... didn't you say you miscarried?"

Lyric's eyes dart between Josh and Matt. "I... um... I did, but it... all... just..." She shakes her head. "Nothing made sense. They all said I was crazy," she blurts, suddenly talking fast. "Josh didn't get there until after I miscarried. He came in while they were working on Jaxon. Dr. Freeman took over, but by that time so much stuff happened that I couldn't even comprehend. I didn't even know how to talk about it because I wasn't sure if I'd dreamt it or not."

"Baby, what happened?" DJ asks, his voice a calming beacon in the storm. Even I'm starting to hyperventilate. Jaxon can feel it and is starting to become agitated himself.

Lyric shakes her head and sniffles. "I can't even describe it, DJ. I swear I heard him breathing. He was pink when he came out. They said it was the blood, but I saw his skin. He wasn't just covered in blood." She hugs herself harder. "I saw them cleaning him. They used a suction thing on his nose and mouth. It was when they had him on the table that it all stopped. He was still. He wasn't moving. He started turning a different color, but it wasn't like that when he came out. He was alive. But they said I was wrong. They said I never saw what I did."

"When we got there, he wasn't breathing," Josh says almost as softly as DJ had been talking. Lyric's eyes snap to him. "They were doing compressions and a lot of other stuff. They rushed him out of the room,

Lyric. And he wasn't a normal color. Dr. Freeman followed them. He's the one who declared him."

"But I told you. I told you what I saw. I guess not all of it, but I told you about the nurse with the different hair color. She had brown hair when she left. When she came back, it was blond."

"I know. I know, Lyric. But I told you then that wasn't conclusive evidence. There were a lot of nurses in that room."

"She told me she'd been there the whole time, though. And she wasn't. They all told me it was the drugs I was on for the pain. I didn't know what was real and not. I talked to Mariah. She filed the report for me because I was so convinced that something wasn't right, but I honestly thought that it had been canceled or something because of the death certificate we got."

"It wasn't." Alex clears his throat. "It wasn't. It was because of that report that we discovered who this little boy is." He nods towards me.

"I never canceled it," Mariah whispers, "because of how convinced you were."

I take a deep breath and use Alex's nod as my cue to turn Jaxon around. I kiss his forehead and smile when he looks at me. "It's okay," I whisper. "They all just want to say hi and meet you. Do you think maybe you could turn around and wave? Just like our brave Jim Hawkins in the book we were reading."

Jaxon nods slowly and hesitantly turns. He keeps a tight grip on me with one hand. With his other, he sticks his thumb in his mouth and carefully wiggles four of his fingers in some kind of a semblance of a wave.

I rest my head against his cheek. "That was perfect," I whisper.

Lyric backs away wide eyed as her breathing picks up. "No… no.. no… It's not possible. They said I was crazy… They said there was no way I saw what I said I saw… They said it was the drugs…"

I watch in horror as she drops to the floor. Her eyes are wild, darting around the room. Tears start streaming down her cheeks. Her fingers tangle in her hair and tug as she rocks back and forth mumbling incoherently.

My chest tightens. Jaxon starts crying as he turns back into my neck and clings to me, understanding there's more going on here than his mind can comprehend. Matt, DJ, and Josh all kneel in front of Lyric.

Mariah sobs into her boyfriend's chest. Alec looks like he wants to strangle someone. Luca is mimicking his expression. Beckett and Layne look as if they don't have a clue what to do. I don't blame them. I feel the same way.

I do the only thing I'm capable of doing. I close my eyes and sway gently with Jaxon, humming soothingly. I don't know if it will work for him, but it does for me. Suddenly, it's like I'm transported to a different time and space. Everything that's happening to the people I love isn't really happening. It's all a dream.

Just a dream.

Chapter Five

☙ Josh ❧

What seems like several hours ticks by while Matt and DJ calm Lyric. I know how fucking shocking it is to have a kid we weren't sure was alive or dead show up on our doorstep. I don't know how she's going to manage with everything else I have to say.

Dallas leans against my arm. The second I heard her sniffle, I was automatically moving to her side. I can't figure out how I heard it above the wailing coming from Jaxon. As soon as I sat next to her, both she and Jaxon calmed down. I want to put my arms around them both and hold them close, but I don't know if any of us are really there yet. I know Dallas is still pissed at me. She has every right to be.

"Ready, beautiful?" Matt asks just above a whisper. Lyric nods her head. She's sitting between Matt and DJ. Both are holding her hands and rubbing her back. Matt looks up at me and simply nods.

It takes me a few moments before words finally start coming out of my mouth. I chuckle. "I spent most of the flight over here trying to figure out how I was going to say what I need to. I guess rehearsal was never going to be helpful because I don't think the way I wanted to say any of this is right." I pause briefly before smiling softly. "First of all, I'm sure you're all wondering what the hell I've been doing about all of this over the past five years."

"I'd like to know," Beckett says quietly as he shrugs. "I guess I don't understand any of what happened, though."

"Well, then I'll start from the beginning. Alex and I got a call that Lyric was going into labor. The thing is, it was too soon. She was only twenty-two weeks. At least, that's what we thought. That's what the doctor she was seeing told her. Dr. Freeman doesn't exactly specialize in pregnancy. Not to say he hasn't studied up." That gets a chuckle out of almost everyone in the room. "Anyway, we grabbed Dr. Freeman and flew down. We were at Ryan's and Ariana's engagement dinner. It didn't take us long to get here. Maybe a couple of hours. By the time we got to the hospital, Jaxon had been born. To me, he looked small, but definitely more than twenty-two weeks. That was the first red flag. The second was the look of confusion on Doc's face. And the third was Lyric screaming things that made absolutely no sense to me."

"What kind of things?" Alec asks.

"She was saying he was alive. Save him. He was alive," Luca says with a sigh. "They wouldn't allow me in the room, even though she was begging for me. By the time Josh got there, I'd been detained by hospital guards, but let go under the condition that I could sit outside the room with two guards. Just to make sure I didn't try to go in. She was in so much pain. They wouldn't give her any pain meds. They said they couldn't because she was in active labor. It was too late for that. It's why them saying shit like 'it's the drugs' didn't make sense. She wasn't on any."

"He was alive," Lyric whispers. "I saw him. But they told me he was stillborn. They called it a miscarriage, but it wasn't. I had Jaxon."

"The doctors rushed Jaxon out of the room. There was so much chaos, I didn't know who was who," I continue. "All I knew was that Lyric needed me. Everyone left her in that room. All the nurses. All the doctors. They left her to bleed out. And that was flag number four."

"Oh my God," Dallas whimpers.

I lean into her and turn to kiss her temple. She needs to get out of here. Anything to calm her down. "Can you get Jaxon something to eat?" I ask her. "Do you still have the list that Doc gave you about safe things for him to eat while he gets healthier?"

She nods. "Yes, sir."

I watch her hurry to the kitchen with Jaxon. It's an open floor plan, so we can see them and they can see us. I smile while she talks to him quietly and settles him at the breakfast bar. Once she opens the fridge, I continue.

"Alex grabbed a doctor. I think he must have been the head of the hospital or something, though, because he about fucking lost it. He saved Lyric, then went on a warpath."

"While Josh was with Lyric," Alex picks up for me, "I went with the doctor. He left the head nurse in charge of Lyric and went to find where they were working on Jaxon. By the time he got there, Dr. Freeman was coming out. He'd called Jaxon's time of death. There was nothing he could do. He'd tried everything. Jaxon's lips were blue. His heart wasn't beating. He was clinically dead. He was non-responsive. There was nothing. No brainwaves. Nothing. He told me there was a needle mark on Jaxon's arm. Tiny, but it was there. The other doctor said it was a shot of adrenaline to get his heart pumping. Dr. Freeman told me that was a flag for him. He'd requested an autopsy. There was nothing off. Tox screens and everything were completely normal, but he'd requested to be the one to do it. By the time he got the okay, it had already been done. All of those test results didn't come from him."

"What's more," I cut in, "is that they said they cremated him."

"When I asked if we could say our final goodbye," Lyric begins, "the nurse who came in was a different nurse. I hadn't seen her before, but she insisted that she'd been there the entire time and was so sorry that this happened. I knew she wasn't there, but she'd convinced me that she was. That they had pain meds dripping into my IV, and I was getting delirious. Josh didn't know if she was telling the truth or not. It was chaos when he got there, and I was so confused. I don't know what I was being drugged with, but I felt the pain. All of it."

"Even still, it was flag number five for me. I'd already decided I was going to investigate what the hell was going on, but it wasn't until Lyric asked to see Jaxon one last time when it all clinched for me. She was denied. She'd been told they'd already cremated him. Neither of us gave permission for that, and Dr. Freeman was pissed because it prevented him from exhuming the body and doing his own autopsy per our request and his. We left a couple of days later with a cardboard box that had ashes in it. When I finally got her to sleep that night at home, I started putting out calls to every single resource and ally both Ryan and I have. International and otherwise. I was asking for information. I never filed an official report, but I did have everyone looking for a newborn."

"You said something about twenty-two weeks," Matt says. "I thought it was more than that. Lyric mentioned that once."

"It was more than that." I nod as I stand. "Dr. Freeman estimated him to be thirty-two weeks. Not twenty-two. I requested her records from the hospital from the OBGYN she was seeing. When I went to question the discrepancy of her records and what actually happened, remember, we had a report with the approximate age by this time. A report by another doctor. When I went to question her, she wasn't there anymore. She'd resigned the day after Lyric gave birth. Every single doctor and nurse involved with Lyric were gone. Including the head nurse and hospital administrator. So, there we were with a report that confirmed what our doctor said about his age, and hospital records that said when she was first seen, she was thirteen weeks. This all happened nine weeks after she was first seen. How can a baby go from thirteen weeks to thirty-two? In just nine weeks?"

"It can't," Layne says. "That makes no sense."

I grin. "You're right. What was even more strange to me, was during all of this, we discovered a NICU nurse was fired for negligence, but not until four weeks later. I had absolutely no idea if it was related, but I couldn't find her to ask her questions, so I sent her information into all my contacts as well. She was never seen again."

"Who was she? What was her name?"

"She had a few, according to what Cole found. I'll have him send what he found to you so you can do some digging on your own." I rub the back of my neck. "Over the years, I just never got information. Until last night."

"What happened last night?" Layne asks curiously.

I smile a little. "Well, Damon got some information. A random as fuck call out of the blue. No idea who the guy is, but he gave some credible information that checked out. We didn't know it would lead to Jaxon, per se, but he said there was a kid being held on a boat. He told us he'd been there for years. Since he was a newborn. He'd tried to get information to authorities several times when they've docked, but something always happened to thwart his plans. Whether it be him being followed or their captain requiring them to go in pairs. He said his captain was being lax this time and believed it's because he has allies here. He told Damon he wants to help the kid but needs protection. He got it. Damon and Gavin mobilized. Damon met the contact at the docks."

"Where were you?" Lyric asks me quietly. She's wringing her hands and looking down at them.

"I was dealing with other matters. Mostly related to businesses. I saw this as something small that could easily be handled without me. Gavin and Damon are good at what they do. They all handled this well. Dane was there with Cole, too. It was a flawless mission. We didn't know who the kid was until later when Dane's team found your missing person's report. Jaxon's DNA matched yours. Mariah has apparently been on this since the beginning because there are updated aged photos based on the picture Dr. Freeman took."

The folder I've had sitting in front of me has all of the information I just told her in it, but Lyric has always been better about hearing it all before she sees it. The visual solidifies what she heard in her mind and makes her feel more stabilized. It makes everything feel more real.

Matt and DJ, on the other hand, like cold, hard facts. They like everything being in neat little files waiting for them to scrutinize. Not that they can't figure shit out on their own. But as soon as they do, that information is getting put right into a file. I'd say it's the cop in them, but I know better. It's really just how they work and process things. Everyone learns and thrives differently.

I pick up the folder and hand it to her. "Everything I just said is in here. I know you'll want to flip through, but I think maybe we all need to discuss the severity of the situation." Without waiting for anyone to say anything or ask what I mean, I jump right off the deep end. "Jaxon is alive. He's right here in the flesh. He's our son, but what's more is that he's the son of a powerful man, the boss of one of the largest mafias in the world. And we have him." I take a deep breath and glance at Dallas before lowering my voice. "That being said, Lyric, you're the mother of my heir in everyone's eyes."

"There's a big target on her back," Matt finishes. Lyric's eyes widen as everything I'm saying dawns on her.

"It's not just her with a target," Alec says, drawing all of our attention to him. He nods to Mariah. "She's the cop who filed the report. It's public record. Not to mention her connection to me. It's not well known, but with a little digging, it wouldn't be hard to find out. Matt and DJ are in danger because they're married to Lyric. And their kids are in danger for no other reason than being their kids. They're seen as leverage."

I can't help but notice he left Luca out of all of that. I know why, but he needs to be included. "Luca can be seen as leverage for both Mariah and Lyric, since he's her brother and Mariah's boyfriend." The words sting Alec. I can tell the second he drops his head with a nod.

"I don't see another option," Beckett says as he sits up. He looks at his parents with a small smile. "We were talking about it, but I think the timeline has moved up substantially. We have to move to Chicago now."

Lyric nearly chokes as she shakes her head. "You both wanted to finish high school here with your friends. Your dads and your aunt and uncle would have to put in for transfers."

"Baby, they're right," DJ rumbles soothingly. "We don't have a choice. We'll have to find someplace to stay and deal with moving and selling the house while we're up there. This is a safety issue. I don't think being apart is a good idea, and if we're going to move there anyway, taking a leave of absence isn't going to make sense. Especially if we have no plans to go back. Which we don't."

"Not only that, Jaxon is your son, and ours by marriage," Matt says. "He's finally home, where he belongs. You're not going to want to be away from him after you just got him back, and none of us would ever ask that. This is a huge safety concern for our entire family, but it's also a family issue."

I smile as I watch them. I've always been happy that she found her soulmates, but it always makes me even more so when I get to observe the way they take care of her. I love watching her face light up when she's with them or her kids. Lyric has definitely found where she belongs, and I couldn't possibly be more proud of her for that.

The more they all talk, the more convinced she becomes. Watching her go from so unsure to that beyond confident girl she's grown into is something that always amazes me. It also convinces me every single time I see it that us breaking up and becoming such good friends was the best decision we could have made for each other. It allowed her to fly like the butterfly she is.

And it allowed me to meet my one true love.

I glance over at Dallas once more and smile a little. I don't know how any of this is going to work, but I do know that she's it for me. This isn't going to be an easy road. Not that I won't keep my promise and try. I do want to be with her, but my reasons for staying away remain. She's way too good for me, and looking at her with Jaxon is proof of that. The way she's keeping him quiet and calm while she plays with him, and the way she made sure he ate. It all proves she's an angel, and I'll taint her wings.

It's not going to fucking work, worthless piece of shit. You know that. I close my eyes and look away just as Dallas starts speaking low to Jaxon and glancing in my direction.

My dad's voice.

It's always in my head. Always telling me I'm not good enough. I don't do enough. Usually, I can fight it away, but the relentlessness is exhausting. All of the memories of what he did to me never leave my mind. And sometimes, I'm lucky enough to have a new one come to light. Something just as horrible as everything else that I've blocked out of my mind.

PTSD.

I don't need enemies to take me out. It's doing a good job of that on its own.

Like I do every single time, I hide it. I choke it down and focus on anything other than letting the darkness take over. Dallas walking over with Jaxon is the perfect distraction. She holds his hand and walks just a step in front of him.

When she gets to the couch, she stops. She smiles down at him encouragingly, and I furrow my brows. Lyric has her head in her hands, like she's trying to will all of this to something normal. I can't blame her. Everything about the past twenty-four hours has been one fucked up mess. I glance at Alec. He shrugs slightly and furrows his own brows as Jaxon lets go of Dallas's hand.

We all fall silent and watch him when he clasps his hands in front of him and puts his head down. He walks slowly to Lyric as Dallas' smile spreads further across her beautiful face. Lyric is still trying to make sense of everything in her mind. Jaxon walks right to her. He stops at her leg and hesitates just for a moment before he rests a hand on her knee.

Lyric's head jerks up, her eyes glistening with unshed tears. She watches Jaxon with just as much wonder as is swimming in his sharp, blue eyes. She tilts her head slightly to her left side. Jaxon slowly does the same. She bites her lip and does it the other way. Jaxon follows her movements.

"Hi," she whispers after a few moments. Her voice cracks, and my heart shatters. I wish for the thousandth time that I could've stopped this from ever happening.

I watch Jaxon squeeze her knee just a little bit. Lyric understands that's his way of acknowledging her.

She smiles just a little. "Can I introduce you to everyone?" she whispers once more.

No one moves for fear it'll scare him. He slowly nods his head before he finally breaks eye contact and looks down at his feet.

"If you look behind you, that's Mariah and Luca." Lyric still keeps her voice barely above a whisper. Jaxon doesn't turn around, but he nods as he sticks his thumb in his mouth. "And on the couch over there," Lyric points, "are Beckett and Layne. They are my sons… Just like you…" Her voice drops even lower. I'd have to strain to hear her if I wasn't so close. "And next to me are my husbands, Matt and DJ. And I'm…" She takes a deep breath. I know it's to try and stop the tears, but they start spilling anyway.

"She's your mom." My voice is stronger than I feel, but I still keep it soothing. Jaxon's eyes widen as he looks at me. "She's your mom," I say one more time, this time barely whispering myself.

I wish I knew what he was thinking right now, but it doesn't take too long before I understand. He takes a step closer to Lyric and hugs her. There isn't a dry eye in the room when he wraps his small arms around her as much as he can, but it's not until Lyric drops her head to bury her face in his hair and wrap her arms around him, that I lose it.

The two of them cling to each other while Dallas walks slowly towards me, that beautiful smile lighting up the entire room. She sits quietly next to me after I sit, and I can't help but put an arm around her. I pull her close to me and kiss her temple.

"I know what you did," I whisper low in her ear. She shivers and leans into me. "And I don't know how to thank you for it, baby."

She looks up at me, smiling adoringly. I swallow the lump in my throat. The fact that anyone could look at me like she does is the one thing that always manages to chip the ice I've built around my heart.

"He kept looking at her," Dallas whispers. "It was like he recognized her somehow, but didn't know how. I asked him if he knew who his mommy is, or what she looks like. He shook his head and looked at her again. I whispered that's his mommy, and it was like recognition hit him hard. You could see it in his eyes." She looks at Lyric swaying gently with Jaxon and leans her head on my shoulder. "I asked if he wanted to give her a hug, and he nodded."

I hug her closer. "You're fucking amazing." I close my eyes and let my lips rest against the top of her head. "So fucking amazing."

Whispers about what we're going to do float around the room. I know I need to address it, but I want to give Lyric as much time with Jaxon as I can. Time I took from her by letting her be alone during her pregnancy. Whether she agrees or not, I let someone get to her and robbed us all of time.

We'll never get it back, but I'll sure as fuck track down whoever took Jaxon from us.

And when I do... Hell's wrath will be a reprieve to what I'll put the fucker through.

Chapter Six

☕ Dallas ☕

(Three Weeks Later)

I close my history book and push it away with disgust. "I feel like I'm going to vomit."

Rosie Knight, my best friend and classmate, closes her science book next to me. "Is it the final project you're working on?"

"Yeah," I sigh. "I don't know why I thought it would be a good idea to do the Holocaust of all things. It already breaks my heart. I should've focused on something totally different. Like the U.S. Civil War."

"Well, if you did that, though, you'd have to focus on slavery. Which also breaks your heart."

"Yeah. And to top it off, the teacher is one of those progressive jerks who tries to teach us that the Civil War didn't have anything to do with slavery."

Rosie blinks. "Okay, what?" she finally asks after several moments of just staring at me.

I nod. "Yep." I pop the 'p'. "I told Alec that, and he went straight to the administrator. It hasn't been mentioned since, and Alec did want me to do the Civil War just to see what he'd do, but he already hates me. I don't want to rock the boat. I don't understand how he feels slavery and the Civil War had nothing to do with each other, but he's very passionate about the Holocaust."

"Oh my God, I'm glad I don't have that guy. I think both of my dads would probably try to kill him."

I laugh. "Not try. They totally would. And they'd make it all look like a figment of their imagination did it because of his stupid belief that slavery has nothing to do with the Civil War. So, the cops would be chasing their tails."

It's my turn to laugh. "Except their boss owns the police and is related by blood to two of them. The cops would just bury it all."

Rosie giggles. "Is it bad that I sort of like that extra layer of protection?"

"Oh God, no. I grew up with the cops always on my dad. When Alec took over and started working with them and becoming one of their biggest allies, I couldn't believe the difference. I lived in fear every day of a raid. It was awful."

"And now you live in fear every day of a gang war," Rosie teases.

I laugh again. "Nope. Because I know the Cranes and Lucinios will drop in and the war will end before it begins."

Rosie smiles. "It's nice. But I still hate so much when they have to go anywhere. I hate the danger."

I wrinkle my nose. "Me too. But it's helpful to know there's an immense amount of backup and so many levels of protection that they use. Alec was gone a week ago. He didn't tell me, but I found out he took a head shot. I had no idea they wore helmets out there. Like actual military grade helmets."

"I'd be pissed if I wasn't told one of my dad's took a hit."

"Oh, I was. Alec is still receiving death glares from me, even though I make sure he gets lots of hugs so he knows I still love him."

"I'm waiting for him to start bribing you."

I giggle. "He actually told me I should start moving all my stuff to Josh's house. Just to see how Josh reacts."

Rosie smiles but looks down at her hands. "How is all of that going?"

I sigh. "Josh is extremely temperamental. I know he's trying to navigate all of this, but sometimes, I feel like he needs to just give in and let it happen. I love how in control of everything he is, but I think there are times he really just needs to let things progress as they're meant to, however that may be. He's also under a lot of stress, though. I definitely get that. His whole life changed."

She winces a little as she looks up at me. "Are you a little uneasy with his ex around? I mean, now that things have changed so much?"

I shake my head. "I'm not. Really. Lyric is amazing, but her and Josh have been over for a long time. She's so happy with her family. Josh has always said that things are so much better between them since they became friends. Honestly, I can see it. They have a very real bond and adorable friendship, but beyond that? There's just nothing there."

She smiles a little. "I've noticed that he looks at you very differently to anyone else."

I blush and look down. "There's always been something there. It's just been hard because of my age. And I really hate how much stuff is going on in the world now about grooming. 'Oh, he knew her since she was fourteen. He groomed her'. But he didn't. At all. And then when I say that, people are all like, 'She doesn't even know she was groomed. She's so damaged. She's just a kid. Her frontal cortex isn't fully developed until she's in her early twenties. She has no idea what's even happening to her'." I shake my head. "He's even tried using that as an excuse on me to keep me at a distance. At least with him, I know why he was doing it, but with other people out there, it's like an age gap just grosses them out."

"I don't get that. Honestly. If it's love, it's love. In my opinion, it wouldn't have mattered if you guys were dating and kissing and all that before. It's really all got to do with the sex. That's the part that so many people have issues with. And there are laws."

"I think it all depends on when people are ready for that. I wasn't. I also think it's the circumstances behind everything, too. There are truly sick people out there who prey on young girls and guys. I understand the reasons for the laws, but to all of the other people out there? I'm eighteen. I'm an adult. I can legally go off to war, get married, enter into contracts, and am treated like an adult in any court of law. Who I love, male or female, or a man who's twice my age is no one's business but my own and the person I am with. People really need to shove their opinions."

"Completely agree. What about everything else? How is he handling being a father?"

My eyes widen. "Okay. Here's something completely between us. Josh is so in love with being a dad. He's always been so terrified of it because of his father. He was afraid he'd somehow turn into him, but he's so far from it. Firstly, he has a heart. At least where his family is concerned. Secondly, he loves kids. He's everyone's favorite uncle. The biggest thing that's bothering him right now is that he can't find anything. The guy they put under their protection gave him everything he has, but it wasn't enough to get any concrete leads. Personally, I think the guy got the kid out because he has some kind of a conscience but doesn't want to give up his boss."

"Eww. Who would protect their boss when he did something so heinous? Gross." She pauses as I reach for my book again. "Oh! What about Jaxon speaking? Has he said anything yet?"

I shake my head. "No. It worries me. I don't think that he's incapable of speaking. Dr. Freeman believes that it's completely trauma based. He said it could take him days to feel comfortable, or months. He said it could even take years. He doesn't know if he'll ever speak."

Rosie sniffles. "That's so sad. That poor boy must've been through so much tra-" She cuts herself off when her phone starts playing her favorite Taylor Swift song, *Shake It Off*. I should say favorite of this week. She picks a new one all of the time. I don't mind. I love Taylor Swift, too. "It's Dylan." She swipes to answer the phone and puts it on speaker. "Hey, girl. Dallas is here."

"Hey, girls." She sounds so sad. Dylan is Rosie's friend from Texas. They met before she was adopted by Lance and Damon and have remained close since Rosie came here. I've gotten pretty close to Dylan myself.

"Hey! You sound so sad," I say.

She takes a breath. "I just… heard something. I don't know what to say or do about it."

"Oh no. What did you hear?" Rosie asks.

"I heard my dad in his office. He was on the phone with someone, but the phone wasn't on speaker. I only heard my dad talking." She sniffles again, and it sounds like she's moving the phone. I imagine she's wiping her eyes.

"What happened, Dyl?" I use her nickname because she loves it as much as she loves dill pickles.

"He just… said that… he never knew she, I think he was talking about my mom, was pregnant when she left Chicago and the wannabe badass biker behind. His words. Not mine. He said he made her believe the kid was his because he knew it could be used to their advantage. And then he said that…" She trails off and chokes on a sob. When she starts talking again, her voice is barely above a whisper. "He said my mom wouldn't have kept it if she knew she was carrying that asshole's kid. He went on to say there's no way it's his because they hadn't had sex at that point. That she was too far along when she found out for it to have been possible to be his."

Rosie and I look at each other with the same confused expression. Finally, Rosie asks, "He was saying 'it' in reference to the baby the whole time?"

"Yeah," she whispers. "He even went on to tell the person on the phone more details about when the birth took place and some details. My mom had a super hard labor with me. When I was born, they tell me all of the time it was in the middle of a hurricane, but it was fitting because of how difficult the pregnancy and labor was. He told that to the person on the phone. I'm certain he was talking about me, but it doesn't make sense. None of it does. The only tie I have to a biker is Drake's boyfriend."

"That's… true, actually," Rosie says.

My mind is racing so fast, I almost start hyperventilating. "Dylan, call Drake. I don't know why, I just… I guess I just feel like you need to be in touch with VV down there. It's better to talk to Drake than it is Blade. I don't know why I feel like that, but I do."

Rosie nibbles her lip. "No… I… I feel the same way. That's so fucked up. Just make sure the guys have your back on this one."

"I'm seeing X later. He's picking me up for a party, but he's using Colton as cover. He said I'm going to his house for dinner and a movie."

I nod. "So, you'll see everyone. Good. That makes me feel better. Make sure Drake can get Blade there."

"I'll talk to him. I gotta go." She hangs up before Rosie or I can say anything.

"Please say that was weird," Rosie says.

"Uh. Yeah." I jump at the knock on Rosie's door.

47

"Dinner, sweetie," Damon's deep voice rumbles. "I don't want to be late. Josh has something he wants to talk about."

Rosie jumps up to answer the door. "Dad!" she calls when she hears him start to walk away.

"Yeah?" He's still next to the door. I grab mine and Rosie's phones and walk to her.

Rosie looks back at me. "Me and Dallas just had a weird phone call."

I watch Damon's entire demeanor change. Suddenly, he's standing straight. His dark eyes narrow. "What happened?"

"It was Dylan," Rosie begins.

"Stop. Come downstairs so Lance can hear, too." He turns and strides down the hall. We both scurry after him. The second we reach the living room, Damon puts up a hand as Lance begins to talk. "Just a second." He turns to us. "What happened, girls?"

Lance is very much on alert. "What? What happened?"

"Dylan called, and it was a weird call," Rosie starts again. She glances at me and then them. "I think she's in trouble," she whispers.

"I think we need Alec. Maybe even Josh," I finish for her.

Damon glances at Lance before pulling Rosie to him. "Okay. We'll talk to Josh. Alec will be there, too. We can pull him into the office."

Both dread and anticipation courses through my veins simultaneously. I haven't seen much of Josh over the past three weeks. I've given him space because I felt like he needed it. Maybe not from me, but I felt like he needed bonding time. While I have seen him, it's never been for more than an hour at a time. I don't want to get in the way of his time with his son.

Once we get to Josh's house a few minutes later, everyone is already here. Alex is with his wife, Raleigh. Gavin and Harleigh are here. Rebekkah is here with her husband, Kent, and her twins, a boy named Jordan and a girl named Harper. It takes a second before I see Dane with Skyla. Lyric is with her husbands, brother, and two boys near the pool. Jaxon is smiling as Josh rides him around on his shoulders. Cole is lounging on the couch reading a kids book. I'd laugh, but I'm too nervous.

I hate everything about taking Josh away from Jaxon when he looks so happy, so I look for Alec. He's with Mariah in a corner of the house. I was young when they dated, barely four when they broke up, but

Mariah was my favorite of all of Alec's girlfriends. No one compared to her in my eyes. Considering he's never settled down, I'd go as far to say it's always been Mariah for him.

I take a deep breath and head for him. All I do is lock eyes and nod towards Josh's office. I don't stop walking. Whatever they are talking about shouldn't be interrupted by me. I hate that it needs to be cut short in any manner at all.

Moments after I'm seated in the chair in front of Josh's desk, Alec comes in. "What's going on?"

I shake my head. "We need Josh and Rosie."

Alec perches himself on the desk in front of me. "Am I about to kill someone?" He smiles just a little. I know he's teasing, but he doesn't know how close to the truth that might be.

I glance over my shoulder. "I honestly don't know, Alec," I nearly whisper. "Rosie and I just talked to Dylan. She was super upset and overheard a conversation that just chills me. My first thought was we need you and Josh. Something is just not right. And what's more?" I continue, cutting off whatever he's about to say. "She asked. She asked for help. Like she knew whatever was going on was too big for her." I look down and hug myself as I shake my head. "I don't know what's going on, but I don't think it's good."

"You gotta give me more than that, Dallas."

I take a deep breath. "We'll tell you everything, but I really think we need Josh. This is… I just… Her dad. He's a Senator. He's really important down there. I think… this is even bigger than us." I haven't stopped whispering because I don't want anyone to overhear.

Alec says nothing for a few moments. Finally, he takes a breath. "Well, I trust your instincts. I guess we'll all have to hear what was said before decisions are made, but if she's in danger, we need to get her out. Just need to figure it out and plan when."

I shake my head. "It's not a matter of figuring anything out. It's not even a matter of when to pull her out. Something bad is going down."

The silence between us weighs heavily. I hear footsteps coming down the hall and know instinctively Josh has assembled his team.

The longer I think about it, the more I'm convinced Dylan isn't safe. We need to take action. Fast.

There is no other option.

Chapter Seven

☙ Josh ☙

"Not that I want to ruin this, man, but we have a thing going on," Damon says to me. He grins at Jaxon, who is happily perched on my shoulders.

I nod. "Not liking the interruption to family time." I head for the backdoor with Jaxon still on my shoulders.

"I know, but this is big enough to have Rosie and Dallas saying we need to be involved. And Alec."

That stops my heart cold. I raise an eyebrow. "What's going on?"

"Office. Dallas just went there with Alec. Rosie is with Lance and Gavin. I just pulled Dane on my way to you. He grabbed Cole."

I let out a sigh. One night. One night a week where all I have to do is be with my family. Unwind from the entire week and just be a fucking person. Not a damn mafia boss. I love what I do. I wouldn't change it for the world, but I've been looking forward to us all being together today. It's been a long time since we've all had the opportunity to take this kind of a timeout. I don't care what anyone else says. Everyone needs this to regroup.

I head for Lyric when I feel Jaxon tightening his grip. He's smart enough to know I'm about to be somewhere he isn't, and he's gotten pretty attached to me. A few times, I've felt like he wants to say something, but stops himself. It's like he's still not totally sure if I'm a good guy or not. I talk to him like I would anyone, and he loves that. He can communicate just fine without speaking, and that's all I need. Everything else will come in time.

"What do you say, buddy? How about some time with mom in the sun? Tell her to stop separating herself from everyone." I grin and wink at him as I pluck him off my shoulders knowing Lyric can hear me just fine. He smiles wide and nods as he reaches for her.

Lyric smiles brightly and takes him from me. Jaxon points to the house with a serious expression, and I about lose it laughing. Lyric, however, isn't so lucky. She cracks up.

"Traitor!" she squeaks out as she tickles him lightly.

I laugh again and turn to Matt. "Keep Kent away from the grill. Food in the house is ready to go."

Matt winks and follows me back to the house. "You got it, boss. Sounds a little bit like my old man. He's convinced he's the master of grills. He's not. Don't let him fool you."

I laugh. "Is he still around?"

"Nah." A small frown crosses his lips before he's smiling again. "Asshole went out fighting, though. I'd expected nothing less."

"You talk like he's still here." I smile a little.

Matt's grin widens. "He is. All around. I know he's watching over us."

My smile grows as I pat him on the back when we enter the house. I follow Damon. We meet up with Gavin, Lance, Dane, Cole, and Rosie. I lead them down the hall to the office as the girls help Matt carry things out and get everything set up buffet style outside. It's a warm, Spring day, and I want everyone to take advantage of it.

The second we walk into my office, I have to fight the urge to take Dallas in my arms. I can see how upset she is, even though she's trying to stay strong. I take a breath to steady my racing heart and put the boss facade in place. The armor that covers the man beneath clinks into place.

I sit in my chair behind my desk. "Okay. What's going on?"

Dallas looks up at me as Rosie sits in the chair next to her. Gavin closes my door as everyone takes a seat around the office. Gavin sits on the arm of the couch. Alec stays perched against the corner of my desk near Dallas.

Rosie reaches for Dallas, and the two clasp each other's hand. "We had a really weird call from Dylan," Rosie begins. "She seemed really upset and was telling us about a phone call that she overheard. She was talking super low, almost whispering."

"She *was* whispering at the end," Dallas says.

"What was so weird about the call?" I ask, hoping my voice is gentle and not as sharp as it tends to get when I'm in business mode. Judging by the way Rosie's head drops and Dallas winces, though, I'm pretty sure I failed. I grimace in apology.

Dallas, though, meets my eyes just like the beautiful, tough woman she's grown into. "She was talking about her dad," she says, her voice strong and confident. She has no idea, but I fall in love with her more. "She said her dad was talking to someone. She didn't know who. She was saying that he said some messed up stuff. Stuff that she believed was about her." She pauses, but her eye contact never breaks. I clasp my hands in front of me on my desk and nod encouragingly. "She said he gave details about her birth. Like she was born during a hurricane, and her mom had a super tough labor. He even said that it was fitting of her to be born during a hurricane, considering the labor and difficult pregnancy."

I furrow my brows and glance at Gavin before looking back at my girl. "So far, it kind of sounds like he was just having a conversation."

"Yeah, I know, but that happened after the really weird part. That just solidified in her mind who her dad was talking about. The weird part…" Dallas looks up at Alec as she trails off. She focuses back on me seconds later, and I'm suddenly very on edge. "The weird part, Josh, is that he said he never knew she was pregnant when she left Chicago. Dylan thought he was talking about her mom because her mom did come from here. And then she said the part that really scared us." I see her squeeze Rosie's hand, who still refuses to lift her gaze any higher than the front of my desk. "He said he never knew when she left Chicago and the wannabe badass biker behind that she was pregnant. And that she would've gotten an abortion if she knew."

Alec runs his hands down his face. "Fuck," he rumbles.

"I… know there's other biker gangs here…," Rosie starts, "but… she… lived in such a sheltered world. She doesn't know any other bikers. And her dad has no idea that Drake is associated with one."

Alec chuckles. "He's not just associated with one, honey. He's in a fucking relationship with the Chapter President of Viper's Venom."

"Which…" Cole leans back in his chair and laughs as he rubs his head. "Which means Dylan is in some pretty big fucking danger."

"Not necessarily," Dane says. Always the one who tries to be the cool level headed one. "We don't know this wannabe badass biker is Viper's Venom. There's a few gangs around here. Ruthless Warriors being one of them. Who's to say it ain't them?"

Gavin shrugs. "That would be even more reason to put protection on her at the very least."

"VV is already thin with all hands on deck looking for Ruthless Warriors and their leader. We know he's one of ours who went rogue," Alec says. "Blade will absolutely spare all he can. I'll send some guys down there from here, but I'm gonna need more for an operation like this. I'm up against a powerful man down there. No telling who he paid off."

"I'll get you guys, Alec," I say. "But we need more information on this before we go through with an extraction mission." I look back at Dallas. "Did you tell her to go to Blade?"

"I told her to go to Drake. Drake can get Blade. I was a little afraid that she might get hurt if she goes to Blade. I didn't want to say that, so I just said I wasn't sure why I felt that way, but to go to Drake. Maybe it's because her dad trusts him or something. I just didn't want her to be seen talking to someone she shouldn't be that could put her in more danger."

"Smart." I couldn't be more proud. She's thinking on her feet and including all circumstances in her decisions. I don't know if she really understands that's what she did, but she made a decision based on the information she had and instincts that came from that information. I tear my gaze away from her pretty blush and look up at Alec. "I'll gather a team and head down there with him. If we need to get her out, I'll be there to do it right then. In the meantime, contact Blade. Tell him what's going on. Get him to mobilize a team right now so we have eyes on her."

"I'll call him now," Alec says, taking his phone out of his pocket.

"Gavin, I'll need you with me on this one. We'll make sure Ryan is on alert to help out Damon and Lance here."

"You got it," Gavin says with a nod as he also takes out his phone.

I watch Dallas' hand move to her chest. She smiles softly, but I can tell it's pained. I furrow my brows slightly. I keep her in my line of sight as I look at Dane while Dallas rubs her chest.

"Dane, you and Cole keep doing what you're doing with the leads you have. I want to know all I can about that cargo ship. I don't care if you're at the point of getting Robby involved. Have him break into the FBI and find records. I'd have Lance do it, but he's busy enough keeping tabs on the DEA, Coast Guard, and the Carabinieri. I'm really interested in what the fuck the Italians want with this cargo ship."

"So far, all we have with that is they offloaded. That came from Damon's contact," Dane says. "We all feel like he's given us enough information to keep us intrigued, but we feel like he's holding onto some because if he doesn't, the protection stops."

I sigh and lean back in my chair. "Maybe it's time to step things up with him then. It's been three weeks. I'm sick of the little tidbits here and there when we hit just the right question. And I'm with you. He knows more. The protection wouldn't have stopped when we got all the information, but it just might now. I don't play games when lives are involved."

Dallas clears her throat softly and stands, leading Rosie with her. She gives me another soft smile that doesn't reach her eyes. Without saying a word, she leaves my office with Rosie following behind her. I don't know what any of that was about, but I know I need to talk to her.

"You want me to call the pilot and get us in the air as soon as possible?"

My eyes still on the door after Dallas closes it, I nod. I shake my head a little bit before looking back at Gavin. "Yeah. As soon as he can, but I at least want this damn dinner. We all need it. We've been running ragged for months now. We need the time to just be humans instead of vigilantes."

"I second that," Damon says, rubbing his eyes.

I stand, suddenly feeling like Dallas is pulling me to her or calling my soul. "We're going to enjoy this night if it kills me. Soak up all the positive energy." I stride to the door and open it quickly as Gavin starts talking to the captain of my plane.

I know Dane, Cole, Lance, and Damon are following me out while Gavin and Alec make their calls, but there's one thing on my mind. I don't know what's happening, but I need to find my girl.

Only when I get out to my living room, no one is there. No one is in the kitchen. Everyone is outside, but there's no sign of Dallas anywhere. In a slight panic, I run upstairs and check her room and mine. She's in neither.

I pause and take a breath. "Focus, Josh. She's obviously upset. She wouldn't want to be around people." And that's when I figure it out. I run to the library. She likes sitting in there just for the solitude, but she also knows it's my favorite room in the house.

I jog down the stairs and head directly for the library. *The fuck is wrong with you?* I think to myself. *Not once have you ever been hell bent and in a panic to find her.* Yeah. I'm going fucking insane. That voice in my head is correct. I've never had this feeling before. Like I need to get to someone before something bad happens. My heart feels like it's being ripped out of my chest.

The second I enter the library, I know instinctively I made the right choice. I close the door and quickly make my way to a crying Dallas. When I reach her, I don't hesitate to turn her towards me and wrap her in my arms.

"What happened?" I whisper in her ear.

She tries to pull away as she shakes her head, but I don't let her. Not this time. Usually, I'd let her pull back just to keep her at arm's length. I might not be the best at intimacy, but I am trying. Every time she tries to pull away, I hold her tighter.

I wait her out. The silence is deafening, but I know when she needs to put her thoughts together before they come out of her mouth. She's been that way as long as I've known her. She never speaks before she thinks. It's why her words often cut so deeply. It's because she's thought about them and knows exactly how she wants to word them.

Several minutes of just hugging her and refusing to let her out of my grip, she finally gives up. I know it's only a matter of time before she'll start talking. Maybe her words will ease the fact that I'm close to a panic attack, or maybe she'll send me right into one.

"I've stayed away so you could bond. I don't want to be selfish and take your time, Josh." Her voice is so low that even with my ear being so close to her lips, I can barely hear her. "That's not my intention. I don't want to sound like a whiny brat, or attention seeker. But seeing you with Lyric is like a stab to my chest. It's obvious your bond with her is far stronger than it could ever be with me, and I know I won't measure up. The problem is, I'm not sure you even care." Her voice drops even lower. So low that I'm not certain she even realizes she utters her next words. "And if you don't care, why should I even try?"

I have no idea what I thought she was going to say, but it wasn't that. I keep her in my grip because I'm incapable of letting her go, but I can't believe she thinks that little of me and herself. "Wait a minute. You think I still have a thing for my ex? Even though you know better, and I've said as much."

She shakes her head. "No. At least I... I don't know. I don't. I don't know where I even fit into this entire thing." She chances looking up at me, and what I see kills me a little more inside. Pain, hurt, and confusion swim in her eyes in the form of unshed tears.

"Dallas, I'm lost. I'm not gonna lie. You're saying I don't care about you or us. It's simply not true. And what I got from that is jealousy over Lyric, who you know is still really close to me and this family. There are no romantic feelings between us. There hasn't been in a long time. So, you need to be clearer about what's going on here, because I really don't understand, honey."

She looks down at my feet. "You're leaving."

I raise an eyebrow. "Yeah. I am. Because you alerted us to something very wrong. Am I not supposed to act?"

"You are. It's just that..." She trails off and places her hands against my chest, but still doesn't look up at me. "I guess maybe it is selfish. Forget I said anything. Really."

It's during the brief moment my grip is loosened enough for her to get loose that she does just that. She pushes against me and turns quickly enough that my hold breaks. She speed-walks to the door and is already pulling it open before I have a single second to react. I don't think I've ever let my guard down like that with anyone but her. I should've known she'd take advantage. She's not like any other woman I've ever been with.

In a flash, I'm on her and closing the door. She lets out an adorable squeak that has my dick solid as steel faster than she can say my name.

"We're not done," I growl low and dominantly, narrowing my eyes. "I'm not letting you go until you talk to me."

Her eyes are wide. Her lips form an 'O' of surprise. I've never done this before. I've pinned her against a wall and kissed her, but I'm usually shoving her away seconds later. Not this time, and I can tell she sees it.

If she wants me to let go and give this a chance, it's exactly what she's going to get.

Chapter Eight

❦ Dallas ❦

I stare at Josh in openmouthed shock. I expect his lips on mine in a kiss that makes the world stop before he inevitably casts me aside and tosses me over a cliff, but it's not what happens. Instead, his intense gaze slices through my very being with such precision, I'm left with my head spinning; my heart beating wildly out of my chest. His hands grip my hips. His thighs meet mine as he pushes me against the wall. Impure thoughts flood my mind, making me forget everything that I had in there to begin with.

"Talk, Dallas." His voice is low and vibrates its way through my body, settling in the pit of my stomach.

"I…" It's all I can get out before I'm drowning in his icy-blue gaze.

"You…" He pushes closer, and I'm suddenly under his magical spell.

I don't know how long I stand mesmerized by him before the subtle squeeze on my hip wakes me from my reverie. Everything comes crashing over me once more, but something's different this time. I feel calmer. More confident. The way he always makes me feel.

I finally submit and spill the words. "It's just that you're leaving. I know it's for Dylan. I know it's important. I know all of that. I guess I just... hoped that maybe... we'd get some time. Things have calmed. Jaxon has a routine. He's been doing so much better. He's happier. His room is complete. Jessa and Jason are working on a house for Lyric and her family. The guest house is set up with a super nice room for him so he feels at home when he's there." I sigh and slump a little as I shrug slightly. "I hoped that was a good sign that things could progress with us. That's all."

In a second, his large hands are gripping my thighs just below my butt. He lifts me up so quickly that I have no other choice but to wrap my arms around his broad shoulders and legs around his muscular waist.

"So, let me get this straight." He leans in so his lips are almost touching mine. All it would take is a tiny fraction of an inch for our lips to connect. My eyes fall to his mouth. "You're jealous of Lyric. And you're being greedy and selfish and want to hog all of my time."

My mouth drops, and my eyes snap to his. "What? No!"

A tiny smile that I'm sure he doesn't think I notice turns his mouth up just a little. "That's what I got from all of that."

My eyes narrow. "I know what you just did."

He pulls back slightly and looks at me curiously. "Yeah? And what was that?"

My eyes narrow further but the slight drawl I hear makes me weak for him. "You reverse psychology'd me."

He raises an eyebrow. "Reverse physchology'd you? We're making up words now?"

I raise my head stubbornly. "Yes."

He leans in and kisses my throat. "Did it work to make you see how ridiculous that all sounded?" The deepness of his growly tone shoots straight to a part of me I've always been too shy to touch. A part only he's ever brought alive. All it takes is being near him. I'm a mess.

I groan and drop my head to his shoulder. "Okay, I know how it sounded, but it's still kind of legit... I really just don't know where my place is right now. I don't want to take any time away from anything that's going on, but at the same time... I... guess... I just..." I sigh. "I don't know."

He kisses the side of my neck. "You're ready for this to become real, like I said, and not some game."

"I don't feel like it's a game." I bring my head up and meet his pretty eyes. "I feel like things just get in the way. I don't think I'm really jealous of Lyric. I love her. But she has gotten to be around you this whole time. I've just been kind of scarce. You haven't really even texted me much. Or called. Or when I am here, your attention is on Jaxon or the family bonding you're doing. And before you say anything, I understand. It's where it should be. I just feel like..." I huff and shake my head as I close my eyes. "Like not sounding like a whiny, spoiled brat."

"Baby, I don't understand why you keep thinking of yourself as a whiny, spoiled brat. You're allowed to have feelings and want things to be different than they are. I have been spending a lot of time with them. I think we're both making up for lost time with him, but that doesn't mean I should be ignoring you."

My eyes snap open again, and I vigorously shake my head. "No, that's not -" I'm instantly cut off when his lips crash to mine. His usual taste fills my being, but this time, it feels so much different. This time, he's not holding back. There's no barriers between us.

I grip his shoulders and press closer, greedily taking all he gives me and stealing more. When his tongue slides into my mouth, mine automatically finds his and starts a dance that only we know. Instead of dropping me, Josh presses closer and angles us both so his jean clad dick is against my center. He swallows my moan and deepens the kiss impossibly more than it already is.

He's so hard. I've seen him like this. I've felt him inadvertently, but it's never been like this. Never felt this good. There are so many tingles running through my body. It's like my core is shooting them everywhere until I feel like I'm a firework ready to explode. His tongue is everywhere and nowhere. His hands are all over me, but they haven't moved an inch.

We pull away from each other abruptly, panting, when someone knocks on the door. "Josh?" Alec's voice rumbles through the door.

Josh gives me a look to silence me. "I'll be right out. Needed a minute."

"Matt's finished grilling. Everything is set up. Tell my sister Matt made her favorite."

Before I can stop myself, I let out a squeal. "Matt made grilled watermelon?" I cover my mouth with wide eyes and look at Josh in a complete panic. Alec's laugh can be heard fading all the way down the hall.

Josh grins. "You know he's going to murder me if anything ever happens to you, right? I'm shocked he hasn't tried yet."

"He wouldn't kill you." I grin a little wickedly. "He'd have Tyler do it. He's the sniper."

"So, I shouldn't break your heart. Is that what I'm getting out of you?"

I nod. "I'm a fragile princess made of glass. Be gentle."

Josh throws his head back and laughs richly as he hugs me closer. "Let's get out there. And after everyone leaves, I'll finish what I started."

I nearly choke on my own spit as he lets me slide down the wall. He swats my ass, and I let out a squawk as I cover it. "Josh!" My cheeks feel hot.

He leans down and kisses me. "Joking aside, I promise that you and I will spend some time together tonight. Alone. We can talk. We can sit here and hold each other saying nothing. I don't care. Whatever you want. But I do need to leave and help down there. If things go down and we have to act quick, I'd rather I'm there instead of getting a phone call about it. I want the jet there for them to use. I don't want my pilot thinking he needs to come back here for any reason. The guy's been with me for years. He doesn't like being split between me and the others unless I have a second jet. Since my other one is having maintenance done, I don't have that. Ryan's been dealing with his own shit, so his are in use. My reasons are twofold."

I turn to him as I reach for the door handle and sigh. "I know, Josh. I don't want you to think I don't understand that you have to leave. I've been around you for four years. And I grew up with Alec. I know that things happen that need your attention. It's not that. I just want to be some kind of a focus in your life again. I feel like you've reeled me in many times only to push me away when I get too close. I don't want that anymore. A balance. That's all. A balance would be nice."

He cups my cheek and leans down. His lips graze mine before he softly kisses me. It's a kiss that makes my toes tingle, but it's far more gentle than the others. "What if I text while I'm down there? Every day. I can't promise I'll be able to talk long, but I can try to call. I can't promise I'll be able to. I don't know how things are going to play out, but I'll at least text."

I nod, the lingering tightness in my chest easing more. "That would make my whole world."

He smiles and kisses my forehead. "And things will be better than they have been the last three weeks, but on that note, I don't know if I'm fucking up unless you say something. You need to remember that this is all new for me. I haven't been in a relationship in a long time, and I can't say I was the greatest with Lyric."

I smile softly and let my fingertips trace his jaw. "I don't think you were that bad."

"You have too much faith in me. There's going to be a lot of failure on my part. And you're going to have to stand up to me when I'm being an asshole."

My smile spreads into a smirk. "I think I got that down."

He laughs again as he opens the door and takes my hand. He leads me out of the library towards the backyard. "I can't deny that. You might be the only one I let do it."

I know he means in my way because I'm not the only one who stands up to him, but the words go a long way. It's his way of confessing feelings to me, even if he can't quite say it. I've learned his code, and I've learned it well. When he wants to say something, but isn't sure how to broach the subject, he says things that mean the same without actually using the words. Instead of saying I make him better, he says I give him flight. When no one else is around, Josh is the sweetest, most kind man. At least if people know how to read him.

When we reach the backdoor, I attempt to remove my hand from Josh's. It's something I've conditioned myself to do because Josh always drops my hand before anyone sees anything. This time, he holds it tighter and locks our fingers together. I look up at him in surprise, but he doesn't say a word. Not even when everyone can blatantly see what's happening.

Once again, I feel my cheeks burning. Josh code. He's showing we're together because he can't fully say the words. Most would think it's because he doesn't care to make the announcement, but I know better. He doesn't trust himself to not hurt me somehow. The tremor no one else would notice in his hand confirms I'm right.

Matt hands us both a plate. I smile brightly at the grilled watermelon. "Just for you, madam," he drawls with a wink.

I giggle. "Thank you. I haven't had this in forever."

"You just became DJ's favorite. He's a big fan of grilled fruit."

I smile more and let Josh lead me to the buffet table as Matt finishes putting the rest of the grilled fruit he made on a serving platter. He puts it on the table and makes sure the grill is turned off before he gets his own plate.

Josh lets go of my hand so we both can dish up. I instantly miss the warmth, but he sticks close to me. I love how he senses when I just need him close. I love even more that he came searching for me. I really didn't know I needed him until I was trying to push away from him. Then, I started pushing him away because I didn't want him to see how foolish and selfish I was being. Now, I just feel like a crazy person.

Leave it to Josh to nip that in the ass. As soon as we're dished up, he takes my plate. "Pick a seat, but make sure I can have you in my lap. No negotiation."

I blink a moment before looking up at him and fighting the urge to cross my legs. "Why do I feel like saying, 'yes, sir. Anything you say, sir', and then saluting?"

I expect him to laugh, but he doesn't. He keeps that same smirk on his face that I find so incredibly sexy and leans down close to my ear. "'Yes, sir' will do just fine."

I gasp inwardly as Matt walks by winking once more, this time very knowingly. I lose the battle with crossing my legs. It's instinctive. "What are you doing to me?" I whisper.

"Holy fuck, am I gonna have fun with you. Walk in front of me."

I glance at the sizable bulk in his jeans and instantly feel the need to follow instructions. That's mine. No one else gets to see it. I turn slowly and walk in front of him, choosing a seat near Lyric because I know he'll want to be around Jaxon before he leaves. He leans over me and puts our plates on the outside table next to the chair. I put our drinks down. He sits down and pulls me into his lap. I'm so shocked, I completely forget how to breathe.

I'm very obviously not the only one, either. Many eyes are curiously on us, but Josh doesn't say a single word. He simply hands me my plate and starts eating from his as soon as I take it. I don't know whether to melt and enjoy where I am, or run.

After a long, very uncomfortable pause, everyone must realize Josh isn't going to say anything, so they resume with their conversations. Before I know it, the sun is setting hours later, and people are getting ready to head back to their own homes. It may have been a warm Spring day, but the nights are still pretty cold. Josh hugs Jaxon and tells him he'll see him in a few days, and it's then that the dread falls over me like a dark blanket.

Alec gives me a hug. "Do what you need to do to be okay for the next few days. Tyler will be with me, so stay with Rosie." His voice is low. I hear the words, but they do little to comfort me. When he lets me go, he gives me an encouraging smile before looking at Josh. "Want me to secure a second plane?"

He shakes his. "I'll take Alex's. He doesn't need it for a couple weeks. Chase is getting his ready for you and your guys. We should be good." Josh sits down on the arm of the couch as Alec nods. "Okay. See you there."

I watch my brother saunter out the door. It takes me a few moments to gain enough courage to turn towards Josh. When I do, I'm so close to crying, and I don't even know why. Maybe I'm about to get my period or something. Stupid rollercoaster of emotions.

"Baby, come here." Josh holds out his hand, and I nearly run to him, but give myself at least some dignity.

As soon as his large hand closes around mine, the show is over. The curtains close, and I'm a crying mess. Unbecoming of a woman who wants to be with a man like him. I'm supposed to be strong. Hold back emotion. Be some type of leader, like Ariana is with Ryan. I'm sure she never breaks down in tears at the drop of a button. Maybe I'm the unworthy one here.

Josh, however, does what he does best. He holds me close while I fall apart and picks up each broken piece, gently putting me back together. Everything I should know how to do for him, he does with such grace and class. Not even a second thought or hesitation. He simply knows all I need and does it without question.

I grip his shirt. "I'm sorry. I don't know why I'm reacting like this," I whisper into his neck.

"Because it's all different this time," he rumbles against my neck. His hands rub slowly and soothingly up and down my back. "This time, you're not just watching your unattainable crush head out for yet another mission. This time, it's your boyfriend. It's new. It's still not completely sunk in yet, but we are a couple after all of these years of dancing around it. Neither of us can deny it's happening. And while we're trying to navigate it all, it's not the same. Before, it was all thoughts in your head. Not easy to let me go, but easier to play off. Now, it's real. I'm not a crush."

"So, I'm not crazy?" I shift a little and slide my arms up his chest and over his shoulders so I can hug him just as tightly as he is me.

He chuckles. "Well, I didn't say that. You're definitely crazy. Having any kind of feelings for me that's more than disdain or hatred definitely puts you in the 'in need of men in white coats' category." He grins against my neck.

I can't help but laugh, but I grip him even tighter. "I'll be crazy then. I'm okay with it."

"Good. Because I think we're both in for a hell of a ride. Twists. Turns. Bumps. Bruises. You think you can handle all that?"

"Does it mean I get to keep you? Like Casper got to keep Kat? Are we in this forever?"

He wraps his arms around me and pulls me as close as he can. "I'm ready for the fight."

I bury my face in his shoulder and breathe him in. Tough. Spicy. Fresh. Like the ocean after a storm. "Me too."

It's a whisper that only he can hear, but it's a promise. The longer the words hang between us, the more I feel our bond strengthening.

Like the spoken words are weaving themselves into the rope that binds us together.

Chapter Nine

☙ Josh ☙

(Two Weeks Later)

"I know, baby. I don't know what to tell you, though." I squeeze Dallas' hand as we walk near the lake bordering our compound. "There's just nothing there."

I just got off the plane and came straight home. Dallas was waiting for me. Instead of telling her at the house, I thought we'd take a walk. I know she hasn't been out much the past couple weeks. Given our text conversations and brief phone calls, it's obvious how nervous she's been for Dylan. Her and Rosie have been holed up together, which gave me some peace that she wasn't alone.

Dallas sighs. "The call, though. I can't stop replaying it. Rosie and I have talked so much about it. She was really scared, Josh."

I nod in understanding. "I can only work with what I have, though. And what I have is absolutely nothing. I'll be the first to admit that it's quiet down there. Too quiet, and I'm on high alert because of it. But all I can do is go off what happens next. Because everything up until right now is nothing."

She shakes her head as she thinks. "There has to be something. I'm not questioning you or anything, but is there any possible way that something got overlooked? Anything at all. Maybe a rat walking opposite other rats."

I laugh because it's adorable, but she's grasping at straws. "I promise. I didn't leave any stone unturned. As fucked up as it is, there's nothing for me to go on. Even my conversation with Dylan at Xavier's house led to nothing. She knows no more than what she told you. Yes, that's scary, and definitely suspicious, but since then, nothing more has turned up. Her dad isn't acting any differently or suspiciously. He's even excited about her upcoming graduation. He's been helping her plan a huge graduation party. He's excited she chose to come here for college."

"Wait." She looks up at me. "No. That's not right. He wants her to go to the University of Texas."

I nod. "Mmhmm. I know. I also asked her about that, and he's the one who suggested she apply for Chicago. She told him she already had and got accepted with several different scholarships, and he threw her a congratulatory party. I got suspicious with that and made the decision just based on that to leave some people down there, but since that phone call, Dylan really doesn't see any reason for alarm."

"Hmm… She has seemed pretty happy lately. She even mentioned she was excited to move here in a couple of months."

I rub my thumb soothingly over the back of her hand, which mine engulfs. "My professional opinion says observe."

She giggles, and I smile. I love that sound. "Your professional mafia boss opinion?"

"Shh! Don't say that so loud. Someone could hear you and ruin my rep as a by the book businessman," I tease.

She giggles again, but lowers her voice as she looks up at me through her lashes. Kryptonite. "By the book of Josh, you mean?" She attempts to dart away, but she must've forgotten her hand is firmly in mine. She gets as far as I let her before I'm tugging her back.

She gasps when she hits my chest, hard, but I don't so much as move. I wrap her in my arms and lift her off her feet. That beautifully, melodic tone comes from her throat again, and I'm gone. She wraps her arms around my shoulders and legs around my waist so naturally that I forget completely it wasn't always like this with us.

"I missed you, " I tell her truthfully. "Never wanted to admit it, but I always have. Every time you're not near me, I miss you."

That pretty blush creeps in her cheeks, and she smiles softly. "Sometimes, I wish you would've told me that. It would've helped during times you were gone, and when you were being a jerk."

I give her a half-smile, but inside, I know I'm capable of letting it happen again. I have a lot of demons I haven't fully coped with yet. "I had my moments, didn't I?"

She nods as she runs her fingers through my hair. "But you always seem to come out of it."

I'm usually the one to initiate kisses, but this time, she leans in and brushes her lips over mine. Maybe it's a moment of weakness on her part, or perhaps it's her exploring. Either way, I've never been so happy to have her do it because it means she's becoming more confident in taking what she needs. The first rule of a dominant man is to empower his woman.

I press my lips more firmly against hers and wait for her to respond. When she matches my pressure, I coax her mouth open with just a touch of my tongue. She closes her eyes and submits to the kiss completely. My jeans get tighter and nearly bust when she softly moans.

"Hey, lovebirds!" Lyric yells from the backyard of the guest house with a giggle. "Jaxon is running towards you!"

I spot him out of the corner of my eye and slowly break the kiss. I let her down gently with a grin as she laughs. The second Jaxon reaches me, I swoop him in my arms and lift him high above my head. No sound comes out, but he spreads his arms wide with a huge grin on his face. Understanding he wants to fly, I turn him in the air so he's facing forward and start jogging with him towards the guest house.

Dallas laughs behind me while I move back and forth across the grass like a maniac. "Dip low! There's a plane coming right at you!" I dip him low then swoop him high again. "And one more!" I move him to the side. "To the other!" I fly him to the other side. "We're almost there! Get ready to land!" He puts his arms above his head and grips something like a throttle. He pulls back on it, and I dip him low so he's just above the ground and stop him right at Lyric's feet. "Phew!" I pick him up and settle him on my hip. "Nice flying, Ace."

He shakes his head and points to my t-shirt. He tugs the sleeve and looks at me.

I raise an eyebrow. "Sleeve?"

He shakes his head again and just points to it.

"Uh… red?" I guess. My shirt is red.

He nods, and I grin. He then looks around. He must not see what he wants, so he spreads his arms again and moves back and forth like he's flying.

"You want to fly again?"

He shakes his head and looks to Lyric for help, but she looks just as confused as I am. Dallas steps forward a little to get a better look just as Jaxon points to my shirt once more. Just the picture on the front this time.. It's of an old style airplane. One of the very first planes that would sit one person and has little protection against the weather. A Lockheed Vega 5B. There are no words on the shirt, but the plane is red, lighter than the dark red color of the fabric itself, though still red.

"Plane? Red plane?"

He thinks for a moment, but shakes his head again. He looks frustrated then points to the plane again, this time poking his finger into it and my chest.

"Bar…on…?" Dallas asks. "Red Baron?"

Jaxon's eyes light up, and he nods victoriously as he points to himself.

I laugh. "Red Baron. You want to be called Red Baron?"

He nods even more enthusiastically.

Lyric smiles. "That actually makes sense. Layne was watching Snoopy the other day, and there was a part where Snoopy was flying his doghouse and being chased by the Red Baron. He was completely fascinated by it."

"Looks like we know what he's getting for his birthday." I grin down at both Lyric and Dallas.

Dallas bounces in place, and I fight the groan rising when I see her tits bouncing in that sexy black tank top. "Can I shop with Lyric for it? There's so much stuff we could get!"

I laugh. "If Lyric is down with it, have at it. I'll even give you my credit card."

"Yes!" She looks happily at Lyric, who I can tell is already plotting. "We have to do this. I have so many ideas!"

69

"It's happening. It's so happening. No expense is too much!" Lyric teases me.

I laugh because I know damn well she'll try to pay for it all herself. What she doesn't know is my girl won't let that happen. She knows Lyric a little bit too well.

"I'm going to leave her in your capable hands," I whisper to Dallas as I kiss her forehead sweetly. I reach in my wallet and pull out my credit card. "Make sure she doesn't try to purchase everything on her own, and make sure you're purchasing the more expensive stuff."

She smiles up at me as I turn and kiss Jaxon on the head. "You and me have a day planned for tomorrow, right? Maybe we can go fly in a helicopter." I widen my eyes like I just came up with the greatest idea ever.

He tilts his head. It's a sign he has no idea what a helicopter is, but he's grinning and copying my own wide eyes, so I know he's excited just by the word fly. I put my wallet back in my pocket.

"Are you sure that's safe?" Lyric asks quietly as I hand Jaxon back to her.

"Yes. I was almost flying by myself at his age. Look how I turned out." I grin with a wink.

"Yeah, not comforting," she teases as she shakes her head.

"I'll be careful. Promise." I drop an arm over Dallas' shoulders and hug her tight to my side. "So, I know we just got in a little while ago. There's been no real progress made with our guy from the -" I glance at Jaxon and don't finish the sentence. I don't want to say ship. He has a serious aversion to them. "I didn't have time to deal with it before we left, so I'm heading there right now. I had them bring him to the -" I cut myself off again. I can't exactly say my own little house of torture. "Uh... the house. Mind if Dallas hangs out and helps with the shopping?"

"Is the sky blue?" Lyric asks with a giant smile. "No. I don't mind at all." She takes Dallas' hand and pulls her away from me. "Be safe! Don't have too much fun!"

I laugh and catch the kiss Dallas blows my way. I make a show of putting it in my pocket as I turn to walk towards our interrogation house. Dallas' laugh fills the air and follows me, keeping me level headed enough to not rip this guy's head off and spit down his neck.

I storm across the compound, and the second I arrive at our interrogation house, the anger and frustration I'd been able to keep at bay, bubbles to the surface. I know I've been being jerked around by this guy for over a month. He's been careful, but he's gotten comfortable and too trusting of the devil. Unfortunately for him, I'm done fucking playing.

I stop at the door and glare up at the one-sided glass that holds the control room behind it as I place my palm on the scan box. Seconds later, I'm asked to enter my code. My eyes never leave that glass. No one knows it, except those who have direct access to this room, like I do, that there are multiple levels of security that needs to be gone through in order to get in. One of them is a body scan, which is happening right now. The other is that guards need to visually verify the person entering the room and make physical note of it, not just through the computer system. I don't take chances. I'm a lot like Ryan. I have backups for backups, and even more backups for those.

"Good afternoon, sir," a voice says over the speaker. "Please look at the eye pad, eyes wide."

I do as I'm told with a low growl. I love the security measures. I don't love the time. "How many guards?"

"Two sir."

"Get Gavin over here."

"Yes, sir. You're good, sir. Just enter your personal code."

I enter a second code. Another security measure is that we have two different codes. One accesses the system. The second accesses the room. As soon as the green access light shows, the door clicks open. A little more violently than necessary, I throw the door open and slam it shut behind me. It makes the room shake just a little, but it's enough to get this asshole puckering in fear.

Good. He should be afraid. Terrified, even.

"Josh! Shit! I'm glad you're here! Get me the fuck out of here, man!"

I watch the fear slowly morph into relief the second he sees a familiar face. I had him picked up before I left for Texas, but I had my guards dressed completely in black and bust in like the fucking FBI's takedown team.

I flick my eyes towards the guards, who are doing their best to hide their smiles and laughs. I do the same. The smile that wants to hit my lips doesn't even get the opportunity to flicker. This guy doesn't take any of the hints, though.

"When did they take you?" I ask, letting my voice project the power and dominance I have over him. He has no idea I already know the answer.

"Man, I don't even know! A couple weeks ago? They won't let me out of this place!"

I glance around like I don't have a clue what's in this place. "Looks pretty clean. There's a bed. Food. Water." I lean a little to my side. "Well, look at that. Even a bathroom."

"With bars on the window, man! You can't get out no matter what you do! The damn glass even zaps!"

"Electric shock." I nod. "Impressive." I cross my arms over my chest. "Maybe I'll get one just like it some day." I look at the guards with a cocky grin. "Must be nice having a place like this to keep your prisoners in, huh?" I gesture with my head towards the door. "I just use the basement. A lot darker. Cold. More dank."

"Oh, you want cold?" one of the guards says with a huge grin catching onto my game real quickly. "Let me just help you out." He uses the watch on his wrist to send a message to control.

I know he's pushed the temp control button that tells them to drop it to freezing, but I'm not letting my prisoner in on that too quickly. There's no fun in that.

Instantly, I can feel the temp shift as soon as the air kicks on. "Damn, check that out? You just push a button, and the house does whatever you ask?"

"That's not even the best part. We can turn the heat up, too. Make him sweat," the other guard says. "But the best part, and my personal favorite, is this." He pushes another button. I grin when the lights dim and watch in amusement when hologram demons appear amidst the suddenly red lights.

"It's like a fucking disco in here!" I say as the holograms dance along the walls. It's when one of them suddenly pops off the wall and flies at us screaming, that my little prisoner loses his mind.

"Shit!" he screams. Several other holograms, like zombies and black-eyed ghosts do exactly the same thing. They fly off the walls and all scream directly at him in front of his face. "Ah!" He rears back and falls off his chair as he screams hysterically. He kicks and slaps at the demons and creatures horrifying him. The guards lose it, unable to withstand my own personal subtle humor. The holograms were completely my idea. I implemented them not long ago. This is the first time we've used them against anyone.

One of the two shuts my little torture device off while they compose themselves. I keep a completely straight face and lean down slightly to help the scared shitless prisoner up and back to a seated position in the metal chair he fell over in.

"Get me out of here, Josh! Fuck! Why are you alone? Where's your backup?" He looks behind me as he tries to dart for the door.

"Hold on, now. Come on. They're coming. We don't just walk into a place without a damn plan." I grip his shoulders and push him back down in the chair. "Sit."

His eyes dart between me and the two guards, but I can see he still trusts me. I chuckle darkly as I turn away once more. "What else does that do?"

"Check this out." One of the guards presses a command. Seconds later, the house is a disco room complete with opera music that's ear piercing.

"Okay, fuck!" I cover my ears in mock horror knowing that was Dallas' idea completely.

She's been coming up with ideas to make this house a true house of horrors ever since she learned just a fraction of the things Jaxon went through. We really know nothing, but her imagination has been running just as wild as Lyric's. This was one of her top ideas.

Both guards laugh as they shut it down just as Gavin comes in. "Thank the diabolical Lucifer himself for shutting that shit down. When the hell did we get that?" Gavin rubs his ear like he's trying to get something out of it.

"Recently. You can thank Dallas. And I'm sure Lyric had a hand in that one. They aren't really the biggest fans of the things that happened to Jaxon."

"Remind me never to cross either of them." Gavin grins.

"Wait…" Our prisoner looks between the two of us and at the guards. "Why… are… the guards…?" He trails off as realization suddenly hits him. We all watch him register shock, then awe, then defeat.

But not enough. He's not there yet.

My suspicions are confirmed when his gaze darkens. It makes me grin from ear to ear. "You figured it out?" I don't wait for an answer. "They work for me. Obviously. And you're a guest in my interrogation house, Morpheus. The game is over. I want answers, and I want them now."

"I don't know what you're talking about. I told you everything," Morpheus mumbles.

"See, I hate liars, Morpheus. I really do." I lean down at his side with one hand on his shoulder and the other on the metal table in front of him. "And I know you're lying to me. You've been playing a dangerous game thinking I'm caught up in your web. But guess what? Where there's a small spider, there's always a larger one lurking behind it. That's me. And I have you caught in my own web. You have two choices. Tell me all you know right now, or I'll pump it out of you. Drop... by... drop. And in good faith, I'll even tell you that I know you made contact with someone a couple of weeks ago. Someone you told me you needed to get away from. That as soon as he knew you'd betrayed him, your life was over. So, tell me Morpheus. Are we gonna keep playing this game? Or are you gonna start being a good boy?"

He swallows. Hard. I don't take my eyes off him. Gavin has moved to his other side. He's just out of Morpheus's reach, but close enough to stop him from the very stupid thing he's about to do. The two guards' playful demeanor is over. They've made their way just behind Gavin. I know exactly what his next move is going to be.

The second he stands and turns towards me, I'm already stepping out of the way. He screams at me like a toddler who didn't get the toy he wanted at the store and stretches his arms out, his hands attempting to grab my neck.

Not that he would've had a chance against me, but I grin when Gavin has him in his grip and pulls him back towards him with such force, Morpheus is nearly wiped off his feet. Gavin's arm is around Morpheus' neck in less time than it takes him to blink. Before he even knows what's happening, Gavin has complete control over him.

"Go to sleep now. Night, night," Gavin says, tightening his grip. "There we go. Don't fight it." Morpheus's eyes close slowly. His body drops further and further until he's completely limp. Gavin, just to make sure, holds on a few seconds later before moving him against the wall where we have shackles attached. He drops him.

"Take care of him," I command. "I'm leaving him a week. Make his life fucking hell. Give him enough water and bread to keep him alive." I grin sinisterly. "Actually. Fuck the food. If Jesus can survive for forty days and nights on nothing but a few sips of water and God, surely this asshole can, right? Let's see who he's praying for in seven days. Me, or the one who so many believe will save them from evil."

"Diabolical, but yes, sir." He starts helping the other guard shackle Morpheus. When they're finished, he looks at me while he stands. "Maybe we should just do the forty days thing. You know. Prove the theory."

"Or disprove it," Gavin says with a shrug.

I laugh. "I like it. But I don't want to waste another month on this fucker. I think after a week, he'll break. And if he doesn't, we'll break him. Be hard on him. No food. Give him one sip of water every twelve hours. Keep the room at a hundred and ten during the day. Drop it to fifty at night. Keep him on the floor. If he needs the bathroom, give him a bucket. No guards in here. Except to give him the sip of water and empty the bucket. At the most random times, like when he feels relaxed, turn the holograms on or just the whispering voice and demonic laughter. No bathing. Let him sit in the same clothes the entire time."

"Yes, sir."

We all leave the room. Gavin chuckles as he closes the door behind us. "Good thing we have strong stomachs because it's gonna reek in there."

"The sense of smell is usually the first thing that ends up making people break. The second thing is a person's hunger. The third is the mind. Do all three of those things at the same time, and the chances of him resisting for long are slim."

I walk with him back towards our houses. He chuckles. "What do we do with him after?"

"After hearing his call to 'Captain'?" It's my turn to shrug. "Kill him."

Chapter Ten

☙ Dallas ❧

"This year needs to be done with," I grumble as I set my book down and rub my eyes. "I'm not capable of doing any more midterms that are half of my entire grade."

"Just wait until finals," Josh says with a chuckle.

I know he's joking, but I completely deflate. "I don't understand. If they expect these giant projects to be so much of our grade, and we have two of them, one for midterms and one for finals, why the hell do we even have homework, lessons, quizzes, tests, book reviews, essays, or anything else throughout the year? They don't count. Midterms are fifty percent. Finals are fifty percent." I drop my head in my hands, close to tears. "I'm exhausted."

I can't see him, but I hear Josh close the book he was reading and set it down. Moments later, his hand is on my back, soothing me. He rubs it up and down my back a few times before pulling me into him and wrapping his arm around me. I sink into him, barely keeping the tears at bay.

"How about we call Lyric and have her and her family come over to babysit for us? I think I still owe you a first date."

I keep my eyes closed and burrow closer. "I never thought I'd utter these words, but can we take a raincheck? I'm so tired."

"Then how about you let me take your mind off all of this for a couple of hours? Jaxon is asleep. We could do a movie. I'll make all your favorite snacks. We can watch one of your favorite horrors or thrillers. And after, I'll take you to bed and give you the best massage you've ever had."

That makes me smile. "Only if said snacks include extra buttery and salty popcorn with pieces of Heath candy bars in it and Mountain Dew for the drink."

He laughs heartily, and I melt. "Room for negotiation on the Dew so late at night?"

I shake my head. "Not a chance. I'm eighteen. I live off Mountain Dew, coffee, energy drinks, and all things sugar at this point in my life."

"Hmm. Well, I'll concede to the Mountain Dew tonight. I'll allow coffee. Energy drinks are out, and all things sugar are definitely being limited and discussed."

I open my eyes, furrow my brows, and look up at him. "What does that mean?"

"You've watched *Fifty Shades of Gray*."

"Uh. Yeah. And you know how much I hate that movie. I couldn't even watch the other two, and I refuse to read the books."

"Well, there are things about that movie that you should probably pay attention to if you want a relationship with me."

I narrow my eyes. "If you think you're about to get me to sign a contract and be whatever Ana was to Christian, I'm not really sure how I'll react, but having Alec beat you up might be included in the plans."

Josh grins and laughs as he shakes his head. "No. He was controlling and a fucking psycho. He wasn't a good representation of a truly dominant man. He came off like an asshole and more a sadist than I think the author of that book truly intended him to be. I get where she was going with it. I never read the books, so I don't know if she fucked up or Hollywood did, or if it was both. What I do know, though, is that while there are some things about that movie that make sense, that's not what a relationship between a dominant man and a submissive woman is all about."

I tilt my head and shift so I'm sitting facing him with my legs folded over each other in front of me. "Tell me. I mean, I've kind of done a little research, but I want to know more. I want to understand what you mean."

He sighs and nods. "I'll be honest. Lyric warned me a couple of years ago that this conversation would come." He taps my legs. I uncross them and settle with them over his lap. He drapes one arm over my thighs and rubs his thumb slowly in circles over my hip. The other arm slides around my waist and pulls me closer to him. "What did you research? And why?"

I purse my lips. "I guess I was just curious. Lyric mentioned something about you being a real Alpha male and dominant. I didn't really know what that meant. She explained a little bit. Like it wasn't BDSM. I didn't know what that meant either, honestly. That's why I watched *Fifty Shades* in the first place, though. She said it was everything you're not. And the way Ana was portrayed was everything a submissive woman isn't. The research I did do, though, was really not conclusive." I look down. "It scared me, actually."

Josh squeezes my thigh lightly. "That's because when people think submissive and dominant, they automatically think sex. Sex isn't all that it is. Being tied up, whipped, spanked with a paddle, ball gagged, barking like a dog, and whatever else they dream up isn't what a relationship is with a dominant and submissive. BDSM isn't the same. What you found was all related to BDSM." He reaches up and tangles his fingers in my hair.

"I still don't exactly understand, but I'm glad."

He kisses my cheek. "Maybe this will help. When you came over today, what was happening?"

"Um. I guess I was feeling pretty chaotic. I had so much stuff to get done, and I can't do it at home. It's just so loud sometimes. I need quiet. And the construction is annoying."

"Mmhmm. You hadn't eaten." He runs his fingers through my hair. "You were telling me about all of this stuff you had to do and how it didn't feel at all like it mattered. What did I do?"

I smile softly. "You had me play a game with Jaxon while you started dinner. Then, you had me go take a warm shower and change into something more comfortable than my uniform."

"Then, we ate dinner. We got Jaxon settled with that movie he's been wanting to see. The Red Baron one with Snoopy."

"And then we made a list," I say softly.

"And you've been checking off things on that list for the past few hours because it brought you order to the chaos."

I nod. "It's been amazing."

"Have you noticed whenever you need order to the chaos, you come to me? Or when you need help with decisions of any kind, you come to me? When you need to feel safe, or when you need something steady, it's always me you come to. Or Alec. I've seen you do all of that with him, too. Also with some of the guys in VV that he's close to. You've done it with Ryan. I've even seen you do it around Matt and DJ. You trust dominant people to guide you while still making you feel like a normal human being, which you are. You don't go to people you feel will judge you. You're not comfortable around people you feel can't protect you or lead you. While you're capable of standing on your own two feet and making your own decisions, which I've also seen you do, sometimes, you feel like you're falling or that you're out of control. That's when you tend to move towards people who can be the guidance you need and give you back that sense of control."

I ponder his words for several moments before nodding. "I think I understand."

"Being with a man who is dominant and the Alpha male, as they say, doesn't mean that man is here to control every aspect of your life. People will have you believe that dominant men are toxic. Alpha males are toxic. They're bad for the world. They think with their muscles and brawn. Not their heads. They don't have a brain. They have too much testosterone. They're controlling and abusers. They want their women to be barefoot and pregnant while slaving all day in a kitchen and cleaning the entire house. Her place isn't outside the four walls of his castle. She has no voice. No one around them takes a stand because they'll crush them. They're cocky. Arrogant. They're unsupportive of everyone else and only surround themselves with other Alpha males. Do you feel like that describes me?"

"Oh my God, no!" I look at him in shock. "You're completely opposite."

"And do you view yourself as a weak woman who will always submit to one of those Alpha males? Those dominant men who would trample all over anyone they view as beneath them? A woman who is meant to stay at home and bear children while minding the household?"

I wrinkle my nose. "No. I mean, I like being home, but that's ridiculous."

"I know women can also be dominant, but in this case I'm using a man as the example." He looks down at me as I nod. I'm glad he said that because that was going to be one of my questions.

"A true dominant man will do all he can to make his woman and those around him stronger and more confident in themselves. He's protective. He's even possessive of what's his. While those can be good or bad qualities, they are something that he's never going to change because they're a large part of who he is. His job is to protect. Defend. Show those he loves that they are his. And while they belong to him, he's never going to clip their wings and stop them from flying. He's going to be the goddamn wind that keeps them in flight. And if they crash, he's going to be the one who catches them. He's going to be the one who cares about everything they do. Be their voice when they can't talk. Their strength when they feel like they don't have any. Help them eat healthy. Sleep. He's not going to some asshole who controls everything they put in their mouths, but things like energy drinks and empty sugars? Not a chance. Health covers physical, mental, and emotional well-being. He's going to be the person who helps to make sure that's happening."

"But isn't that a form of control?"

"No. It's a form of guidance. I can't stop you from drinking an energy drink. Will I like it? No. Will I tell you I don't like it? Yes. But I'm not going to pull a Christian and put shit like that in a contract, make you sign it, and then abide by it and punish you if you don't. That's fucked up. You'll know I'm disappointed, and being who you are, that's going to weigh on you. You know they're unhealthy, and putting them in your body will cause nothing but a sugar crash, high anxiety, and physical issues, potentially even a heart attack."

My eyes widen, and I nod again with a blush as I look down in shame, suddenly completely understanding. "Sorry. That does happen a lot. The sugar crash…"

"I know." He cups my chin and tilts my head up. "When I mentioned *Fifty Shades*, it was because there are some things in there that I kind of do. Like rules. Nothing ridiculous, but I have two and they come with punishments."

I furrow my brows. "Rules...? Like, I can't be out past a certain time?"

He smiles a half-smile. "No. It all goes back to what I said about real dominants lifting their partners up and helping their confidence and everything else so they can be the best version of themselves. Rule one. You will not disrespect yourself. I won't allow you to call yourself stupid or a failure. I won't allow you to talk down about yourself by saying things like you look like shit or hate your body. Rule two is you won't disrespect me or anyone else. I've only seen you do one of those things when you shoved me in my office. I've spent my entire life disrespecting myself, being disrespected, being beaten down, shoved around. I've seen others be disrespectful to themselves. I've seen others disrespect each other and push each other around. I don't expect you'll ever push me like that again."

"I understand. I'm really sorry I pushed you. I felt bad about that right after."

"I know." He smiles as he lets his hand trail down my arm, leaving goosebumps in its wake and making me shiver as I melt into his gaze. "I know you're sorry. And I know it was in the heat of the moment. I know you won't do it again. But if you do or if I catch you talking down about yourself or others..." His hand drops to my hip, and he squeezes it, making me jump a little. "You get five spankings, but I promise you'll enjoy every single one of them and everything that comes after."

The heat starts somewhere between my thighs and rushes to my face. I'm certain my entire body is blushing. I have to take a deep breath to keep from panting. "I saw a video," I whisper. I can't meet his eyes.

Josh rumbles from deep within, succeeding in making my body react in embarrassing ways. "You're not telling me you watched porn, are you? My innocent girl?"

I turn my head and hide in his shoulder. I don't say anything simply because I can't. The next thing I know, he's standing and tossing me over his shoulder. "Josh!" I squeak.

He swats my ass, making me jerk into him but loving the sting his hand leaves behind. "Shh. You'll wake Jaxon."

I giggle but put a hand over my mouth to muffle it. Once we get to the kitchen, he sets me on the counter. He starts making popcorn and crunches up a Heath candy bar to put into it. I love that he keeps a couple around for me. Josh is a very healthy person. He works out and eats right.

He's mindful of what goes into his body, but he doesn't starve himself and isn't afraid to put food in his mouth. He snacks sometimes, but never overdoes anything. His motto when it comes to all of that is everything in moderation.

So, I'm not surprised when he indulges in the movie night junk food with me, but I love even more that he not only allows the soda, but takes one for himself. And as we watch *The Exorcist* followed by *The Witch*, I find myself relaxing more and more into him. His hand caresses my arm. He leaves light kisses randomly on top of my head. And when it's time for bed, he leads me by the hand to his bedroom instead of the one I've claimed as mine.

I've fallen asleep with him before, but I've always either woken up in my own bedroom or alone in his bed or on the couch, usually without him since he always wakes before I do. I'm not sure where I'll end up this time, but I'm so content that I don't care. At least I get him for a little while...

"Mmm... Josh...?" I mumble softly when I feel the bed move. He doesn't answer, but my eyes fly open when I hear him groan. He lurches and rolls to his side, curling into the fetal position and covering his head. "Josh!" I reach for him, touching his shoulder with wide eyes.

"No!" he yells so loudly I'm sure everyone in the compound can hear him and is going to come running.

I jump to my knees as his body tenses. I recognize what's happening. He's having a night terror. I've heard that waking a person having one isn't the best idea, so I pull my hand back and try to think of what I can do for him.

"Josh?" I ask as calmly as I can. "Josh, I'm here. It's okay."

He's trembling. I watch his body jerk and him curl into himself more and more. It's like he's being punched or hit and is reacting to them. I hate that if that's what he's dreaming, he can also feel it. That's the only reason I can think of that his body would be doing what it is.

"Get off me!" he screams. He's facing away from me and is on the edge of the bed, but he punches out, his fist hitting the nightstand. The alarm clock and his lamp go flying. "Get the fuck off me!"

And just like that, he's in a fight for his life. He rolls onto his back and starts kicking and punching the air. I leap backwards off the bed to avoid being inadvertently hit. He flails, turning from side to side.

"Get off!"

Tears are streaming down my face. I try to brush them away, but they flow even faster. "Josh, I'm here, baby. I'm right here." I choke back the sobs, trying to be strong for him. My eyes snap to the door just as Josh flings open his nightstand drawer. There's a nightlight in the hall Josh put in just in case Jaxon needed him during the night. The dim light peeks through the door.

"Daddy?" Jaxon's soft voice splits the air. Considering that's the first thing he's said since we've had him, it sounds like an atomic bomb.

Josh points something. I notice the glint of something shiny and start running. "Jaxon!" I scream. "Josh! It's Jaxon! It's Jaxon!" I know I'm not being calm. I'm being hysterical, and it probably doesn't help him at all.

"Da-" Jaxon cuts himself off as soon as I reach him. My arms are around him in a flash, and I'm lifting him in my arms as I run.

"I said get away from me!" Josh screeches.

I don't know if he's gotten up. I don't know if he's giving chase, but I run to my bedroom and slam the door behind us. I lock it and quickly take the phone I left on my charger last night. I run to the bathroom and lock the door as Jaxon, knowing something is wrong, starts crying hysterically.

"Shh… It's okay, sweet boy. It's okay," I whisper to him as I bounce him soothingly on my knee once I sit down on the edge of the jacuzzi tub. "It's okay, baby. I promise. Daddy is just having a bad dream." I quickly dial Alex's number. He's the only person I can think of right now who can help. "Please, please pick up. Please. Please, Alex. Please pick up."

So many thoughts are rushing through my head right now. I pray to anyone listening, God, Angels, Demons, Lucifer, anyone who can hear me to please not let me hear a gunshot. Please just keep letting him scream. At least I know he's safe that way.

"Yeah?" Alex grumbles into the phone. I don't blame him. It's three in the morning. I'm sure he didn't even look at his phone to see who it was.

"Alex!" I nearly scream into the receiver. By the grace of who knows, the scream is more of a whisper. Jaxon is still wailing. I keep bouncing him soothingly.

"Dallas?"

"Alex! Please, please get here! Now!" I'm still scream whispering.

"Dallas? What the fuck is going on? I'm throwing on jeans. Is Jaxon crying?"

"Yes! Alex, Josh is having a night terror. It's bad! He's gotta be in a fight for his life. He grabbed his gun!"

"Oh fuck. Okay. Okay. Where are you? I'm coming."

"We're in my room in the bathroom. I locked the door. He's still screaming at them to leave him alone!"

"Did you hear a gunshot?"

"No! But I'm scared, Alex. I'm scared I'm going to hear it! He really believes he's being hurt! He looked like he was taking hits and kicks. He punched out and hit the nightstand. He didn't even wake up! And then, it was almost like he got away and got his gun. Jaxon came in at the same time and actually said 'Daddy'! And now he's so scared, he's crying hysterically. I'm trying so hard to calm him!"

"I'm coming, honey. I'm almost there." I can hear him running. He doesn't sound out of breath, but I know he's running.

"He pointed the gun at Jaxon, Alex. I think he thought he was someone in his dream or something."

"I'm here, honey. Stay where you are. Calm Jaxon down. Call Lyric. Matt or DJ need to come get him. Call Alec to come get you. Don't argue. Just do it."

"Yes, sir." I nod. I hang up the phone and immediately call Lyric. I can hear Alex pounding up the stairs.

"Hello...?" Lyric answers groggily.

"Have DJ or Matt come get Jaxon. It's an emergency. Josh is having a night terror. I can't explain right now, but someone needs to come get Jaxon now." I don't give her a chance to respond. I'm about to break down. I call Alec and hug Jaxon closer and tighter. His sobs are slowly subsiding, but silent tears are streaming down his face, just like they are mine.

"Dallas? What's going on? You okay?" Alec answers. I can hear in his voice that he's just woken up or is just going to sleep.

"No..." I choke on a sob and take a deep breath. "Come get me. Josh..." I trail off, not being able to say more. I bury my face in Jaxon's neck.

"I'm on my way. What happened?"

"He's... h-having a n-ight t-terror."

"Oh hell. I'm coming, honey. I'm on my way."

I hang up with a nod and hug Jaxon. I sway gently with him whispering 'it's going to be okay' over and over again.

But I don't know if I'm saying the words for his sake...

... or mine.

Chapter Eleven

☙ Josh ☙

(One Week Later)

I've been leaning against the metal table in the center of the interrogation house with arms folded over my chest for most of the morning. Turns out Morpheus passed out sometime during the night and didn't wake up. I poured a bucket of cold water over him. He woke up, but he didn't look healthy enough to answer the questions I need him to. Dr. Freeman, the incredible soul he is, gave him just enough food and water to perk him up enough for me to continue what's about to be some tortuous fun. He won't survive it, but at least the aggression I've pent up over this past week will be released.

It won't be enough.

There's only one thing, one person who can truly talk me down. And after what happened, I don't trust myself anywhere near her. May whatever God the next people who end up in this house pray to really listen to them. Because I won't. No mercy. I never got any. Why the fuck should people who hurt innocent people or take innocent lives get it when all of those innocents were never shown any? I'll never let what happened to me happen to another soul. I'll stop the whole world from turning into a monster if it kills me.

"You ready to talk to me now?" I ask, my voice dangerous. He's just finished the last of his water.

"Fuck you."

I roll my eyes. "I get that offer a lot. I have no issues with the way you swing, but you don't have the right parts for me."

"Your girl, then. I'm sure Cap would have lots of fun with her. Right before he throws her off the ship in the rough waters like he did to that bitch nurse he hired to deal with your spawn."

His words make my blood freeze. It'll be a cold day in hell before anyone gets their hands on my girl. "He'll die trying. And I won't blink a fucking eye." I sit on the table and lean forward slightly. He's still shackled to the wall where he's been for the past week. "But we're getting somewhere. It's just us. Tell me about this nurse."

"No."

"Do you really think you're in a position to fuck with me?"

"Well, you need information. I have what you need. You have to negotiate to get it out of me. So, give me another bag of Cheetos."

"No. You seem to forget who holds the power here." I look around the room. "There are no guards. None of my guys are. There's no one to hold me back from carving out your spleen and feeding it to you, and then choking you with your large intestine. Not a damn person to hold me back. I can either make your death quick, or painful as fuck. Your decision. Tell me about this nurse."

He looks like he's at least contemplating his fate, but his decision is very wrong. "You won't do shit. You want the information."

"You're right. I do. And I have several means at my disposal to make you give it to me." I reach down and take a knife out of the pocket of my black BDUs. "I'll start with the spleen." I jump off the table as I ready my knife. It's a large switchblade. "I keep this extremely sharp. Sharper than a scalpel. Should be enough to carve you up."

Keeping just out of his minimal reach, I grab the chain we loosened so he could move enough to eat and drink what he was given. I firmly yank it hard enough so his weakened arm flies to the wall and slams against it, making a sickening sound that just might be a bone breaking."

"Ah!" Morpheus shrieks. "My shoulder! My shoulder!" His other hand moves towards his shoulder, but I'm quicker.

I secure the chain above his head and jump to his other side, doing the exact same thing with his other hand. He screams again, trying to struggle to keep his arms from ending up above his head. It's really no use. His legs are secured so tightly to the ground that his ankles are bruised and cut from all of the moving he's attempted to do over the week. His wrists are the same, but I don't give a single fuck.

I connect his wrists to the chain in the middle of the wall so he can't possibly move an inch. Once I have him exactly how I want him, I squat in front of him. He's still screaming, so I wait for him to realize he's not getting any help or sympathy.

After a little while, he starts panting. Tears are streaming down his face. "Okay. Okay." He takes several deep breaths. "It was Meeka. Meeka Jakowski." He sounds defeated, and I'm quite disappointed. I wanted a bigger fight.

"Tell me about her. What did she do? How did she come to be the kid's nanny?"

"What the hell do you want all this information for?"

"Because I'm a fucking nosy prick." I grin cockily as I put the knife to his throat. I make a slight mark, just enough to make his jaw bleed. He grimaces but glares at me. "So, tell me the tea? Is that how it's said? Spill the tea? What's the gossip?"

He sighs. "Fuck," he groans as I hold my knife against my thigh, tapping it menacingly. "Cap blackmailed her. When she was in nursing school, she went out one night partying. There are a lot of pictures of her in some fucked up situations. She was snorting coke and engaging in a gang bang. She thought she buried the pics, but they weren't that hard to find. She changed her life around. Turned out to be a pretty good girl. Got married to a doctor. Had a couple kids."

"So naturally, you had to ruin her life. Why?"

He shakes his head. "Man, you're fucking stupid."

I punch him in the face. Hard. Blood spurts from his mouth. He coughs up blood and a couple of teeth. My father and his guards called me stupid all of the time. No one will ever have that chance again. "I didn't ask for your fucking opinion," I growl. "Keep fucking talking."

It takes him a few minutes to recover, but time is all I have. Once he manages to breathe through the pain, he shakes it all off and attempts to return my glare. Like the coward he is, his gaze quickly drops. "He found them so easily because she was his ex. Broke it off with him after she finished nursing school in Texas. Moved here and got a job immediately. She was married less than a year after graduation. Cap was pissed."

"So, you blackmailed her."

"Yep."

"What next? You took the kid from the hospital."

"We blackmailed a lot of people. Even the bitch she used as her OBGYN. It wasn't hard. We had her tell the brat's bitch she was further behind what she was. We had the exact weeks. We knew when we could poison her enough to induce labor. We had orders to not kill either of them. We didn't care. We just wanted her crotch goblin anyway. We didn't give a shit what happened to her, but we needed her alive, so it didn't matter. She had to give birth. We blackmailed Meeka's husband, too. Used her for leverage. Neither of them knew. We told him if he didn't drug the brat with what he provided, we'd kill his wife. And we told her that if she wasn't a good girl, her kids would be left with no parents and sold to a sex trafficking ring. They both did exactly what they were told."

With every word he spills from his lips, I feel myself hardening more and more. I don't take what he did to Meeka and her husband lightly. Nor do I enjoy the threat against her kids. But call my kid a brat and crotch goblin and Lyric a bitch, and I can feel my blackened soul darkening even further. I don't know how I restrain myself, but this motherfucker is lucky I'm not tearing him apart.

Yet.

"How did you poison her?" Lyric rarely left her house. She lived in a secured building. Her best friend was a cop, and her brother was a protective motherfucker. Still is.

"Her last appointment. We had her OBGYN tell her she was a bit dehydrated and gave her some Pedialyte. It was laced with some kind of labor inducing drug. I had no part of that. Was only told about it."

"Okay. Get to the ship."

"We kept the brat in the hospital until he could survive outside. Bribed a NICU nurse with a lot of fucking money. Once we could take him, we went after Meeka again. The NICU nurse, we got her fired and killed her. No loose ends. We forced Meeka to tell her husband she was leaving him and the kids. Told her if she didn't, we'd kill them all in front of her." He gets a sickening grin on his face. "She played like a good girl. We boarded the ship. She cared for the little crying asshole while we sailed around the world continuing our own drug trafficking and human trafficking business." His grin brightens. "Best part of the job was fucking all the men, women, and children before selling them."

I let out a low growl. My hand shakes slightly at my side. It's not because of nerves. It's because I'm doing all I can to keep from stabbing him in the dick. "What happened on the ship." It's not a question. It's a fucking statement, and if he says one word about anyone assaulting my kid, I'll rip all of his insides out with my bare hands.

"I'm tired. I don't want to talk anymore." He hangs his head and lets his eyes close, but it's a mistake.

Never fucking stop paying attention to your enemy.

Without a moment's hesitation, I slam the knife into his knee cap.

"Ah!" he screams. I twist. "Ah!" Louder. I twist it again. "Ah!" Even louder. He's trying so hard to move his leg, but it's not going to work. He's immobile. I doubt very seriously he'd even be able to walk right now even if I hadn't fucked him up. "Ah!" The scream turns into cries, but I'm more than fucking done.

"Tell me what happened to that kid on that ship, Morpheus. Or I'll stab your other knee cap followed by your dick. Do *not fuck* with me."

Through his tears, he continues. I leave the knife buried just so I can use some pain management tactics against him. "Nothing. Nothing to him. Physically. Okay? He was well taken care of. She even tutored him. He's really fucking smart. But he saw a lot of shit. Nothing was hidden from him. That was our orders. He saw Meeka being raped. He saw us taking the people being trafficked. He saw us high and drunk. He saw us kill. He never talked to any of us. Meeka was the only one he said anything to."

That answers a lot of questions, but not near enough. "Why the fuck would anyone order that and you obey?" For the first time, fear crosses his face. He doesn't answer, but it's all the answer I need. He's afraid of this Cap person. "Why did you call us?"

That makes him shake his head. "I never did! I'm not that fucking stupid. I went to meet Damon because the person who did call him had been caught. He set up an entire damn meeting with your guy. Cap caught him. He heard the whole thing but never stopped him. The plan was he'd meet Damon. He'd get the kid and the girl off the ship. He told your guy about the kid. He didn't get a chance to tell him about the girl. He called from a satellite phone. Said when we'd be there and everything."

"And you all knew we'd be right there surrounding you guys the second you docked."

"Fuck. Yeah. Okay? We had to call him back with a change of plans. Cap volunteered me. Said to meet Damon and get the fuck out. It didn't go as planned. You guys had the place swarmed. We planned to ambush you. We thought you'd come in small. It was just for a kid off a ship. Nothing more. After we dropped him as bait and put our guys on him, we thought we were good. We didn't think you'd come in with force like that. We had no one else to hit you with. You took out everyone who had been on the ship and even some of Cap's other guys. You were never supposed to get the kid. I thought I'd call Cap after a few weeks and tell him where I was so we could make a plan to get the kid back."

"Really thought I was an idiot, didn't you? But you know my rep. I'm more ruthless than even Ryan Crane, the fucking modern day Dark Knight. I'm even worse. Scarier. So, why test me?"

"It was my orders."

I shake my head and chuckle. "Mistake on your part, I guess, huh? What happened to the original contact and the girl?"

"They were thrown still alive and naked off the ship with weights to make sure they hit bottom."

I'm disgusted, but I don't show it. That's not the way I am. Instead, I grin sinisterly. "Good choice. But you should've cut them open. Superficial wounds so the water stings. No telling what's really in it, but the blood will definitely attract predators. Would've been great if some of them immediately swarmed while they were drowning."

I see the glimmer of desire in his eyes. He doesn't know I've just found his weakness. He gets off watching others in pain, though he doesn't like pain himself. Too bad I won't be able to exploit it. I have almost all I need.

I chuckle when his eyes follow every move I make. I reach forward and grip his shirt. It's soiled. I'm certain it's not just sweat. He smells worse than just some body odor. He definitely puked all over himself. Probably a few times. I pull my knife out of his knee, making blood spurt and him jerk and groan. I start cutting down the middle of his shirt. Slowly.

"You know. One of my favorite things about being who I am is that I have more money at my fingertips than even my father did. I have more resources than he did. More contacts. I have more alliances. I even have governments around the fucking world on my side. Did you know if I asked, the military would show up and join in whatever war I had going on with anyone at all?"

"Whatever. If you're so powerful, why can't you stop all wars? All crime syndicates? Why not eradicate us? You're nothing."

I get to the bottom of his shirt and rip through it. "Now, that's not nice. I've shown you hospitality. Revived you from near death. Who knows. Maybe you were dead." I shrug and press my knife against the top of his chest. He hisses when I press enough to draw blood.

"I gave you what you wanted. Just let me go."

"One more question." I look him dead in the eyes. "Who's Cap?"

He blinks, and I know I'm not getting anything more out of him. "My boss. And he's coming for you."

I laugh. "Good. I love a good fight. Helps me release all my demons."

His eyes widen a little bit. "Come on. You got what you wanted. Let me go."

I laugh again. "I'm sorry. I think you misunderstood what's happening here. There's no surrender or escape. You're done. I don't think you know who your boss actually is. I think you only know him as Cap. And I even believe you were following orders. But you're not getting out of here alive. You lost that privilege the second you made the decision to fuck around with my son, his mother, and threaten my girl." I start moving the knife down his chest, not taking my eyes off his.

To his credit, he doesn't scream. His eyes fill with tears at the realization that he really isn't getting out of here alive to fight another day. "Josh…" It's a whispered plea.

When I get to his belly button, I stop. "Let me tell you a little something about me. I'm going to kill you. It's going to hurt so much, you'll go into shock. You'll feel every fucking second, but you won't be able to scream. You're going to be locked inside your mind writhing in agony and praying to whoever you pray to for them to just let you die so you don't feel the pain anymore. They won't. No one is going to hear your cries. I'm going to collect your fucking soul and not feel a damn thing. I'll get up, walk out of here, and go back to my house. I'll shower. I'll eat. And then I'll spend time with my family and fuck my girl. I won't think of you. Not for another second. You won't haunt me. But for the rest of eternity, I'll be the last face you see, and the one who haunts you in your afterlife."

I say nothing more, but as I speak, my words sink in deeper than my knife has any hope of doing. I jam the blade into his stomach and watch as his mouth opens and forms a horrified 'O'. I don't move it. I simply allow the pain to sink in deep, frolicking with my words. The second his eyes start to close, I move the blade up, slicing through his flesh.

Once more, his eyes fly open, but he doesn't scream. I can tell he wants to. His eyes scream for him, even as they dim. I keep moving the knife up slowly. Blood spills from him along with other parts of his insides. His intestines, mostly. When I get to his chest cavity, I stop. His eyes are open, but there's no life left in them. They were already gray, but now they look glossed over, making them even more dull. His head has dropped to the side.

I pull my knife from his body and stand. I'm dripping in his blood. It's not the first time I've been covered in the fluids of another person when I've left this place. It won't be the last.

I walk out of the interrogation house and close the door behind me. Two armed guards are standing on either side of the door with AR-15s strapped to their chest.

"Looks like you had some fun," one of them says to me.

I chuckle. "Get our cleaners in there. Warn them it's a fucking disaster."

"Yes, sir."

I walk towards my house knowing I need to brief my team. It can come later. Right now, I need a shower. Thankfully, my house isn't close enough to the guest house for Jaxon to see me. He's afraid of me enough at this point. No wonder, considering what he's been through and the shit he's seen. The only person he trusted was murdered in cold blood right in front of him.

I strip my clothing and toss it all into the washer. I don't even know how much blood has gone through this thing. I throw in detergent and start it. Walking naked through my house, I head for the shower in my bedroom. After getting it ready, I step under the hot spray.

As promised, I don't think of Morpheus again.

Chapter Twelve

❦ Dallas ❦

I close my book after finishing my homework for Math. Not like it matters anyway. I'm sure it's being done because the stuff will be used in the final. We need to know how to do it, but it still feels pointless to me. Maybe because we could have the entire last half of the year to work on our projects instead of having to do them at home. School work at school. What a concept.

My History teacher said he'd like us to focus on something other than WWII for our final. I'm sure that has something to do with the fact that everyone in my class is fascinated with that particular period of time. So, because we're all Seniors and all upset with the entire school for thinking it's okay to still do homework and all of this other stuff and making it count for nothing, my entire class is focusing on WWII.

I chuckle a little. Different aspects of it, of course. Some are doing things on how the auto industry switched production to things for the war. How so much manufacturing switched to things like building weapons. Others are focusing on the clothing industry and how some switched to uniform manufacturing instead. And one is focusing on the nursing aspect of it all. Their role.

I've chosen to go a lot darker with my project. Even darker than I did for my midterm. The whole thing is going to be focused completely on Auschwitz, and I'm ending it with how they were liberated with no resources at all. How so many of them had to start their lives over after experiencing so much trauma while having absolutely no support. How they were just told they are free and can leave but felt abandoned by everyone. The way their families were torn apart. How so many of them had nothing. Their entire family had been murdered. They had no one to return to. No home.

I'm almost completely done with it. I'm nearly done with all of my projects because not focusing on them allows my mind to wander. And when it wanders, it lands back on Josh. My home. Thinking of Josh causes me to cry. I cried for the entire day after Alec picked me up because Josh ignored all of my calls and texts. I still don't really know if he's okay. Alex said he's trying. That he's dealing with stuff he really doesn't understand or know how to deal with.

I know he's talking about me and Jaxon. He doesn't know how to deal with having us in his life when he experiences night terrors on top of the other dark thoughts that plague him constantly. I don't know anywhere near the entire story of the hell he rose out of, but I do know that it irrevocably changed him.

I shake my head, but it's a futile attempt to keep Josh's face out of it. I dive into another project, but I'm suddenly not able to concentrate. I haven't allowed myself to think about what happened that night since after that first day. I wanted to be the strong one for once. The one who held him up when he needed me.

Only, he never ended up needing me. As the minutes, hours, and days go by with zero contact from him, it's more and more evident that he doesn't need me. He doesn't need anybody. And when people want to be there for him, he pushes them away because he really doesn't need them. Josh only allows people around him who he wants to be around him. It's become obvious I'm not one of those people.

I'm probably nothing more than an annoying brat to him. Someone he'd been trying to be nice to even though he never needed to be. He was trying to let me down easily this whole time, and I never listened. I kept pushing and pushing.

After hours of getting nothing else done, I finally give in and decide to try and sleep. Not like I've been able to do that much this week. Every time I close my eyes, my heart cries. And when my heart cries, my eyes try to. I refuse to let them. My stupid heart keeps his image close. I can't get a moment's peace because it always feels him near and holds on to him.

Alec has tried to get me to talk to him. Even Rosie and Dylan have made valiant attempts. I just can't do it. Everything is still so fresh in my mind. The hurt for him. Knowing he's struggling and not being able to help him. It's all I want. I don't even care if I don't get to be with him in any other capacity. I just want to ease his internal suffering.

Suddenly feeling exhausted, I take a deep breath. I strip my clothes and put them in my hamper, and then walk to the bathroom. I make sure I have a fluffy towel ready when I get out. I turn the water on and set the temp before closing the door. I start brushing my hair so I can put it up. It allows me to focus on it instead of my thoughts, which are steadily dropping into low territory. Not thinking about Josh once I've started isn't easy.

The glass starts to steam up as I start putting up my hair. It's long and thick. It's one of my personal prides. I get lots of compliments on it. I'm a small woman, very petite. I'm not often noticed, but when I am, it's for my hair. The girls in my school ask me all of the time how I make it so healthy. I love telling them my routine.

Once I think I have my hair dealt with, I wipe the mirror with my hand to make sure it's all up. I don't really want to wash it right now. I don't have the energy. It is nearly four in the morning, afterall.

It's the moment I see my reflection that I feel myself begin falling apart. There are dark circles under my eyes. My cheeks are flushed. I look pale and sick. I think my cheeks might even be sunken in a little bit. The tears I've been doing so well at fighting back this entire week flow freely.

Suddenly, the song *Cry Pretty* by Carrie Underwood is on repeat in my head. The words are so spot on. I don't often show emotion outside of my very small circle, but this is who everyone has seen this entire week. The line that hits me hardest is, *You can't hide it. You can't fight what the truth is. You can pretty lie and say it's okay. You can pretty smile and just walk away. Pretty much fake your way through anything, but you can't cry pretty.*

It's exactly what I've been doing for the past week. I put makeup on and hide it all. I smile and avoid questions about if I'm feeling okay. I lie and say I'm fine. I've been faking my way through all of this and shutting down. I haven't allowed myself to feel any emotions at all past day one.

So, as my tears flow, I force myself under the spray of the water. I fall completely apart, each broken piece of me flowing down the drain with my tears. For the first time, I truly let it all out. All of it. The pain from being kidnapped when I was fourteen by Josh's father, Matthew Lucinio, though I didn't know it then, seizes my heart. The terror from that entire period of time grasps at me. The humiliation of being stripped down and kept shackled to other frightened and naked women who would have a fate different to what I knew mine would be clutches at me.

I scream out and cry harder as all of the memories I've worked so hard to keep deep inside explode to the surface. I think of the fear of having a bomb strapped to my chest in the basement of Matthew's house. Jessa was so calm and collected the entire time, even though she was having a hard time, just like me. I know I wouldn't have survived as long as I did without her. Her confidence that we'd be rescued is the only thing that kept me alive.

The relief when Josh showed up with so many people to help flowed through me that day, but I never felt it through the fear. I still wasn't sure I was truly alive for months afterwards. It's why I stuck so close to Josh, the man who literally saved my life. The one who kept the bomb from exploding and killing us all.

I scream into the shower louder and pound my fist against the wall. The anger from the day releases with every punch. I turn my back to the spray and beat the wall with both fists as I scream and cry.

"Dallas?" Alec asks in a low voice I barely hear over my own screams.

It doesn't stop me, though. I can't stop the screams any more than I can stop the tears. I'm sure I'm scaring him. I'm certain every single thing happening right now is terrifying to him. It's just as horrifying to me, but my body has a mind of its own. I hit and kick the wall as the screams and cries get more painful even to my own ears.

Eventually, the anger lessens until all I feel is my strength leaving my body. The punches slowly stop. I sink painfully down the wall until

I'm on my knees on the shower floor. I collapse into a heap and draw my legs up to my chest as I curl into the corner. My voice is hoarse from screaming. I don't think it's possible for me to cry anymore, but the tears continue to flow anyway.

I don't fight them anymore. I don't fight the thoughts. I don't fight the emotions. Everything just seeps out of me with each tear. The fact that I'm too emotionally damaged for Josh. I'm too damaged for anyone. No one is going to want me, which is fine, because Josh is it for me. I may be young, but the second I realized I was in love with him, that he was more than just my hero, I knew there'd never be another person. He is my soulmate; the other half of my heart. I know that just as much today as I did then.

I'm so stupid. I never should've believed for a second I was good enough. I'm nothing more than the princess of VV. I'll probably marry a biker to help Alec grow his alliances. That's my fate. It's the fate I grew up believing before Alec took over. That's what people whispered about me. My dad never said a word about it, but he was killed at Alec's hands because of an alliance he'd made with someone.

I know Alec would never do that to me. He proved himself when he took out our father and the small gang I would've been married into. He'd never do it to me, but I would do it for him. He'd never have to ask.

Maybe I naively thought that wouldn't be my life. Maybe I thought I'd get my fairytale with Josh afterall. Knowing that's not happening now, I've come to accept the fate I've been handed. To be VV's princess forever. Whether it's on purpose or not, that's what will happen. I'm not good enough for anything beyond the confines of our compound. I've never wanted to go to college, but it wouldn't matter if I wanted to. I'm not smart enough and will always be tied to this life somehow.

Viper's Venom's princess.

The tears keep flowing. I find myself hitting the wall again. Only this time, it's only a couple of times. My heart knows everything I just thought is completely false, but it doesn't matter. My head is screaming a lot louder and drowning out everything else.

I hug my knees even tighter and let the tears keep streaming down the drain with the water. I don't even know if it's warm anymore. I feel empty. I don't feel anything at all.

I don't know how much longer I stay curled up in the shower crying, but eventually the water shuts off. I feel myself being wrapped in a towel and picked up off the shower floor. With numb hands, I manage to get the towel secured around me. I'm too weak to stand, but when I start to slump, strong arms grasp me and lift me once more.

"She okay?" a deep voice asks. Tyler. I've known his voice my whole life. I know it as well as Alec's. I don't need to see him.

"She will be," Alec says resolutely, but even I can hear the uncertainty he portrays.

And he's right to feel it. I might never be okay again. Not after letting years of emotion out like that. Emotions I didn't even know I held deep within. This goes farther than Josh and what happened. Its roots run deep.

"I'll go let the others know. Everyone is worried."

"Thank you."

Moments later, Alec is towel drying my hair. I don't say anything. I can't. I can't even look at him. I can't explain what happened in there. I don't even know myself. I haven't fully grasped any of it.

He takes my hands and starts applying something to my knuckles. I look down and see my knuckles are bruised and cut. I hadn't even noticed. I don't feel the pain. I watch him intently as he bandages my hands like I've done with his wounds so many times. He says nothing at all. He doesn't ask me what happened. No questions. Just does what a big brother does and takes care of me.

No questions.

No talking.

Just love, understanding, and respect.

Once he's finished with my hands, he lifts me once more and carries me to my bed. He sets me down on the edge of it and walks to my dresser. He pulls out my favorite dark pink sleep pants and the tank top that matches it.

He holds them out to me once he reaches my bed again. "Think you can put these on?" It's the first words he's uttered since talking to Tyler. I take them and slowly start dressing, the towel still wrapped around me. I know tears are still falling, but I don't feel them. I don't have the will to stop them.

As I dress, Alec walks back to my bathroom. Once I finish, he reappears. He puts my brush and detangler on the bed and takes my towel. He walks back to the bathroom and comes back moments later. He shuts out the light in the bathroom and closes the door. Sitting behind me on the bed, his legs on either side of me, he sprays my hair with the detangler and starts gently brushing my hair.

Once again, he doesn't say a word, and he doesn't know how grateful I am for that. I'm still being tortured by all of the thoughts running through my mind. I don't know how to articulate anything right now. I feel so weak, like I've just had a psychotic break or something.

When he finishes, he shifts and helps me to lay down. He takes my brush and detangler back to the bathroom. He comes back with a glass of water and sets it on my nightstand.

"I'll be right back, okay? I need to check in with the guys, but then I'll come back."

I nod. He knows I want him near but don't want to talk. I'm scared to be alone, so I sit up until he comes back. He leaves my door open so I can hear the chatter coming from downstairs.

I'm not alone. I'm not alone. I keep chanting the words in my mind, but the longer he's gone, the more I feel like I am. I quickly become a paranoid wreck. My head swivels between the bedroom door and the window, certain someone is going to take me. Before long, I've got my eyes everywhere at once. The door, the window, the closet, the bathroom, under the bed. To me, they are all legit places for people to hide and attack me.

Out of the corner of my eye, my standing lamp in the corner of my room flickers. I whip my head to it. My heart stops when I see my dad's face followed by Matthew's. I try to scream when they loom towards me, but nothing comes out of my mouth.

Alec chooses that very moment to come back. Dressed in sweats and a t-shirt, he wraps his arms around me. "Shh… shh… shh… It's just shadows…," he whispers. "You're okay. You're safe."

I grip him with everything I am as I tremble. When he starts to stand to shut out the light, I tighten my grip. He keeps a hold of me as he flicks it off, then helps me lay back down. He crawls in with me and wraps me in his protective arms.

I cry more.

I let him hold me and keep me safe as I fall apart. My mind is spinning with everything that's ever happened in my life, but Alec keeps me safe.

Eventually, long after the sun has risen, I fall asleep. It's by no means peaceful. It's an exhausted sleep that only happens because I can't fight my body anymore.

I can't fight anymore at all…

Chapter Thirteen

☙ Josh ❧

(One Week Later)

I throw a left hook. Lyric blocks it like an expert. I'm both impressed and a little pissy it all seems so easy for her. It kind of means I have nothing left to teach her.

"You've been practicing. Matt and DJ helping you?" I ask, giving her a quick jab. She blocks it and pushes back, throwing several punches of her own. I easily block them because neither of us are doing anything more than sparring.

"Yep. They even taught me how to throw a grown man."

I grin. "Impressive." I go at her like I'm not fucking around and back her into the wall of my gym. I cage her in. "Don't actually kick me in the balls this time, huh?"

"I won't."

When I back off and turn, thinking that was a good enough sign for a break, Lyric attacks. She has her arms locked around me. The next thing I know, I feel her body shifting and my feet lifting off the ground.

"Holy shit!" I bark when I hit the mat under us hard. I lay on my back blinking. "When the fuck did you master that?"

"Marine. Army Ranger. Now up. That was fun. I wanna knock you on your ass a few more times. There's still some asshole left in you."

I crack up and take her hand she offers to help me up. I jump to my feet. "Calm down, brat. I need a drink. And so do you." I point to the bench along the wall where our water bottles are. We're both drenched in sweat.

"I'd roll my eyes, but I'm sure you'd spank me."

I laugh. "I might not be your boyfriend anymore, but damn right I'll spank your ass for that bullshit." I take a drink of my water as she giggles.

"So, Dallas. You've allowed yourself time with Jaxon. Why not her?"

I watch her carefully as she sits down and adjusts her knee pads. "How do you know I haven't?"

She raises a bratty eyebrow as she looks up at me. "Please. She hasn't been around. I'm not the only one who hasn't seen her. Even Jessa is worried. All she knows is that Alec has been with her."

I sigh. "Lyric, you know better than anyone why I'm not relationship material. I'm still navigating how to be a father with all the shit I have going on in my life. You really want me to add an already fucked up relationship on top of my very fucked up life? Dallas is far better off in the light. I don't live there, and I don't want to dim her because I live in the shadows."

She stands. "You're wrong, you know." She speaks softly, but she looks right in my eyes. It's something she never used to be able to do, even after I spent years working with her on her confidence and place in this world. It's one more thing that makes it clear she's with the right people and far better off than she was with me. "You're so much more than you think you are."

I take a long swig of my water and shake my head. "You always had me on a high pedestal. I'll never forget how hurt you were when I failed you in the worst possible way."

She narrows her eyes. "You mean how you kept me from killing myself after I thought I miscarried our child? Or do you mean how you single handedly gave me the strength to trust my instincts that something

104

wasn't right? Or maybe it was the way that even after we broke up, you still found ways to look out for me and make sure I was safe. Was it how you always made me feel like I had a family even when I felt like I had no one? Or perhaps when you -"

I hold up a hand. "Okay! Okay. Point taken, but it doesn't change my decision on this. You're far better off without me now. You never would have stood here like this with me before. You've stood up to me, but you've never stood here looking in my eyes while you've done it. That's not on my account. That's all your husbands."

"Who I wouldn't have met without you, Josh. Had you not gotten me in that club and felt like I was ready for it, I never would've been there and met them. Do you really not understand the impact you have on people?"

Before I have a chance to retort, I hear someone ringing the doorbell. Feeling like I've literally been saved by the bell, I start to leave the gym to answer it, but Lyric isn't done. I should've known she wouldn't just let this go.

"She loves you. And I know how you feel about her. Don't be an idiot. Everyone can see you're meant for each other. You're just too fucking stubborn to admit it to yourself."

"Oh, I've admitted it. I just know she'll find someone a lot more in her league than me."

I hear Lyric sigh as I head for my door. I'm only wearing shorts, and I'm sweaty. I hope this isn't important because my massaging shower is calling my name.

I open the door to see Alec. I haven't seen him all week, either, but after what Lyric said, I know why. He's been with Dallas. Why he looks like he hasn't slept or had a shower in a week is beyond me, though. It's kind of alarming. Alec is usually well-groomed, but his hair is disheveled, and his facial hair is definitely overgrown.

"You look like shit. You okay?" I ask. "Want a water?"

"Need something a little stronger than that, man."

I step back and let him in. Lyric comes out with her gym bag slung over her shoulder. She raises an eyebrow at Alec, who slumps in a chair. He closes his eyes and rubs his head. She looks at me. I just shrug because I don't have a clue what's going on. I can only assume it has to do with

Dallas, which raises my protective instincts, whether I want them to be or not.

"I'll grab coffee," I say, heading for the kitchen.

"Whatever," Alec grumbles.

"Um… I'm gonna head home…" Lyric says. I can hear the concern laced in her words.

"Have a good night, Lyric," Alec rumbles.

"You do the same," she says softly, squeezing his shoulder on the way by. He makes no move to pat her hand. He doesn't even stand up to hug her. Which is odd because he adores her.

I get a cup of coffee from the kitchen as Lyric closes the door behind her. Once I'm done pouring it, I grab my water and walk back to my living room. I hand him the coffee. When he doesn't take it, though, I set it in front of him.

"Alec, the fuck is going on?"

He leans forward slowly and rests his elbows on his knees. He drops his head in his hands and rubs his palms against his eyes. "She had a psychotic breakdown, Josh."

"What?" My heart stops beating. "What happened?"

"She was upset the entire week after your night terror. She was upset that you never got back to her. I told her to give you time and space to figure it out. I know you needed it. I know how you get, and I understand it. She did. She gave you the space. Gave you the time. It hurt her because she wanted to be here for you through all of this, but I think she understood. She threw herself into school to pass the time. I was going to tell her to call you over the weekend. If you didn't answer, then the plan was for me to come by and talk to you."

I furrow my brows. "Okay. But you didn't." I start putting the pieces together, and it breaks me.

He shakes his head and runs his hands through his hair. He locks them behind his neck as he sits back in the chair. "No. I didn't. Because at four in the morning, the entire club was woken up by her screams. Fuck, bro. I thought she was being murdered. The screams were so loud. Everyone in the clubhouse went running to her room. Ink had to stop everyone from charging in. I went in with Ty. Hawk was right behind us. The screams switched somehow. It went from pure fucking torture to the worse fucking pain you can imagine. Heartbreaking shit. She was screaming. Crying. Banging on the shower wall. Then she sat down and cried. It was all I could do not to haul her out of there."

"Jesus." I fall back and close my own eyes. I did this. I fucking did this.

"That's not all. This went on for an hour. Once she was all screamed out, she sat on the floor in there and cried until the water turned cold. I sat outside the damn shower listening to her release all of this agony. A few times, she went back to screaming and hitting the wall. She barely noticed that I was there when I shut the water off. She almost collapsed when I had her on her feet trying to get the towel around her. She didn't say a goddamn word when I was drying her hair or brushing it. She barely had the strength to get dressed on her own. I don't know how she did it. She didn't even feel the pain of her busted up knuckles."

"Fucking hell, Alec. I -"

"Shut-up, Josh. I know what you're thinking, and it's not that. Just listen. I'm nowhere near done."

I swallow and nod. "Okay." My heart still hasn't resumed a steady beat. It sounds like a fighter jet to me right now, and it's racing just as fast.

"I left her alone for less than ten minutes. I told Tyler to tell the others she'd be okay. She just had a lot of pent up anger. Something. Anything. I didn't care what he said. Just make up an excuse. And then I went and threw sweats and a t-shirt on. I didn't want to leave her alone. I grabbed a blanket and pillow. I was going to sleep on her chair or the floor. I just needed her to know I was there, and I knew she needed me there, even though she hadn't said it. She hadn't said anything. When I came back, she was looking in the corner where her stand up lamp is. She looked fucking terrified. Her mouth was open like she was screaming, but no sound was coming out. She was so scared, she couldn't speak."

"Like, Jaxon," I whisper to myself. I doubt Alec hears me.

"I wrapped around her and just held her. She cried for hours after the sun came up until she finally fell into an exhausted sleep. Over the past week, she won't eat unless me or Tyler feed her. It's like she doesn't have the fucking energy to move her arms. When she goes to the bathroom, she needs help walking there. Once when I was going to get something to drink, I came back and Tyler was helping her off the bathroom floor. She fell. Just collapsed in a heap and sat against the bathroom cabinets hugging herself. I've gotten very little out of her, but I know it has to do with everything she's gone through that she's shoved down and never dealt with. Like her feelings when she found out I killed our father because of his plans to marry her off to another biker gang to form an alliance. She murmured something about how her own dad could do that to her. I questioned her, but all I got was marry. Just one word. Marry. It fucked me up. I thought she was saying he married her. I fucking made Tyler check everything and get Robby to help."

It's my turn to rub my eyes. I know now it's not all me, but none of what he's saying eases my mind at all. "Fuck."

"Yeah. Fuck. It gets even worse."

"That's not fucking possible."

"That's what I said. Usually, if I can't get something out of her, Tyler can. She's just as close to him as me. She didn't have a lot of friends before Rosie. She had Raleigh, but it was never quite the same as with Rosie. Before that, though, her best friend and only friend was Tyler. Neither of us can get anything out of her but one or two words every couple of days. Like Matthew and bomb. Trafficking. Jessa saved her. Sometimes, she'll murmur your name before she starts crying again. She won't sleep unless I'm with her. I can't even get her to clean up for me. She's tried, but she can't. I've given her sink baths, but all she's able to wash on her own is her privates. I have to do the rest. I had a doctor come, and she started screaming and crying all over again. It took me the entire day to calm her down." He pauses and takes a deep breath. "Josh, I… I don't fucking know what to do. She's broken. She's being haunted by shit that I can't even comprehend. I only know what you've told me about what happened to her. She won't talk to me about any of the other stuff. I'm at a fucking loss. You have to help me. Please. I don't know what's happening between you or if it'll ever be fixed, but I honestly think she's begging for you."

I take a deep breath of my own. "Jessa said she never let anything happen to Dallas. She always hugged her and made her turn away from the sights, but shit happened that she could definitely hear. Rapes and beatings of the other girls, mostly. One of them was killed trying to escape, and blood spatter hit Dallas." I lean forward and glance at Alec. "I'm not good for her, man. I don't know what would've happened that night if she hadn't grabbed Jaxon. When Alex got to me, I still had the gun in my hand. He tackled me to the ground. I woke up just as he took it and threw it away from me. I don't remember anything that happened. I don't remember Jaxon coming into the room. Nothing. I've never had something like that happen before. I've had night terrors, but nothing where I've grabbed a fucking gun."

"Then, you take fucking precautions. You're already doing that, according to Jess. You've let Jaxon stay here since that night. He's even started talking again." He runs a shaking hand through his hair. "If you don't want to be with her, Josh, fine. I don't fucking agree that's what you want, but I won't stop you, and I'll pick up the pieces of her broken heart. But I honest to fuck believe that you're the only one who can get through to her. Help me get her help. Please, Josh. I can't stand seeing her like this."

"Alec, come on. You know I'm not leaving her in that state no matter what the fuck my feelings are. Let me get dressed."

I jog upstairs and quickly shower. Five minutes later, I'm dressed in jeans and a black t-shirt, and ten minutes after that, Alec is pulling up in front of VV's clubhouse. I follow him inside. I've never seen the place so quiet. Everyone looks very much down, almost like they lost a major person in their crew. It hurts my chest because I know how important Dallas is to everyone here. It's almost like her smile is what holds them all together. Fuck. It's what holds me together most of the time.

Rhys, also known as Chaos, stops Alec before he starts climbing the steps. "She just had another screaming fit. Tag is wrapped around her. I was just grabbing her some chicken broth. He said she's freezing."

Alec nods and glances at me sadly. It breaks me even more because I know this isn't him. I've never seen him look so beaten down.

I follow him up the stairs. He leads me to Dallas' bedroom, and what I see shatters me. Wrapped in Tyler's arms is a shell of the woman I fucking love with everything I am. I'll beat myself down later about how badly I messed all of this up with her, but that's not my concern right now.

My concern is my girl. She's trembling and gripping Tyler's arm so fucking tightly, I can see the marks. To his credit, he doesn't move. He just holds her.

"Why? Why? Why?" she chants over and over again. No other words, giving little insight into what she's wanting to know the answer to. Her cheeks are streaked with tears. The bags under her bloodshot eyes stab me. She's pale.

"Shh… Dallas, shh… You're safe." Tyler's voice cracks.

"Fuck," I whisper. I don't waste another minute. I have no control over my body anyway. My heart does. And my heart belongs to hers.

I quickly stride across the room until I'm behind her. I don't know if she even saw me, but it doesn't matter because I know she needs me. The second Tyler spots me, though, a relieved smile crosses his face.

"Josh," he whispers to her. "Josh is here."

I take that as my cue to reach for her and pull her to me, but I don't get the chance. She turns and is in my arms where she belongs before I have a chance to say her name. I hug her tight, lifting her feet off the ground, and swaying with her.

"Never again," I whisper in her ear. I kiss her neck, tasting her tears. "I'm never letting you go again." I kiss her neck again and keep my lips pressed against it as I speak the words I should've said a long time ago. "I'll spend the rest of my life making it up to you, baby. I'm so sorry. So fucking sorry."

I've been a fool, and the guilt I'm always going to feel not being here for her when she needed me the most is the bitter price I'll be paying for my very stupid actions.

I'll never make that mistake again.

Chapter Fourteen

🍎 Dallas 🍎

(One Week Later)

No matter what I do, the memories I locked down won't let me out of their grip. One second, I'm a child running in our backyard. The next, I'm hearing glass breaking, yelling, and gunshots.

While I stand frozen in the backyard, more people run towards the house. The gunshots are deafening. I cover my ears, but it's like they're whizzing by my head along with the broken glass.

Before I know it, Alec is running towards me with Tyler hot on his heels. He picks me up without stopping and takes me to his own house. I feel safer than I ever have, but I'm uneasy because I can feel he is. I know there's a whole chunk of something missing. Something I can't quite grasp.

Suddenly, I'm not a little girl anymore. I'm a teenager being taken from school by men I've never seen before. I scream, but everyone just looks at me like I'm crazy. The person taking me is wearing Viper's Venom's cuts. Everyone knows I'm VV's princess.

"Ah!" I scream. I lurch out of bed. I'm dripping sweat and panting, but I wasn't sleeping. I haven't slept in days.

"Shh... I'm here, baby." Warm arms embrace me and pull me closer to a large body and hard chest. They envelop me like the most comforting hug.

Josh.

He runs his fingers through my hair and presses his lips against my neck. Each caress of his fingertips and lips soothes me more and more. This entire week, Josh has been my anchor. And with him, I've gotten stronger and stronger.

But I still can't force myself to speak. And the thoughts screaming through my mind won't shut up. Now that Pandora's Box has been opened, it won't close.

"Keep fighting for me, sweet girl." He sways with me. "Fuck, I wish I could get you to talk to me. Let me help you fight this better. Give me an idea of what's going on in your beautiful mind," he whispers.

I can't.

I want to talk, but the words don't come out of my mouth. I know what I want to say, but something stops me. Something keeps it all locked inside. Keeps me locked inside.

I look down, disappointed in myself.

Josh gently grips my chin. "Hey. Don't do that to me," he says with a half-smile. He kisses my forehead sweetly. "I'm gonna love you no matter if you're mute or the most talkative being in this world. You're everything to me. My whole world, Dallas. I'm so fucking sorry I wasn't here for you when you needed me the most, but I'm here now. I want to help you through this, baby, but I have very little to go on. If all you need from me is what I've been doing, I'm okay with that, but if you need more, you need to find a way to..." His voice cracks. He lowers his head until his forehead is resting against mine.

Love me. I close my eyes against the tears threatening to fall and focus on the words. *Love me. Never stop loving me.* I have to be stronger than whatever is keeping my voice hidden.

Josh holds me as close to him as possible. I bury my head in his chest as he lays down in my bed with me. He hasn't left my side this whole time. Ever since Alec brought him here. He's apologized profusely. He's helped me shower and been incredibly respectful of me, never taking advantage. He's helped me eat. I've even gained more and more strength so I can eat myself, but he's always next to me just in case I start to drop something. He's proven with each second that he means everything he says. He really is sorry and really isn't going to leave my side.

Every time I snap out of my head, however briefly it is sometimes, Josh is always right here holding me and helping me fight whatever it was I saw in the carousel of my mind. Whenever I want to run to him, I don't need to. He's already here.

He stays.

I let my eyes drift close because I'm so tired. I can't keep them open for long, even though if I had my way, they'd never shut. I don't like what I see when they aren't open.

I take a deep breath and breathe Josh's cologne in. I clutch him a little tighter just to convince myself that he's here. He's real. He'll keep me safe in his arms. No one can hurt me. Not with him here. I'm safe.

And with that, I'm sucked back into the darkness. I don't see Matthew. I don't see the bomb strapped to my chest. Instead, I see things I've never seen before. Women assaulted. Killed for trying to run.

The next instant, before I can make sense of everything, I'm pulled back in a whirling cyclone and dropped into that same backyard. That same little girl.

I bend to pick up a dandelion. I'm wearing my favorite yellow sundress, and I love how the dandelion matches it. I giggle and dance in a circle with my face up to the sun. I let my eyes close as the sun warms me. I've always loved Spring days. They're my favorite.

In an instant, my eyes are snapping open. I whirl towards the house. There's arguing. Something breaks.

"You're not fucking touching her! Got me?"

Alec? Was that Alec? Touching who?

I curiously make my way towards the house. I tilt my head just a little and furrow my eyebrows at more things breaking. Is Alec okay?

"It's not your decision, asshole! She's not your daughter! She's mine! My property!"

Daddy?

More breaking. The closer I get, the more scuffling I can hear. I quicken my steps.

"You're going to have to go through me to get her! And we both know how that'll turn out!"

"I own this club! You're not the goddamn leader yet!"

I reach the backdoor and slowly open it. Alec and our father are locked together in a fight. Alec slams him against a wall. Dad gets a hold of him somehow, though, and shoves him back. Dad quickly grabs a knife and charges.

With wide eyes, I scream, "No! Daddy, no!"

Alec looks at me, and just that brief second gives our father the access he needs to get Alec into another hold. Alec manages to pull out his gun, and I scream again. I run towards them and grab onto dad's arm.

"Dallas, no! Go outside! Go outside, honey!" Alec yells.

"No! Daddy, no!" I scream again, trying to get his arm holding the knife away from Alec.

Alec manages to shove him back again, and I stay attached to his arm, hoping I can make him drop the knife. I don't see it coming, but with his other hand, our father slaps me so hard that I have no choice but to let go. I hit the floor hard and slide across it.

Dad flies once more at Alec, knocking his gun away. He slams the knife down, but Alec moves. The knife grazes his arm, but I immediately see the blood dripping down his tattoos. Before I know what's happening, our father has Alec on his back on the ground. The knife is dangerously close to Alec's neck.

I look down at the floor. Alec's gun slid across the floor and is resting at my feet. I stare at it and look back at Alec. He's struggling to get dad off him. I can tell his strength is lessening. I'm sure it's because the gash on his arm is probably deeper than he thinks. His arm looks more bloody than it should for just a small gash.

Shakily, I pick up the gun. I have to help my brother. The knife is too close to his neck. It looks like it pierced his skin. His other arm is bleeding a little from another gash.

All I hear from them are grunts and groans. Our dad isn't paying attention to me. I'm sure he thinks I was knocked out or something. I wasn't. I was just dizzy for a few seconds.

I've never shot a gun before. At least not without help. Alec helped me once. He knelt behind me and held my arms. I remember my arms shot up. I dropped the gun after I shot.

"Get off..." Alec groans.

I walk towards them slowly. Alec fights for his life. Just when I think he gains the upper hand, our dad has him in his grip again.

"You did this, boy. You had to interject yourself where you don't belong," my dad grunts.

"You're not marrying off a fucking kid!"

Dad manages to slice down into Alec's shoulder. Alec yells out in pain. Dad takes the knife out of Alec's shoulder and raises it above his head. Alec's movements aren't as quick. He grabs our dad's arm and stops him from slicing down quickly. He tries to push him off with his other hand, but it's weakened from the stab wound.

Our dad punches Alec in the face, and the knife gets closer and closer to his head. Alec's eyes meet mine. They're wide and hold a fear I've never seen from my big brother. So, I waste no more time. I raise the gun and get closer, as close as I dare. Dad doesn't see me. He's too focused on Alec.

I shoot. "Ah!" I scream. The gun goes straight up in the air and flies out of my hand.

"Alec!"

I look up and see Tyler running towards us with his gun out. He locks eyes with me as my dad slumps to the ground bleeding profusely from the middle of the top of his head.

Tyler looks over his shoulder and back at me. "Run, Dallas. Go outside. We'll come for you." He nods towards the door as he kneels and grabs the gun I lost control of.

I nod and run to the backyard. I turn back to the house when I hear more gunshots. I'm frozen in fear, terrified some of my dad's men got Tyler and Alec, but then Alec runs out of the house. He scoops me up with the arm that isn't as wounded and runs towards his house, Tyler hot on his heels.

"Ah!" I scream. I fight against the strong arms holding me as I scream.

"Shh… it's me, baby. It's me."

Josh.

My body seems to know I'm safe. It stops fighting and starts melting into him, but my brain is still locked in itself. "Ah!" I scream again. Tears start running down my face, but I grip Josh with all I am. "I killed him!" I scream. "I killed him! I killed him!"

"What? Who? Killed who?"

"I killed him. I killed him!" I grip his shirt hard. I hear my door open. Moments later, another body is pressing behind me. "I killed him…" I don't bother trying to wipe the tears. For the millionth time this week, I soak Josh's shirt.

"Alec, what the hell is going on?" Josh asks, pure concern and alarm lacing his deep voice as he holds me tight.

"I'm not saying anything. Not until I know what she remembers," Alec says quietly.

As if something inside me unlocks, the words rush out of me. "I killed him! My father!"

"Fuck," Josh whispers and buries his face in my hair.

"What do you remember, Dal?" Alec asks softly. He rubs my back.

"Everything," I whisper. "Everything. I remember him trying to kill you. Him knocking your gun away. No one else being there. I remember trying to help you. I remember him hitting me. I remember grabbing your gun. I remember shooting him. Tyler came right then." I don't take a single breath as I speak. I don't know if I'm still crying or not. I don't even know if he can hear me. I'm speaking into Josh's chest with my eyes open so all I can see is him. "He told me to run."

"Jesus Christ," Alec murmurs. "Fuck, Dal. I didn't think you'd ever remember. I was hoping you never would. It was like you went to sleep that night and all of the memories of the day before erased. All you remembered was playing outside and hearing arguing and gunshots. Then me and Tyler running to you and taking you to my house. The next morning you asked what happened. You asked where dad was."

"And… you… told me…" I let out a long breath and sniffle. "You took the blame. You took the blame for what I did. You got arrested."

"But I was let out right away, Dallas," Alec says. "You remember that. It was self-defense. There was overwhelming evidence of that. And with you on your knees standing so close to him, it helped me. It went in my favor. As far as anyone is concerned, I did it. Not you. I'll take that to the grave. It's in the past. It's been resolved, and we've all moved past it. The reason for it never changed. He was trying to kill me."

"Because you wouldn't let him marry me off," I whisper. "It's always been my fault."

"No," Josh rumbles. "No. It's never been your fault. It's not your fault he was a sick fucking man who thought it was okay to live by barbaric rules that came into existence during a time in human history where women were viewed as property. You're not property and never should've been treated like it. You did what you did to protect your brother. Your family. Yourself. That's really the end of the story. How it came to be is irrelevant, but if you need it to make sense in your mind, then you need to place the blame where it belongs. On him. He's the one who thought he could do what he planned for you. Alec protected you. And you, in turn, protected him. You did exactly what you should've. Yes, you were young and never should've been placed in that situation, Dallas, but you were. You were, and you made the right fucking decision."

"I'm proud of you, little sis," Alec says. He hugs me as he takes a deep breath. "But I still wouldn't change what I did. No one knows what really happened that day except us and Tyler. No one. And no one is going to because it doesn't fucking matter. He's gone. You're safe. And I'm alive. Those are the only things that matter."

I nod. The more they talk the more I know they're right. It doesn't matter who pulled the trigger that day. What matters is Alec and I survived.

After a long while, Alec gets up and leaves the room with a promise of bringing back food. For the first time in two weeks, I'm actually hungry and looking forward to eating.

"How did this happen, baby? What broke?"

I shrug lightly. "I don't really know, honestly. One minute I'm thinking about you. I was upset that you hadn't called. I was upset you'd pushed me away again after promising to try. But I think I understood, to be honest. I felt like Alec was right. You needed time. It didn't really stop me from thinking some of the worst things. Like how I'm not good enough or strong enough for you, but I never really got the chance to correct the thoughts and put myself right because the next thing I know, it was like a switch in my mind was activated. I went from thinking about everything Matthew did when he'd kidnapped me to thinking about my dad and how he never loved me."

"I'm so fucking sorry, baby. I know words are empty, and I have a lot of groundwork to lay before I have any hope of your forgiveness, but I really am sorry I wasn't here for any of this. I should've been."

I shake my head and snuggle myself closer to him. "It's not your fault that this happened so quickly after what happened with you. The more I'm able to think about things, no matter how few and far between the lucid thoughts are, I sort of think maybe it was all the push I needed to… deal… with it all. I never really did. I just shoved it down. I never talked about it. At least not all of it or in much detail. Not even to Jessa, really. She was there. And she tried to get me to open up, but I wasn't ready. And eventually, a lot of stuff, I just… forgot. Repressed." I look up at him. "I didn't want to think about it, so I didn't. Then today, something felt like it just snapped. Like whatever was holding it all back broke. Suddenly, I was blurting it all out, but I don't really know how, given I haven't been able to force myself to talk this entire week. I've tried to."

"I'm just happy you were able to get that out at least." Josh runs his fingers through my hair and kisses me softly. "Not that I'd ever push, but if you want to get the rest out, I'm here."

I take a deep breath and lay my head in the crook of his shoulder. "I'm not ready for all of that yet," I whisper. "I feel like I need to process this first."

"That's understandable."

We fall silent for a while before I look up at him once more. "Josh?"

"Yeah, baby?"

"I do forgive you. I don't blame you for anything. And I've been wanting to say this for this entire week. You kept saying you love me. And you kept asking me what more you could do to help me. And my answer is…" I trail off. Josh's eyes darken a little, but it's with his unconditional love for me. "I love you. And all I want is for you to love me and never stop."

He smiles. "Baby girl, loving you is something I'll never be able to stop and never get enough of. Nothing would ever make me stop loving you."

"Even though I killed my dad?"

He chuckles and pulls me tight to him. "Your body count has a long way to go before it reaches mine. You know what I do. You still love me, right?"

I nod. "Always."

"Then, stop worrying about that. If you hadn't killed him, Alec might not be here right now. That's what you need to think of. You may have taken a life, but you saved one that day. You saved two. Yours and your brother's. Don't think about the life lost. Think about the lives saved because that one is gone."

"Is that how you justify it all in your mind?"

He chuckles a little again and kisses the top of my head. He hugs me tighter. "I'm different. My justification comes from a deep rooted need to protect my family. The lives I take are lives that could take someone I love from me. And if they don't take someone I love, they'll take someone someone else loves. That's my justification."

To love and to protect.

The words are the definition of the man who holds my heart.

Chapter Fifteen

ૐ Josh ૐ

(One Week Later)

I turn and look over my shoulder when I hear my door open. I continue to wash my dishes as I look to see who's entering. Only a small number of people have the ability to just walk in here. Whoever it is has a code and full security clearance in the compound. Which means it's any member of my family or Dallas or her brother.

I smile when I hear Dallas sigh and drop her backpack. I turn back to the dishes. I know she's taking off her shoes. Then, she'll hang her backpack on the coat hooks nailed to my wall that I don't use for any other purpose except for her hanging her backpack. She'll put her shoes in the closet on my shoe rack, and she'll make sure they're next to my sneakers.

It's been four years. She's never deviated from the routine once. And as soon as she's done all of that, she'll stand next to the door, close her eyes, let her hair down, and breathe. In and out. Five times. It's her too adorable way of letting everything that happened at school go.

I put the last dish in the drain wrack just as I hear her start walking. Her steps are soft. Confident and sure, but still light and gentle. Much like she is.

"Josh?" she calls.

"In the kitchen, baby." I turn, wiping my hands with a towel after draining the water. I grin at her when she turns the corner and sees me. She's still wearing her school uniform, and my mouth is instantly watering. Not because of the uniform, but because of the peek of skin I get near her neck. My favorite place to kiss. "How was your last -" I narrow my eyes when I see her tears, and then almost snap the moment I see the bruise on her arm. I cross to her in seconds and gently take her hand to inspect the bruise. "What happened?"

She shakes her head and jerks her hand away. I hang onto it, though. She really should know me better than that. She shakes her head again and doesn't look up at me. "It's nothing. It's over. I made it through the year." Her voice breaks, putting me on high alert.

"Dallas, what happened? Who grabbed you? And what do you mean it's over?"

"Nothing... Please, Josh. Just... I don't want anything to happen."

I choke down the explosion about to occur. She needs me to be calm. Her rock. I cup her chin and gently force her to look at me. "Baby girl, please tell me what happened."

She searches my eyes, but I don't know what she's looking for. Sincerity? A promise I'm not sure I can make yet? Without knowing what's going on, I don't know what the hell I can do to help, but if someone hurt her, I'm not just going to leave it alone.

"It's just..." She trails off and tries to look down again.

"Dallas. No, baby. If you can't tell me what's going on, who can you tell? I assume you haven't told Alec or Tyler. You know I'd know if you had."

She sighs. "I don't want you or anyone else doing anything, Josh. I... it's over. I'm done with school. I have no contact outside of those walls with hardly anyone. It's really over."

I pull her hand to my lips and kiss it, not breaking eye contact. "Go sit down," I whisper against her silky skin. "I'll grab you something to drink. And then you are telling me what's going on."

I let her go slowly as she nods. Dropping her head once more, she slinks to the couch and slumps into it, making absolutely no noise. Keeping an eye on her, I start heating up milk and a Heath bar. I know my girl well. I made Heath hot chocolate for her a few times, and every time it puts a smile on her face.

Once it's finished, I pour it into a large coffee mug for her. I add whipped cream because she loves it and bring it to her. The mug is insulated, so she won't burn herself when she holds it, something she loves to do. It's a comfort for her. That and inhaling the scent.

I sit down and hand her the mug. She takes it and smiles softly. "You made Heath hot chocolate?"

"Is there another option for a situation like this?"

She shakes her head and focuses on the mug. "No. There really isn't."

I put my arm around her and pull her closer. Carefully, she cuddles as close as she can, tucking her feet underneath her and leaning her head on my shoulder. "Tell me what happened, baby girl." I start running my fingers through her hair. It's relaxing to her, and she loves it.

She lets out a breath. "Do you remember Zack?"

I narrow my eyes as I glare at the wall. I shouldn't be pissed about him. I'm the one who pushed her towards him. "The jackwad who escorted you to the gala a couple of months ago? How could I forget?"

"Well, I wish you would've stopped me. Seriously said anything at all. Took me yourself. Told me to go alone. Anything at all, Josh, because he made me so uncomfortable the entire time. And even though I wouldn't respond to his advances and pushed him away more than once, he still started telling the entire school that he took the v-card of Viper's Venom's princess."

I nearly choke as I look down at her. "Are you saying that he just started bullshit rumors? Or that he took your v-card against your will and bragged about it."

She looks up at me wide-eyed. "Holy hell, Josh. No. Not that. That I would've been screaming for help about. There were so many people there. It's just stupid rumors." She tucks herself back into my side.

My heart slowly slows. "Fuck...," I rumble. "I would've killed him."

"I know. A lot of people would've killed him."

"I'm still not promising I won't. What happened? He's just been spreading shit for the last couple months or what? What happened today?"

She takes a sip of her hot chocolate before taking a deep breath. "I switched classes. Which really sucked because since Rosie was moved up a grade, we had all of our classes together and loved that. But the upside was I didn't have a single class with him. It didn't matter, though, because he constantly harassed me. He tried to kiss me on several different occasions. Alec got a call once because I punched him in the balls. He stopped them from expelling me by threatening them for allowing him to touch me in the first place. I never told him about anything more than that. He just thought I was defending myself, told me good job, and brought me and Rosie to dinner to celebrate. It was a couple days before you got back from Texas."

I can't help but chuckle. "You should've told me. I would've taken you anywhere in the world for that."

She giggles softly, and I grin at getting that out of her, but the smile quickly fades. "Anyway, it didn't really stop. He was just more subtle about it. He'd walk with me to my classes. He'd meet me at my locker. He'd touch my hair. Tell me I looked hot and how much hotter I'd look with the buttons on my shirt undone more. I ignored him the best I could. He said we were going to our Senior Prom together. I said no. He said he'd pick me up. So, I had the crew stop him before he got close to the club and didn't go. I didn't want to anyway. I couldn't exactly go with you, and you're the only one I wanted to go with."

"I never went to my prom. I was on a mission in Alex's place so he could go."

She looks up at me as I tangle strands of her hair around my finger. "You never went?"

I shake my head. "No. I didn't really want to anyway. That's why I told Alex to go. I was being drugged by then, so the aggression was already setting in."

Her eyes widen, and I realize this is something she didn't know. "Drugged?"

I look down. "Uh… yeah." I'd already decided to tell her about everything, but it might just be sooner rather than later.

"Oh, Josh." She sets her drink on the table and wraps her arms around my waist. "I'm so sorry." She kisses my chest in the most tender of motions that if I could physically melt, I just might actually do it.

"Don't be." I kiss her head. "I wouldn't be where I am now if not for all I went through."

"I don't know if I believe that."

I hug her tighter. "Tell me what else happened. How did you get the bruises?"

She sighs. "He was pissed about prom. I was also gone for two weeks. The week before and the week after because of... everything... He was too busy with finals to mess with me, but today... well, I guess he wasn't as busy. He cornered me before lunch. He grabbed my arm really hard. I told him he was hurting me, but he didn't care. He was seething. He told me I'm going to be his and need to stop arguing with him about it. He said we're going to the same college and going to be college sweethearts. I told him I wasn't going to college, and he told me I was. I was going to Chicago State with him. One of his friends got him off me, and they got into a fight. We got released early, so that was the end of it."

"Well, I'm gonna be honest. I don't think it's the end. Just because school ended doesn't mean much. I know that he's not a danger to you from a mafia or biker standpoint because I had him checked the second you mentioned his name. Doesn't mean he's not dangerous, though. There are a lot of crazy fuckers out there."

"I know..." She buries her head in my chest. "Can he be a tomorrow problem? I'm so sick of him." She lightly caresses my stomach.

I do all I can to will my dick to behave, but I know I have no hope. "Yes. Because that gives me a day to figure out how to fuck up his life."

She looks up at me with a smile and doesn't stop caressing my abs. I'm just about to kiss her, but her next words stop me in my tracks. "Will you tell me about the things that happened to you? If I promise to finally open up about everything that I went through over the past couple of weeks? And years, I guess."

I groan and let my head fall back on the couch. "Baby, it's not a happy story. It's fucking hard to talk about." And just those words have my dick deflating. I close my eyes and press my thumb and forefinger to the bridge of my nose.

"I think… maybe… if… you tell me… at least some of it, maybe it will help me to… tell you everything." She looks down at my chest again and starts tracing along the top of my belt.

Something inside me stirs, though. The need to finally tell her all she wants to know. I hadn't intended to do it this second, but if it helps her, I'll do whatever I can. If we're really going to make a go of this, like I want to and know she does, then I can't hold this back.

I lean forward and grab her mug. I hand it to her again just so she has something to do with her hands that doesn't make me envision her mouth over my cock sucking with my fingers tangled in her hair. She, thankfully, takes the cup and starts sipping like she's about to watch her favorite movie.

I pull her closer to me. "For our entire lives, Alex and I believed he was the older one. He was the one taking over for our father. He was the one being groomed for it. Our father didn't need me. He only needed one son. Alex. Only, the older Alex got, the more he didn't want anything to do with the mafia. He saw a lot of shit our father was doing that he didn't like. He knew when he took over, he'd have no hope of changing a damn thing. Not as long as our father was still alive. The short version of the story is that our father hated me. Alex was the golden child and the one who protected me all of our lives. Until he left for Italy to get away from our father and the woman who broke his heart. The day he boarded that plane was the day I lost complete fucking control. Not that I had any to begin with, but the small shreds I did, the ones that Alex helped me hold onto, were gone with him. He kept me sane. Without him, I was lost."

"And that's when you started going after Jessa? And when everything with her happened?"

"Yes and no. Again, the short version is that I became obsessed with her. I believed I was the only thing keeping her safe from our father. Without Alex, all she had was me. The obsession grew. The violence grew. Next thing I know, she's gone. After Alex left, she was the one piece that kept me from completely falling off the edge of sort of sanity to completely insane. I'm not proud of anything that came after that. I'm lucky she saw the man underneath because if she hadn't, I wouldn't be here today. I would've been killed either by my father, at the hands of Ryan Crane, or at the hands of Alex himself. And I can assure you. That's a pain he never would've survived. Thanks to Jessa and her faith in me, though, we found out a lot of shit. I was being drugged by our father. We found family we never knew we had. We even discovered the truth of our birth. Alex was never the older one. I was. Am. We ended up killing our father. I took over the mafia. Turned it legit with Ryan's help. Our father came back from the dead. We killed him for real. That's the short version."

She nods as she focuses once more on her hot chocolate. I run my fingers through her hair because I know that's not what she wants. She stays quiet while I try to formulate my thoughts.

After several moments, I finally decide to just let it out. If this is what she wants, she'll get it all.

"There were beatings. A lot of them. So many that I still don't think I remember them all. They started when I was a kid." Once the words start, I can't stop them. "Alex took the brunt of them, but I still got my fair share. More so when we got older, and he was away more. He wasn't around to protect me. I never resented him for it until later on in our teens. And that was because our father was injecting me with an experimental drug that was meant to control my mind, make it easier to brainwash me, and turn me into a killing machine. He couldn't make Alex do what he wanted, so he tried to model me into what he wanted Alex to be. The thing was, I was the one who wanted control of the mafia anyway. He never had to do any of the shit he did to me. I was willing and eager to learn everything. It didn't stop him, though. The beatings intensified when Alex was in college. The drugs intensified. Eventually, I had no fucking clue who I even was. Large chunks of my memory were gone."

Dallas sniffles and curls as close as possible. I tug her hair just a little as my hand shakes. I don't like going down this rabbit hole, but I keep telling myself that she needs to know.

"Sometimes, I'll have dreams that end up being actual memories. Shit that happened during those periods of time where I'd blacked out. The longer I'd been being drugged, the longer it took me to remember anything. For a while, I remembered almost killing Jessa. But the longer I'd been off the drugs I was being given, the more some things just went fuzzy. That memory came back in force the day I was locked in my office that entire day after Dane had taken his team into the compound for protection. I saw Amy in that room covered in glass. Seconds later, I was right back in Jessa's apartment. Everything. I remembered everything. Everything I did to her then."

I slowly move my arm from around her and lean forward. I squeeze my eyes closed and shake my head a little as I rest my elbows on my knees. I don't expect it, but Dallas starts soothingly rubbing her hand up and down my back. Almost instantly, I'm calm enough to continue.

I let out a breath and stay in the position I am. "During those blackouts, it was after the drugs. I'd sometimes be out for days. Others, I'd come to and face more beatings for weeks on end. And then I'd get another dose. After the dose, I'd be out again, but when I came to again, it was almost like I was superhuman. Invincible. I could do fucking anything. And I often did. I'd get sent on missions and get high praises from everyone. Never him, though. Never our father. It was never enough for him. Or maybe it was too much, and I terrified him. The truth is, though, I was what he made me. The weaker he made, the stronger I felt like I was. I think he noticed that, though, because a lot of shit happened from then on. He killed his second in command right in front of me because I'd managed to get him on my side. I was planning a takeover. I had a lot of guys with me who would've been happy to take him out. After Keith was killed, though, I spiraled. That's when I lost the little control I had. That's when everything happened with Jessa. And it's when I went after her again in New York. For a long time after, I didn't know if it was me or not. I didn't know who I was anymore. I hated everything. I hated her. My brother. I fucking hated my father, but I craved his damn approval. I hated the whole damn world."

I'm shaking, but I wouldn't be able to stop myself even if I wanted to. Dallas sets her almost empty cup down on the table and wraps her arms around me once more. I can feel the love and support pouring off of her and through me. I don't know how long I've been talking; how long she's been listening.

It's at that moment that I lose it. I don't remember the last time I actually let tears fall. I don't think I ever have, but I do with her. I turn and wrap my arms around her. I pull her down to the couch with me and bury my face in her hair.

I've never felt safe enough with anyone but Alex to truly let myself go like this. Not even Lyric, which was something I've always thought was both unfair to her and proof that we never had a future with each other. We were brought into each other's lives to help each other heal and make a beautiful child together. Beyond that, our future's held something more. She found her happy ending.

And now I've finally found mine.

My home.

Chapter Sixteen

❦ Dallas ❦

It takes over an hour, but the pain Josh was holding inside dissipates more and more. Not that I believe he's absolutely cured, but I know it's helped him to feel better, and that's all I care about. I hold him close the entire time. His head is resting on my chest as I run my fingers through his hair.

"Never tell a soul about this," Josh rumbles. I smile a little because I know he's teasing. His grip on me is tight. He loosens it slightly, letting me know he's okay again, but doesn't let go.

I kiss the top of his head. "Never," I whisper.

My heart starts beating a little bit faster because I know it's my turn next. I don't really want to, but I'll never break my promise to him. Especially after he was so vulnerable with me.

"Want dinner first?"

I take a deep breath and shake my head. "I'm not sure I could eat it. I'd probably throw up."

He nods slightly and kisses my chest, just above my breast bone. I shiver at the intimacy as he shifts so it's me who's being held by him instead of him who's being held by me. "Probably best to just let it out as fast as you can and know I'm right here to catch you when you break."

I smile softly and turn so I'm facing him. We're both still stretched on the couch. This is the best way. When I start bawling my eyes out, which is inevitable, I can do it in his chest and hide just a little.

It takes me a long while to find the words, but when they come, they flow like a waterfall. "I guess I should begin with killing my dad. I remember everything so clearly. I was playing outside. I picked a dandelion. It matched my dress. It's so weird because I'd been dreaming different things about it. My dress was different colors. The flower was a different flower. The one thing that was always the same, though, was I heard the commotion, gunshots, and then Alec came running outside with Tyler. He wasn't hurt. There was no blood on him. He picked me up. We ran to the house, and I was safe. I felt safe. Everything was fine."

"But that isn't exactly what happened," Josh coaxes silently as I trace the tattoo on his arm. It's intricate. I never really noticed how detailed it was before.

I always just thought it was a bleeding heart on his forearm, but it's so much more. It's wrapped in barbed wire. The date is his date of birth. I know now that its significance is so much more than just a bleeding heart. It's his. It represents him. His heart was just as trapped as he was. And no matter what he did to get out, the barbs just kept digging in.

I move as close to him as possible and wrap my arms around his middle as I close my eyes. I love the way he smells. So strong. Confident. "No," I whisper. "It wasn't." I take a deep breath and steam ahead. "That dream brought it all back. Alec's confirmation sealed it all. My dress was yellow. Alec fought our father. Up until then, I'd heard rumblings of what my fate was. Rumblings that I was going to be married to someone to form this alliance. My dad always said no. He always said that wouldn't happen. But then, I started to believe what I heard. And he started getting mad when I asked him about it. I needed reassurance. And I guess he couldn't lie anymore. One day, it came to a head. He'd made a deal. Alec found out and confronted him. That's what the fight was about. I didn't know it then, but the deal that was made was for right then. I was to be sold that very day."

"Oh fuck, baby." He hugs me tighter.

I sink into him, using his strength to keep going. "I found out a few days later that Alec had Chaos and Hawk take a team with them and kill the guy who had wanted the deal. That crew ended up in an alliance with Alec anyway. Eventually, they were just absorbed by Viper's Venom. They're just part of the crew now. Those that were left anyway. There were some that fought alongside their leader. They died that day, too. The others didn't fight because they hated what was happening. They wanted to leave but didn't know how. I wasn't supposed to know any of that, but I'd overheard Alec talking with Chaos and Hawk about it. So, while they were battling the other crew, Alec and Tyler stayed back. Tyler was rallying people behind Alec because he knew the plan. He knew Alec would end up killing our dad. He didn't expect it to go down so quickly, and no one expected Alec would have all of the support, except for the very few that were loyal to our dad. That was more stuff I wasn't supposed to know. Getting back to that day, though. I remember all of the details. Small and large. Everything that happened that day. And I remember that I actively made myself forget."

"Honestly, baby, that's pretty normal. Especially something traumatic like that. You were also very young."

I nod but keep my eyes closed. I focus completely on him. On his hard body next to me. The way he smells. How his heartbeat sounds. "I used to love the color yellow. I hate it now. I can't wear it. I don't even like seeing it. I never fully understood why, but now I remember it's because that's the color I was wearing that day. I still will never wear that color again. When my dad was on top of Alec with the knife to his neck, Alec was already bleeding. He had a deep gash to one of his arms. The other was trickling blood." I shake my head when the image of my brother bleeding takes over my mind. My eyes snap open so I can reorient myself using Josh as my anchor. "When I shot him, the blood and brain matter from his head shot out at me. I was so close to him so I didn't miss. I knew the gun recoiled because I shot it once with Alec. It was his gun. I shot our dad with it because dad knocked it out of Alec's hand." Tears sting my eyes, and I try to will them away, but it's no use.

Josh rubs his hands up and down my back. "I know, beautiful. I know how hard that had to be for you."

"I j-just kept th-thinking that h-he was k-killing Alec!" The waterfall of words turns into one made of tears that I thought I'd already cried. "I'm n-not even s-sorry!" And it's because of that single reason that I let the floodgates release. "Wh-what kind of m-monster isn't sorry f-for th-that!"

"Sweet girl, I said it before, and I will again. It was self-defense. Never ever be sorry for saving a life. Especially if that life is yours," he whispers in my ear. "Never be sorry for protecting people you love."

I take several deep breaths while the memories from that day play over and over in my head like a song on repeat. "I remember being covered in blood. Things were dripping off my dress. I didn't know what anything was, but I know now it was parts of his head. I think I went into shock. By the time we got to Alec's house, I was even more covered in it. Alec's blood had mixed with what was already on my dress. Alec got me to the shower and helped me rinse off. Then he got me into the bath. I don't know what he did with my clothes or his or what Tyler did with his, but when I got out, everyone was changed. I had clean clothes. It went a long way into helping me make myself forget it happened at all. By the time the next day started, I'd pretty much forgotten, but I think my brain also worked some magic because I really didn't remember. I wasn't just actively trying to forget. I really didn't remember. I remembered knowing I was meant to be sold to someone. Alec said he protected me. He got into a fight with dad about it and killed him because dad tried to kill him, but he assured me it was over. I was safe. A couple days later, the police came and arrested him."

"But he was back not long after."

"They never pursued charges. They did the investigation. They arrested him, but only because they had to. The DA dropped charges against him after being presented with his account of what happened and all of the evidence. Everything made sense to her then. He was gone for maybe two days. Tyler was with me. As far as I was concerned, it was over. Alec didn't mention it. I didn't. No one did. And if anyone brought it up in conversation, Alec just reaffirmed he did it. I guess I know now that the only people who knew the truth then were him and Tyler. And now me and you."

"Like Alec said, it's staying that way. You don't need that. So many years have passed. It doesn't need to be rehashed. Let people live thinking the truth is what Alec gave them. And if you start struggling with that, then we talk to him about it and figure out what to do."

I chew on the words for a few moments before deciding. "It's better in the past. I don't want to know what could happen with my confession this many years later. Maybe it's selfish on my part, but I really just want to protect him. It's been dealt with. If I were to come out with the real truth, maybe he wouldn't be as respected as he is. Maybe they'd try to overthrow him based on a lie. I don't want that for him or anyone. It's at peace. I want it to stay there."

"Knowing the truth allows you to heal as a person. You may feel guilty. Maybe sorry later, but the real truth is that you protected yourself and your brother. And Alec wouldn't have second guessed himself for a second. He'd have done the exact same thing if the roles were reversed. To him, they were. He went after your dad and ordered a hit on the other guy because that's what the situation called for to protect you. For you, there was no other option to save your brother. That's really all there is to it, baby."

I nod and keep a tight grip on him. It's another long while before I finally let out a long breath. "About... what... happened... with Matthew."

He senses I need him to hug me tighter and doesn't disappoint.

Once I'm relaxed, at least as much as I can be, I begin. "It started at school. I was waiting for Alec. I'm used to other crew members coming to get me, but Alec always texts first. And I know everyone. So, if someone else comes and I haven't heard from Alec, they wait while I text him. Or call him. They all know the rules, and why they're there. That day, there was a blacked out SUV that pulled up. I honestly paid no attention to it because lots of people get picked up like that. I figured it was for someone else. I went back to scrolling my Instagram, but after a few minutes, a couple of people stepped out. They approached me. I saw VV cuts, but didn't recognize them. Not only that, their cuts were all wrong. It said they were Prospects, but the patch wasn't the right color. It wasn't even the right font. I know our cuts. Alec let me help design some of the patches. So, I started running back to the school to get help from security. Only, I never made it. They were faster. They grabbed me. I screamed."

"No one came to help you?" He tangles his fingers in my hair as he runs his fingers through it.

"Well, they started, but then they saw the cuts. They don't know them like I do. They didn't help me. Why should they? The people, as far as they were concerned, were VV. They didn't understand why I was screaming for help. I don't know when Alec got there that day, but during the struggle, I dropped my phone and backpack."

"Alec came to us a couple of days later. He somehow figured out that our issue crossed with theirs."

"I'm… uh… I… don't think I've ever been more grateful for that. I had no idea who these people were, but they were bigger than us. As a faction. A few days went by before Jessa ended up with me, but by then, I'd been in the basement of this house for what I believed was maybe a week. I lost count of the days because I never saw the sunlight. I couldn't even go by when we were fed because sometimes, we weren't. That wasn't really the worst part, though. It was the threats to everyone else, but not me. I lived just as they did. I was stripped of clothing and all of my dignity, but they never touched me like they did them. I wasn't assaulted, physically or sexually."

Josh takes a deep breath. "Thank fuck for that," he rumbles. His hug becomes far more protective, and I feel it seep into my bones. It gives me the bravery I need to continue.

"Things really changed when Jessa got there. I was given clothes, for one. And I suddenly went wherever she did. I didn't know it quite then, but she told me later that whatever plans they had for me changed the second she told them she'd tell Matthew. I still don't know what the original plan for me was, but I heard whisperings that I was meant to be sold specifically to someone who requested me. I did tell that to Alec, but there haven't been any leads. At all. And it didn't take me and Jessa long to realize we were related. All it took was me telling her my last name and the name of my mother and father. She was trying to comfort me after she got there. When she found out, that's when she started making demands and when everything changed for me."

"She's a smart girl. Always has been."

"I'm really happy for that. I don't know where I'd be without her. Anyway, though. It wasn't easy. Before they moved us, there was a lot that happened. Girls were raped right next to me. There was a girl who was shot in front of us for trying to escape. Another was killed for fighting off one of the attackers. When we got separated from them, we found out we were going directly to Matthew. I didn't know who he was, but she told me. I knew he was a bad guy, but I also saw him as a savior of some sort. Anything to get us out of there. I never saw the guys who took me again.

And when we were separated, the ones who were at the house were never seen again. It was different people. We were treated kind of decently. Even when Jessa got caught trying to leave messages for you to find us. They never touched us. We never got punished. It wasn't until we ended up at Matthew's that we found out what the real plan was."

"To lure me and Ryan."

I nod. "Yeah. He kept telling us that the bombs were fake. They were just a ploy to get us out. He said that you guys were the bad guys, and he was just saving us. But Jessa kept asking him if that were the case, how come he didn't just leave? Why stay if he knew you were coming? She kept telling me not to believe his lies. Not to fall for his charm. His wife was the worst. She'd bring food to us and throw it so it landed on the floor. Jessa said to leave it because Matthew would deal with it. And he did. He always got pissed and punished her for it. He'd always make her bring us the food and give it to us like a maid would. Her resentment grew, but he got a kick out of it. It was pretty obvious he had no respect at all for her, but she definitely was head over heels for him. The night you guys came was the night I realized something was off. He was acting differently. He kept telling us that it would all be okay now. That we were going to be okay. Jessa and I never understood the switch. I don't know about her, but I still don't get it. He was kind to us the entire time. Even the night you came, he told us that everything that was about to happen was to keep us both safe." I take a deep breath. "This is easier to talk about then I thought. Maybe I've just cried so much that I don't feel anymore."

"No, baby. It's easier to talk about this because it's never been repressed. This didn't just hit you. It's not that you don't feel. I can tell that you do just by the way your nails are digging into my back. But you've had a long time to process all of this. It's not something that just dropped out of nowhere. You probably started thinking about it more when the memory of your dad came back, but this was something you've had four years to process and deal with. You just feel safe enough to let it all out now."

I nod, but I'm silent for a while until I realize that he's right. I never suppressed this. I've always remembered it all. I didn't talk about it because I didn't know how. Alec and Tyler have asked about it. So has Jessa. I just never really felt like I'd processed it fully enough to really talk about it. So, I didn't talk about it at all.

"I think the part that scared me the most was the bomb and not knowing what would happen. Just before that, he told us we had to strip. He needed us to help him really give you guys a total picture. We were already dirty. He thought that would be the best way for him to show you how bad it could be and make you believe that's how it actually was. When you showed up, I fully expected Alec to storm in with the army of what I envisioned you and Ryan were. When I didn't see him, I honestly thought that was it for me. I'd accepted my fate. Jessa was so calm. I tried to be. I think it was when Taylor had the guy he worked with on the phone that the calmness just left my body. Matthew and Renza were gone, but I was so scared, I couldn't move. When you were talking to me, I don't even know how any words came out of my mouth for me to respond to you. Motions of any kind. It was like I was a whole other being, and I was watching myself from out of my body. Like I was just floating in the corner of the room. And then, when the bomb was supposed to go off but didn't, I became completely numb. I felt the tears falling, but couldn't comprehend them."

"I can't say I really blame you. I don't think my heart started beating again until I had us all safely out of the building."

I sigh. "I know I've said it before, but thank you. Thank you for everything that night. Thank you for saving me. Thank you for giving me some of my dignity back and covering me. Thank you for being so protective of me and making sure I got to Alec. But mostly, thank you for blowing up the house. It might sound silly to some, but it was like that chapter of my life was truly over. It gave me closure. When it was burning, I was just crying into Alec's chest. I think it really helped me to heal and be able to move forward."

"You're welcome, baby. We did that for the same reason. It gave me and Alex closure. A true ending to a fucked up chapter. And now, it's just closing up loose ends with him. Ruthless Warriors was tied to him in some ways, but those ways have been tied up. Hopefully, anyway."

"He still haunts you from the grave," I whisper.

Josh chuckles. "Maybe. But it's getting better. He's getting buried deeper and deeper."

I smile into his chest. The longer Josh holds me, the more comforted and protected I feel. The more loved I feel. The more at peace I feel.

For the first time in my entire life, I fall into a deep, completely dreamless sleep. One of those sleeps that people long for. The one where you wake up energized, like it's an entirely new day.

Like the past is dead and gone…

Chapter Seventeen

☙ Josh ☙

Long after Dallas has fallen asleep, I find myself unable to follow. Something she said is eating at me.

VV cuts.

It's new information to me. And if what I'm thinking is true, then it means Ruthless Warriors has been working with Matthew for longer than any of us thought. And if that's the case, then it means they're bigger than we thought. We already know they've expanded. We know they have an unnamed leader who we suspect is named Ethan, though we can't confirm that. We still don't know how deeply involved with Matthew they were.

A lot of questions run through my mind. If she told Alec, why didn't Alec tell me? Is it a detail he forgot about? I don't blame him. He was beyond stressed the fuck out for a long time after we found Dallas. His head was on a swivel. He tried to get her to stay home from school and get a tutor. I'm positive he forgot completely about it, but we still need to talk about it.

I kiss Dallas's forehead gently before getting up. I pause when she shifts, but she simply snuggles into the back of the couch like it's me. I carefully get off the couch. I hate leaving her right now, but I have to get things moving. It's only midnight, so I know most of my team will still be up. I need to compose my thoughts first.

I quickly walk to my office. I turn on the lamp on my desk and sit down in my chair. I leave the door open so if Dallas wakes up, she'll know where I am right away. Not like she wouldn't know anyway. She knows this is the first place I go if I can't sleep.

I pull out my folder on Ruthless Warriors. There's a lot of information, but not nearly enough. Way too many pieces are missing. I open and take out the page regarding the leader. We don't know a lot about him, but I think we're starting to narrow it down. We know he's based in Texas. Our theory is that he was the rogue Viper's Venom prospect, Ethan. We just don't know anything else about him because the name he gave Viper's Venom is fake.

That was all confirmed the more digging we did. At face value, he came with a mother out of Mexico. He has a rap sheet a mile long. The problem is that Lance figured out the file Viper's Venom had on him was all planted. Viper's Venom confirmed everything he said, but everything they had was completely fabricated. It was entered into the court system and Law Enforcement system, but Lance has ways of confirming further. Whoever planted the information on him didn't know that there are ways to cross reference everything. Which is exactly what Lance did. And then had Robby do just to make sure he was right.

We know that Ethan Ricardo Vasquez is a real person with a mother named Maria Romero, who was married to a man named Ricardo Vasquez. Ethan had his name, but when they divorced, Maria went back to her maiden name. Ricardo's name isn't on Ethan's birth certificate. It's just Maria's. It's something that bothers the fuck out of me, and I hate that I can't figure it out.

We know he went to school in Mexico. We know he ran away when he was sixteen, but that's all the further he goes. As far as anyone knows, he disappeared in the wind when he was sixteen and reappeared with a rap sheet when he joined Viper's Venom. We don't know his actual age for sure, but according to the fake shit, he'd be just thirty-years-old.

Which put us back at square one. Ethan, if that's even his real fucking name, is a fucking ghost. I rub my head. I'm hoping that Dallas will be able to recognize the cut and tell me if it matches the cuts of the other fake VV members we have caught. If it does, it implicates a much larger picture and puts a lot of pieces in place that are currently missing.

I send a group text to everyone on my team to meet me in the morning in my office. They know everything I found out from the asshole from the cargo ship. We think we identified who Cap is, but I need to confirm it. And the only way I can do that is with Jaxon's help.

Not something I'm looking forward to in the slightest.

I rub my hand down my face and let out a sigh before texting Alec.

Josh: Hey, can you meet with me and my team in the morning? My office.

I set my phone down and wait for him to answer as I flip through the file. It's something I've done countless times. Not once has anything more struck me. Not like tonight. All the new stuff in here was added after my talk with Morpheus. We know Ruthless Warriors were involved with kidnapping Jaxon but don't have a damn clue where the orders to leave Lyric alone came from, and why it was that they didn't care to follow the rules they were given. It's like we find out something, but it opens a whole other mess that I'm too tired to unravel.

I look down when my phone vibrates. I see Alec's name, so I open his text.

Alec: Yeah. But give me until at least 8. Need to get Aero. Fucked up. Long story. Explain tomorrow. Keep my sister with you. I sense something bad is about to happen.

Of course he does. Son of a bitch. I feel the adrenaline start pumping through my veins, but I know I need to stay calm.

Josh: Fuck. Come on, man. Are you kidding? We don't need more shit.

Alec: Well, buckle up, bro. It's coming.

I put my phone down and sigh. I don't need more on my plate right now, but if he's going to get Aero, it means something big is going down.

"Do you ever sleep?"

I grin as I look up. I expect to see a sleepy Dallas in her rumpled school uniform. What I actually see is enough to stop my heart and make swallowing an impossible feat. When I was deep in thought, she must've gone upstairs to change because she's not wearing anything but my LA Rams Matthew Stafford t-shirt.

My eyes wander slowly down her body. She's leaning against the doorframe with her arms crossed over her chest. Her feet are bare, and her light pink painted toenails match the innocent pink of her panties. At least the small peek I can see of them. Her hair is a mess, but her face is bare of any makeup. I can't even tell she'd been crying for hours in my arms not long ago.

I clear my throat, hoping to gain some type of control over what she's doing to me. I can't talk. I've forgotten how to breathe. I'm pretty sure I don't even know my own name. The way she's looking at me makes my stomach tighten, and my dick stand at attention. If I'm not released from these jeans soon, I'm going to end up buying a new pair because I'm about to cause irreparable damage to them.

I drop my hand over my dick to try and make it calm down. It doesn't work, so I squeeze a couple of times just to relieve some of the ache.

Another mistake.

I clear my throat, never more thankful for my desk being a barrier between the two of us. "Sometimes. Why aren't you sleeping, little sparrow?"

She tilts her head as she slowly walks into the room. "Little sparrow? You've never called me that before." Her voice is heavy with sleep and sexy as hell.

I have to squeeze myself a little harder, enough to cross over the threshold of pleasure to pain, just to keep myself in control. "It's fitting. Sparrows symbolize love, devotion, and companionship. They represent hope, strength, and resilience. All things you represent."

The more I speak, the more she blushes. I can't help the grin that finds my lips, but it falls very quickly when I see she's not stopping in front of my desk like she usually does. Any second, she'll see what I don't think she's ready to. I let go of my cock and try to casually place my hand over it instead as I watch her.

"I never knew that."

"They also have beautiful voices. So do you." I don't know why those words come out of my mouth, but I don't bother taking them back. They're true.

Her blush deepens. Her hands fall to her sides as she smiles softly. "I woke up. You weren't there. So, I thought I'd keep you company." She lightly bites her lip before releasing it.

I don't know if it was something natural or not. I've never told her my aversion to lip biting, but I can't help but think she felt my displeasure. I hate when women bite their lip. To them, they think it's sexy. To me, it just makes me think they're hurting themselves. It's not alluring.

When she starts biting the inside of her cheek, I realize she wasn't trying to be sexy at all. She's nervous. I can't exactly blame her. There's no way she missed how hard I am. Even though I'm trying to hide it, it's not easy to hide my length.

I reach for her. Instead of taking her hand like I usually would to guide her to me, I grip her hip instead. "Is that all that's on your mind?" I gently pull her towards me. When she's close enough, I move my chair back and move my hand. I watch her eyes fall to my dick as I lift her enough to set her on my desk in front of me.

"Uh...um... I...," she stutters. I grin a little wider. I like that she can't focus on anything else, but that she's way too shy to say it. She shakes her head a little, like she's coming out of a daze. She looks at me. "I just missed you."

"Well, you got me now." More words sit on the tip of my tongue, like asking her how she wants me, but I don't say them. I settle between her legs with her feet on either side of my thighs. I look up at her as I wrap my arms around her. She becomes so content, and I love that I can do that for her.

"I think I just woke up a little startled at you being gone. I thought maybe it meant you'd gone back to not trusting yourself with me or something. And then I thought maybe you'd fallen asleep and woke up with a nightmare again." She reaches up and runs her fingers through my hair.

I chuckle and let my thumbs rub circles near her tailbone. "No, honey. Nothing like that. I never fell asleep. You mentioned some things when you were talking that got me thinking. I didn't know you were taken by anyone wearing VV cuts. It's new information for me, and I think it's getting me closer and closer to solving my Jaxon mystery. A lot of shit was put into play. I just need to sit down and figure it out."

"Oh." She nods. "Can I help?"

I smile before laying my head in her lap. I kiss the inside of her thigh as I hug her a little tighter. "Yeah. You can. But I don't really want to work anymore tonight." I kiss the inside of her thigh again.

She giggles softly as she rubs the back of my neck. "So then, why are you hiding in your office?"

I grin and nip her thigh. She moans softly, and it's over for me. "I was taking notes. Organizing my thoughts. But you just fucked them all up, and now all I can think of is you."

"Good. Then my evil plan worked."

I laugh and kiss her thigh as I look up at her. She's smiling so big, I fall even deeper into her snare. I'm never getting out of this alive. I don't even want to. She's mine. All fucking mine. Forever.

"There are so many things I want to do with you right now." It comes out more like a growl than I mean for it to, but it does something to her. I feel her shiver.

"Maybe you should," she whispers.

The underlying confidence scares the fuck out of me. I watch her questioningly, but she simply searches my eyes curiously. She gives nothing to me other than pure love, desire, and surety. My hand automatically finds my dick once more. I haven't been with anyone other than my hand in a long time. I know the second I touch her, I'm not going to be able to fight off my own orgasm. I'm good at control. I've trained myself well. Dallas is the only one who's ever made me lose it like I'm about to.

I know I need to do this slow and at her pace. There's no way I'm taking her virginity on my desk, but that doesn't mean I can't give us both some relief.

I pull her to the edge of the desk as I watch her. Her eyes grow wider, but she steadies herself by placing her hands on my shoulders.

"You can say stop anytime you want, and I will. Okay?"

She nods, that confidence waning just a little. "O-okay."

"I'm not going all the way with you." I pause and smirk. "Yet."

Relief washes over as she nods again. That confidence returns once more. "Okay."

I grip the hem of my shirt that she's wearing. "Can I take this off?"

Her pretty eyes widen even more. "I'm... not wearing... anything under it."

I smirk again. "Good." I slowly pull it up, though it's torturous to me. I want to rip it off and bask in all she is, but I take my time. It's what she needs. I stand as I raise the shirt until I can pull it off her arms. "My God, you're beautiful," I whisper as I lean in and kiss her.

Dallas's body is everything I imagined it would be. Tight, though she has soft curves in all the right places. Her thighs are a little thick, but just as perfect as she is. She may be small and petite, but she's not skin and bones. She has places I can grab onto. If she wanted, she could be small enough to be a Victoria's Secret model, but I'd never allow that kind of an unhealthy weight or diet. Thankfully, she enjoys food as much as I do.

It's her tits that are slightly disproportionate to the rest of her. While they're not large enough to slap her in the face if she runs, they are fairly big. I know she's a D-cup because she asked me to help her shop for a bra once. I tried to do everything I could to get out of it, but in the end, I couldn't let her go to school in a broken bra and in pain from the snapped underwire. And with her brother and other people she trusted out of town, I was the only one who could help her. She was sixteen. Since then, it's taken every ounce of control I have not to stare at her chest or wonder what kind of bra she's wearing underneath her shirt.

Not that that's worked at all. Ever.

After kissing her breathless, I toss the shirt and let my hands roam her body like I've wanted to do for longer than I'm willing to admit to myself or anyone else. I kiss down her collarbone to her perky tits before looking up at her. Her eyes are closed, and she has a smile of pleasure, but I have to make sure.

"Is this okay so far?"

She nods. "Yes, sir."

Sir. I never should've told her that *sir* was a good thing to call me because it forces my body to do things she's nowhere near ready to hear about. Or see.

I lower my head a little more and take one of her sweet peaks into my mouth. It instantly hardens under my tongue, and the moan escapes without me being able to stop it. She gasps when I suck and flick it with my tongue while my other hand cups her other one. I massage her soft breast as my thumb flicks her nipple. She arches into my hand, and I take that as my sign to switch.

I lavish both of her tits with equal attention from both my mouth and my hands before continuing a trail down to the part I'm craving. I lick and kiss my way to her panty line as I sit back down. I spread her legs more to give myself access to her, but stop once more.

I look back up at her. "Still doing okay, little sparrow?"

She nods, though a little more hesitantly as her breath hitches. "I'm okay," she whispers through a voice thick with emotion.

"You sure? Just tell me to stop. I will, Dallas. I'll never do anything you don't want me to."

"I know." She clears her throat so she can speak more clearly. "I'm okay. Keep going... Please?"

I smile. "Okay, but I mean it, baby. All you have to do is say stop. Or enough. Anything. I'll stop."

"I trust you." Her eyes prove her words, and for some reason, that makes me feel a whole lot better about continuing.

I lean down and kiss both of her thighs before I nudge my nose against her panties. I've been trying to be good and not dive right in, but her sexy as sin scent is making it hard. I close my eyes and inhale. Her panties are already wet. She's ready for me, but I'm taking my time with her. She's way too special to me to do anything else but make this as perfect for her as it can be.

I kiss her pussy over her panties and smile against her when she moans. I glance up at her. Her head has fallen back. Her lips are slightly parted, and her eyes are closed. I gently press my thumb against the crux between her thighs and rub up and down the fabric. I want more than anything to rip them off, preferably with my teeth, but I know the fabric is driving her crazy enough. She arches a little into me and trembles just enough for me to know the answer to my next question.

"Still okay?" I rub my thumb in a gentle circle over her clit.

She jerks and nods, her breathing quickening. "Yes, sir," she whispers breathlessly.

I let out a slow breath of my own. Unable to take another second, I unbuckle my belt and the button on my jeans. "Lay back, baby. Relax." My voice is deep and commanding, but still gentle enough to not come across like I'm barking at her.

She does what I say, propping herself up just barely with her elbows. It's enough for her to see what I'm doing, but not enough for her to be uncomfortable. She's not going to last in this position anyway. Not if I have my way.

I unzip my jeans with one hand while pushing her panties aside with the other. I lean in and lick her from her sweet little pussy up to her sexy little bundle of nerves.

"Oh!" she moans with another jerk of her hips. As I predicted, she's on her back and grasping at anything she can hold onto. She settles on a pen and the desk itself.

I pull my cock out and start stroking with a low moan of satisfaction against her clit that makes her shiver and arch closer to my mouth. I flick her clit with my tongue. Her arching becomes a slow thrust complete with sexy panting and moaning. I keep licking her clit and sucking it into my mouth before sliding my tongue down to her pussy and licking her before pushing it inside over and over again until she's a writhing mess.

"Doing okay?" I ask with a low rumble I know damn well sends shockwaves through her.

"Josh!" she screams. Her ass comes off my desk.

I grin before moving back to her clit. I'm close, but I need a little more. I let go of my dick as I suck and nip her clit. Thinking completely of her and her comfort, I don't start fingering her with two fingers like I normally would. Instead, I tease her pussy with my index finger. Her thighs tremble. I know she's close.

"Oh, Josh!" Her hips move on their own.

I slide my finger inside her and thrust as I lick her. She's so fucking wet and tight. I bury my face in her and shake my head back and forth while my tongue shoots across her clit. Her pussy pulses and clenches around my finger. I pull it out slowly and slide my middle finger into her just to coat it with her wetness.

Everything coming out of her mouth is somewhere between sexy whimpers and moans to complete jibberish, but I love every second of it. How silky she feels. How sweet and tangy she tastes. How wet her pussy sounds, and the beautiful pleasure sounds leaving her lips.

She's not lasting much longer. She's losing complete control, and I'm living for it. I crook my finger against her G-Spot as I flick and roll her clit with my tongue while I suck it.

"Ah! Josh!" she screams again.

I growl possessively and unashamed. "Mine."

"Ah!" She clamps tight around my finger as I'm slowly pulling it out of her. "Josh!" Her hips jerk as she writhes.

"Let go, baby girl. Come for me," I rumble against her as I grip my cock once more. With her essence all over my fingers, I stroke myself hard and fast. I'd close my eyes, but I don't want to miss a single moment of her orgasm.

The pen she holds goes flying, as does the folder on my desk. Her nails grip the desk, and she leaves scratches. She arches into me again just as her release hits her. Her eyes close tight. Her thighs clamp around my head, and she comes so hard, she slides back on the desk, taking me with her.

But I don't stop.

I keep licking her with all I am as I jerk myself.

"Oh my... ah! Josh! Josh, Josh, Josh!"

"Fuck, baby...," I moan into her.

Just as she starts coming down from her high, and after I've licked her clean, I stand slowly. I'm going to come, and I'm not doing it in my fucking jeans. I make sure her panties are back in place as she tries to catch her breath. I let go of myself long enough to grip her hips and tug her back towards me. When her ass is at the edge of my desk, I take hold of my cock again and keep stroking hard and fast, rotating my wrist.

She looks at my dick and what I'm doing with wide eyes that are filled with a kind of curious lust I'd expect from a woman who hasn't ever seen an actual dick before. At least not up close and in person. Her eyes never leave it, and it's the biggest turn on for me.

"Oh fuck, Dallas!" I shout out through clenched teeth as I start my release. My come hits her stomach. Instead of being grossed out like I half expect, Dallas's head falls back once more. Her eyes close as she moans again and arches up towards me. "Fuck," I whisper as I finish on her.

I watch her breathe. Her smile is so content, so soft. I can't fully grasp that it's truly me who put it there, but I know one thing for certain.

She's mine.

And I can't wait to show her every day just how mine she is.

Chapter Eighteen

❦ Dallas ❦

I look up when I feel something against my stomach wiping away Josh's come. When I see he's actually cleaning me, my heart simply melts. I watch him because the tenderness in which he does it is something I don't think he shows many people. It's so beautiful to see that I almost cry.

Josh smiles, seeing I'm watching him. "First rule of a dominant man is to do all he can to lift his girl up when she needs it while encouraging and supporting her to be the best version of herself she can be and chooses to be. To love her and guide her while being her stability." He takes both of my hands and slowly pulls me to a sitting position. "The second is to always take care of her." He wraps his arms around me and pulls me close to him. "Before, during, and after sex, and also throughout her life. To take care of all of her needs."

"So, if I *need* that again and again, your rules force you to have to do it?" I tease.

Josh laughs. "Trust me when I say there's no force necessary." He pulls back a little. The wolfish grin on his face sends heat between my thighs once more, and I blush. "All you'd have to do is spread your legs."

The blush deepens, and I hide in his chest. I hug him a little harder and shiver, actually a little cold. "How about if I say I need warmth, sleep, and to be near you?" I ask, a little shyly. I haven't asked to sleep in his bed with him since that night. I've wanted to, but I didn't want the rejection.

"I say your wish is my command." He steps back and lifts me in his arms. He carries me bridal style up to his bedroom. As I hold onto him, he pulls the covers back and lays me down with the utmost care.

"I'm suddenly exhausted," I whisper shyly.

Josh kisses my head. "That means I did a good job." He winks as he stands and walks to his dresser. I smile and giggle. "So, I saw you stole my t-shirt and almost gave me a heart attack when I saw how sexy you looked in it. Want another one to sleep in?" He turns to me with that cocky smirk that I fell in love with a long time ago.

"I didn't steal it. I confiscated it from the dryer in the laundry room. I was even nice enough to fold the rest and carry it all up here. I put your clothes on your table thingy by the door."

He glances towards the door. "Table thingy? You mean the shoe seat?"

"Sure. That." I giggle.

He shakes his head as he grabs a t-shirt out of his drawer. "Pretty sure confiscate is a different word for steal." He leans down and kisses me as he hands me the shirt. "Put this on before I end up ravishing you all night long."

I blush even deeper at the thought of him doing just that but obey and put on the shirt as he shuts off the light. I lay back down as he crawls into bed. He wraps his arms around me and pulls me close. I didn't expect him to crawl into bed in nothing but his boxer briefs. I gasp a little but snuggle as close as possible.

I fall into a peaceful one hoping he does the same this time. He really needs it.

When I slowly open my eyes, I'm not sure what time it is. I don't expect Josh to still be in bed, so when I feel his hard body against mine, I smile. I try not to shift at all. His arms have me feeling so snug and safe that I don't want to ruin it.

Unable to stop myself, I start lightly running my fingers over Josh's muscles on his back. I've seen him shirtless, but I've never dared touch him like this. Explore him. Josh breathes steadily but doesn't move. The only sign I get from him that he's awake is his hardness against my stomach. I look down but can't see it in the darkness of the room with the blankets over him.

I feel his lips on top of my head as he hugs me a little tighter. "As much as I want to let you continue, we do have a meeting at eight," he rumbles raspily.

"Why do you always smell good?" I ask as I look up at him. "Even after the gym. It's like your sweat just smells like your cologne. You defy logic."

He furrows his brow before grinning. I can see just enough of him and the room to make out what he's doing. "Maybe I'm just that talented. So talented that I don't sweat normal sweat. I sweat cologne. Maybe I don't even use cologne. Maybe it's just all me." His smile grows wider as he pushes the blanket back and starts getting out of bed. "Maybe I am cologne."

I laugh before shivering. "Nooo... I was warm," I whine teasingly.

"Come join me in the shower." He waggles his eyebrows. "Bet you I can make you warm again."

I giggle and pull the blankets up to cover my blush. "I don't think I'm ready for that."

He smiles and walks around the bed until he's behind me. He turns on the lamp and leans down, caging me underneath him. "You know I'm teasing you. This is all at your pace."

I nod. "I know."

"Good girl." He leans down enough for me to know what he wants. I lower the blanket enough so my lips are revealed to him. He kisses me sweetly, but the sparks and electricity I always feel when his lips are on mine ignite. I never want him to pull away and always hate when he does.

I sigh quietly when he starts walking to his ensuite bathroom. He doesn't close the door, but I resist taking a peek. I'm not sure what I'll do if I see him completely naked. Probably something embarrassing. Like pass out.

When I hear him close the shower door, I get up and hurry to my room. I hurry through my morning routine as quickly as I can. It always takes so long with my hair, and I hate that it takes away from time with Josh or anyone else.

Once I finish drying my hair after my shower, I brush my teeth and rush to get dressed. May is still a finicky month, and I hear raindrops hitting the window. I haven't opened the shades, but I kind of don't want to. I put jeans and a hoodie on before quickly finding slipper socks to keep my feet warm. If it's raining in May, it's probably a cold rain, but just to be sure, I check my weather app and see it's only in the forties. It makes me happier with my clothing decision.

I hurry down the stairs knowing Josh is already there. When I get to the kitchen, my clothing choice suddenly freaks me out. Josh looks amazing, but he always does. He's wearing black dress pants, unusual for him, and a navy blue dress shirt. I'm quickly questioning everything.

"Um… I'm going to change," I say softly.

He looks at me with a raised eyebrow as he puts milk into the blender with the berries he has in there. "Why? You look stunning."

"I feel very underdressed suddenly. What's going on? You never wear that kind of stuff. I mean, you look incredible, but am I forgetting a wedding or something?"

Josh laughs. "Baby, no. We have a meeting with my team, and then I have CEO shit to do with a couple of my companies. You look fabulous, but I don't care what you wear. I'm always going to think you're beautiful."

I blush as he smiles, drops ice into the blender, and starts it. I watch him because I never get tired of it. It doesn't matter what he does. He's the most interesting person in the world to me. I sit on one of the high chairs at the breakfast bar as he finishes blending. The concoction is thick and dark purple. He takes the cover off and pours it into two bottles I've seen him use for protein shakes. He puts the lids on them and hands me one.

"Berry shakes?"

He grins and glances at the door as the doorbell rings. "Yes." He leans down and kisses me on the forehead as he walks by to answer the door. "Drink it all. I know your aversion to finishing things on your plate because you don't want me to think you're eating too much."

My mouth drops. "How do you even know that? I've never said a word. I could just be full."

He shakes his head and winks. "I know fucking everything. You should know that by now."

I can't help but giggle as I get off the chair. Josh answers the door and lets Dane and Cole in.

"Damon and Lance are on the way. Gavin was right behind me," Cole says.

Josh looks at his watch. "It's okay. It's still a little early. We're waiting on Alec anyway."

"I saw his truck," Dane mentions. "He was coming in the gate."

"Good. Head to the office. I have breakfast coming." Josh nods towards the office as I turn to the oven.

I'm just starting to smell something delectable. Until I smell the peppers. I make a face. "Peppers and onions?" I ask.

Josh taps my bottom as he walks to the oven. "Yes. I made some breakfast croissants. I have some ham and cheese in the fridge for later for you and Rosie." He bends down and takes out the breakfast croissants.

My eyes fall to his ass. I lick my lip at how sexy it looks in those dress pants. Almost better than jeans, but nothing will beat the way he looks in those. He sets the croissants on top of the stove.

"I think I fell in love with you a little more."

He smiles. "Yeah? What did I do to deserve that?"

"You made a shake for me and for yourself because you know I don't do well in the mornings and eating breakfast."

"You also hate eggs."

I make my way to him, a little teary. I set my shake on the counter next to his and wrap my arms around his waist. He shifts and wraps his arms around me. "I love you. I never really paid attention to all of the little things you've paid attention to over the years. I was more focused on your other actions, like how you left my *Treasure Island* book in your small office. And how you found a first edition of it for me for my fifteenth birthday. How you always let me be near you, even when I'm pretty sure it was annoying."

He tilts my chin up to look at him. "First, I've paid attention to a lot more than I'm ever going to admit to another soul." He leans down and kisses me softly. "Secondly, there was never a second that I thought you were annoying. I've been in love with you for a long time, little sparrow." He leans down and kisses me again, but this one is different. His tongue slices into my mouth in a show of dominance that makes me swoon. It's not overbearing. It's loving and makes me feel wanted and desired.

He pulls back slowly and hugs me again. Without words, I help him put the croissants on a serving platter. He takes it to his office just as Damon and Lance show up. I let them in. Alec follows closely behind them, but helps me bring drinks to Josh's office. He's with Aero and a little girl, who is fully attached to Aero. It's obvious she refuses to leave his side.

I grab some juice for her in one of Jaxon's cups since she looks somewhere around the same age. Together, Alec and I carry the drinks to the office just as Gavin arrives.

"Are we waiting on anyone?" Alec asks when we enter. I quickly and quietly start handing out drinks.

"Nope," Josh answers. "We have everyone. Everyone, take a seat. There's a lot to discuss."

Everyone sits after taking a paper plate I hadn't seen Josh grab. Maybe he has them in here for meetings. He's always prepared.

I kneel in front of Aero with a smile. The little girl is curled into his neck. "I have some juice for you," I say softly to her. "It's apple juice. Want to try it?"

It takes her a few moments, but she finally nods, though she doesn't look at me. She holds out her hand. I give her the cup, handle first. She brings it to her mouth and hides while she takes a sip.

"She's probably pretty hungry," Aero says.

"What's her name?"

"Justice. Justice Addison."

"What a pretty name." I give her foot a squeeze as I get a plate for Aero with an extra sandwich for Justice.

Once everyone has drinks and food, I settle on the edge of the couch next to Lance with my shake.

I hear Josh chuckle. "What are you doing?" he asks me.

I blink, confused. "Sitting… down…? Or… did I misunderstand something…?"

"Oh, you definitely misunderstood something, sweet girl."

I look at him and then around at everyone else. No one is really paying attention. Aero is helping Justice and removing the peppers and onions from her sandwich. Damon and Gavin are comparing something. Dane is pointing at something on Lance's screen. Alec is looking at something on his phone. Cole is doing the same thing. Josh is looking at me intently while he sits on his chair behind his desk.

"Am... I not supposed to stay? I thought that's what you wanted," I say quietly, starting to feel flustered and completely embarrassed.

"Josh, fuck. Stop torturing her," Cole rumbles. Josh just smiles. I look at Cole for help. He points to Josh. "Lap. You belong next to him, or in this case, on his lap."

I hear rumbles of chuckles throughout the room. Even Alec is hiding his own laugh behind his phone. I glare at everyone as I stand. "I hate all of you. You're all mean." I try to be serious, but as soon as everyone starts laughing out loud, I laugh as well. I pause near Alec. "How are you okay with this?" I almost whisper.

He smiles. "You're his queen. Your place is at his side."

The blush I knew was already there darkens. I drop my head as I hurry behind Josh's desk. "What do I do?" I ask in a near panic, not at all confident in my role.

Josh takes my hand and pulls me into his lap gently. His lips meet my ear. "Sit here. Make me look good. And if something pops out at you, say it. You know everyone in here, but if you don't feel comfortable saying it to everyone, then whisper it to me." His arms snake around my waist as he turns to the group.

I let out a slow breath as I settle into him. I notice the folder and pen I knocked to the floor last night are neatly on his desk. The memory of us makes goosebumps appear on my arms.

I wanted him to be serious about us. I wanted things to progress with our relationship. I wanted him to dive into the feelings and push the fears away.

This one simple gesture is all of that and so much more. Letting me be here, with him, while he's leading a meeting with his team... I know the significance of it. Trusting me to be here while this is happening is a huge step.

It doesn't seem like much, but it's everything to me.

Chapter Nineteen

Josh

I rub Dallas's hip soothingly. I can tell she's both nervous and a little excited. She knows that me not only letting her be here, but also asking her in the first place, is a very large step in our relationship. It's me telling her I trust her completely.

And I do. When I opened up to her about everything that happened and let all of my emotions release, that was the clincher. Her just hugging me and letting me be vulnerable was all it really took for the ice dam I built around myself to shatter. I've rarely let myself be that open with anyone. With Dallas, though, it's all different.

"First thing," I begin as I look at Alec. "Alec. You said there's something big going down that we need to know."

"Yep," Alec says. Dallas turns to him with wide eyes as she tenses. "Aero had a breakthrough last night. I'll let him tell you about that, but the big thing is we now know with certainty, not speculation, who the leader of the Ruthless Warriors is and where his hideout is."

Dallas relaxes, but only slightly. My heart starts beating a little faster. My blood pumps hotter. "Who?" I growl.

"I'm actually surprised you don't know," Aero says. My eyes snap to his and darken. He's feeding his daughter, Justice, but he's locked onto me. "His name is Ethan. When he was in Viper's Venom, he was known as Twitch. Name he goes by is Ethan Ricardo Vasquez."

I look at Alec as Lance furiously types. "One mystery solved."

"Oh, there's a lot fucking more than that. Aero, tell him the rest."

"Okay. I had a complete breakthrough last night. I remembered everything. I hate that it took this long, but it's nice to not just have bits and pieces coming at me randomly. Anyway, I was sitting on the couch watching a movie with Justice. It all came at me. I was really excited and got up. I went to tell my wife. She didn't seem as excited as me. She actually seemed scared, but it struck me as weird. She seemed afraid of me."

I raise an eyebrow. "I don't like where this is headed."

Aero chuckles. "Nope. She was cooking dinner. I helped her, but she told me to go finish the movie. She'd bring it out. She said she wanted me to process everything. I agreed with her, but it still struck me as odd. I went back out but I watched her like a fucking hawk. She checked dinner. Disappeared from the kitchen. I went after her. She'd gone into the bathroom. The door was closed and locked. No light on. I could hear her almost whispering. She was saying something about me remembering. She was quiet for a little bit. Then, she said she doesn't know what the plan should be because of the scramblers. She couldn't give her location and didn't know where she was."

"Who the fuck was she talking to?" I ask.

"Ethan," Cole says. "Alec called me. I was serving a warrant last night on a guy he tipped us on. I was working last night doing the paperwork that comes after. He asked me if I could track. I didn't have the equipment with me, so I called Lance. He stayed up to see if she made another call while I got her call history. She's only called three people. Skyla, Dane, and an unknown number that I gave Lance to trace. I left it at that, but after Aero left, I got a call from Lance. She was on the phone with Ethan saying he drugged her and she just came to. He was gone. All trace of him was gone. Justice was gone. The guards were gone. The house was completely empty and dark except for her stuff. She kept saying his name."

"Lucinio Mafia is good," Dallas says softly.

156

I kiss her shoulder and squeeze her hip just to show her it's okay for her to speak. "That we are. So, I assume Ace and our team got you out."

"Yeah, but shit went down before that. She came out of the bathroom after agreeing to something and confirming that she will take care of it. I silently went back to the kitchen when I saw the light come on and heard her go silent. It sounded like she put her phone down on the counter. I finished the movie with Justice. She finished dinner. She brought it to us. She didn't want me to help. I saw her fill mine and her glass with Pepsi. She got Justice juice."

"I'm done, daddy," Justice says quietly, pushing her plate a little away from her. "Read?"

"Okay, baby. Grab your book. It's in your bag by the window over there." Aero lets Justice down. She makes her way to her bag and sits down to ruffle through it. We're all quiet while she finds what she wants. She takes out a coloring book and a Barbie kids reading book. She settles with both.

"What next?" I ask, a little quieter. I sense she really shouldn't be hearing this, but I know she's not going to go far from her father.

Aero leans forward as he glances at Justice before looking back at me. He lowers his voice. "I saw her drop something in my drink."

"Oh no…" Dallas slumps slightly and lets her hand fall to mine.

"Yeah. So, I found another movie. I don't know if she did anything to the food, but Justice asked me for a drink of my Pepsi. She freaked out and nearly shrieked 'no'. It was too late for her to have a drink like that. I chuckled and told her I hadn't planned on giving her one and to calm down. She sat down on the couch. Justice was very confused about the outburst. I helped cut up her food. When I got to mine, though, I asked her for ketchup. She smiled and said she'd grab some and apologized for forgetting it. I don't eat a lot of ketchup, but certainly not with a steak. She left her plate and drink. I switched it. When she got back, I watched her. She dug in. Took a big drink of her Pepsi. By the time she was halfway done, she looked like she was starting to feel a little drowsy. She shook her head a few times. I didn't touch a damn thing on the plate or touch the drink even after I switched them. She didn't finish before she passed out. So, I cleaned up. I got Justice upstairs to her room and packed up her stuff. I packed mine. We both came downstairs. She was still out. I took her upstairs and laid her in the bed. Your team took the rest of her food and glass."

"We tested it," Gavin says. "Date rape drug. Double the dose."

"So, the leader is for sure VV's rogue. Ethan," Dallas says. She leans against me before looking at me and lowering her voice. "Didn't you say the cargo ship had something to do with RW?"

I grin and nod. "Good girl," I rumble in her ear before turning back to Aero. "We know Ethan is the rogue and leader of the Ruthless Warriors. Correct?"

"Yes, sir. He is. How long, I don't think anyone really knows, but I did my research. I narrowed it down to just before you killed your guy's old man. I had a lot of shit on him, but I gave it all to the one person I thought was on my side."

"The wife," Dallas says with furrowed brows. "Wait, though. You said 'your guy's old man'. Alex's and Josh's...?"

Aero looks between me and Dallas before looking at everyone else. He clears his throat as he focuses his attention on Alec. "Does he not know? Or are you guys fucking with me? Because this is fucking huge, man."

"Nope. Not fucking with you. He really has no idea. None of these guys do," Alec answers. "I didn't either until you told me. Keep going."

Aero hesitates before he leans back against the couch, eyes falling on me and Dallas. "Uh... well, to answer her question." He points to Dallas and clears his throat again. "The cargo ship. I assume you're talking about the ship they used for trafficking drugs, guns, and people?"

Dallas nods. "Yes, sir. We -" I cut her off by squeezing her hip. She looks at me, and puts her head down.

I kiss her shoulder to reassure her that it's okay. I just don't want to give too much information. I want him to tell me. "What about the ship, Aero?"

"To begin, Josh, that was information I'd intended to bring to you. The deal with the ship and the kid all started before my time. What I know and learned about it, though, was that the kid was Matthew Lucinio's grandson. Matthew wanted to protect the kid. He talked to Ethan. He wanted help protecting the mother and the baby from his known enemies. He knew you'd also be protecting her, but he wanted the extra layer. Ethan had other plans. He would drug the mother and steal the kid. He had a plan to have a doctor help with the swap, and tell the mother she miscarried. Ethan and his team were supposed to give her an already dead baby, but the one they planned on giving her actually survived. They had to forge documents. The ashes they gave weren't from the kid. I don't know where they came from, but they took the kid and a nurse. The nurse became a nanny on the ship. Whenever I was on the ship for any reason, they all behaved, but I know shit went down when I wasn't the one leading the voyage to whatever the hell destination Ethan had us going to. He was never on that ship."

I don't know how to process half of what I heard, so I focus on questions. "Who was? Who did they call Cap?" I ask.

"He wasn't RW. He was an actual captain who had a co-captain. His name, if it's the same guy, was named Enrique Lopez. His co-captain was named Fredrick Peterson."

"The Feds have both of them in custody," Dane says. He turns to Aero. "They searched the ship and found some girls in the cargo hold along with some guns and a lot of drugs."

Aero nods. "Good. You'll have to tell me how you caught them someday." He turns back to Dallas and me. "They were paid a lot of money by Ethan to keep the kid on that ship until he was seven. He was never given a name. The nurse was the only one who called him by his name, and she did it quietly and made sure he knew not to tell them she taught him that. The only reason I knew is because Jaxon mentioned it to me one day. He trusted me and the nurse. I promised them both I'd get them off the ship. I just needed the time. I only found out about them about a year before Ethan went after Skyla. Jaxon was educated, but he was also forced to watch a lot of shit meant to harden him. Break him. By the time Ethan got his hands on him, the plan was that he would raise him in his image. He'd get him to trust him but train him how to kill without a second thought. No conscience."

"Fuck me," I say pinching the bridge of my nose. "I got a lot of this from Morpheus when we grabbed him and Jaxon. Thought a lot of the shit he said was a flat out lie. Hearing it from you just makes the truth of some of that sink in even more. I can't believe how fucked up this is." I really can't. Knowing my father's intent was to protect Lyric and Jaxon is something I don't know if I'll ever be able to come to terms with.

"At least we have names and someone to verify them," Cole cuts in. "Means we have the right people."

"A plus," I agree. Time to go back to questions. I can't dwell on the Matthew shit. "What else you got, Aero?"

"His hideout. It's in Mexico, the country. Not New Mexico, the State. I can lead you right to it. Show it to you on a map. And the last thing, Josh. He's your brother, man. Matthew Lucinio is his father. His last name is an alias. It's Lucinio."

I can't stop myself from wrapping my arm far more protectively around Dallas than I need to. I squeeze her close as my other hand balls into a fist. The ocean rolls through my ears like a fucking tsunami in the middle of a hurricane. I can feel my eyes darkening, but if I didn't know they were, the way everyone is looking at me would tell me all I need to know. Gavin is very much on guard, but everyone else is watching me closely. Even Lance has stopped typing.

Gavin is the one who breaks the silence with a low rumble of a chuckle as he stands in disbelief. "It never fucking ends, does it?" He shakes his head as he runs his fingers through his hair and looks at me. "He's never going to stop torturing this family, is he? Even from the fucking grave." He starts pacing back and forth.

Dallas turns a little bit and buries her face in my neck. "I feel like I just got hit by a bus. Like I just figured so much stuff out and can't handle it."

"I know, little sparrow," I whisper. "Fuck, I know."

"I have a lot of verifying, Josh. I'll work with Aero directly," Lance says to me.

"We all have a lot of work to do," Dane says as he looks at Cole. "We need to get the Feds to let us talk to the two fuck ups and the others that were on the ship."

"Yeah, agreed. But I have one question," Cole says as he looks at Aero. "Are you saying Ethan went against his father? What happened when Matthew found out?"

"Ethan threatened him," Aero flatly states. "He said if he wants to fuck around and find out, he'll just off the kid."

"I don't get it. Why? Why risk going up against him at all?" Alec asks.

Aero blinks a few times before he finally answers. "Because when he had Jaxon under his control, he intended to go after you, man. But Matthew fucked it all up for him. He wasn't supposed to go after Jessa and Dallas. That was Ethan's future plan for when he was going to go after you." He nods to Alec, and I already don't like where this is headed. "He intended to get you on his side, including Matthew by using his grandson as leverage, then use all of you to go after Josh, with his own son leading the fight." My chest tightens. Dallas stiffens. Everyone pauses and looks to Aero. "Man, I'm so fucking sorry I couldn't remember this shit earlier." A long breath whooshes out of him.

"It's okay," Alec assures him. "We all understood. We'd knew you'd tell us all you could. We hoped this day would come. but we can't exactly fault you for the hit you took. You saved Skyla's life."

He nods but stays quiet for a few moments before continuing. He leans forward and rests his elbow on his knees as he looks up at Alec. "He wanted to go after VV. That's when I joined him. I was following orders. I want you both to know that. I was following orders, and I was never told the entire fucking story. I was told Jessa and Dallas were your sisters. Nothing about Josh at all. He told me he wanted them both alive and unharmed. That his plan was to use them both as leverage to take over VV. He hadn't infiltrated VV at that time. That came after because of his colossal fuck up in underestimating Matthew fucking Lucinio. I don't care what anyone says about the guy. I'd fucking agree with it all, but they can't deny he was smart."

I chuckle. "Yeah." No one would disagree with that statement. He was so smart that when everyone figured the simplicity of his plans, they all felt fucking stupid. I should know. I was one of them.

"The plan was to take Dallas and Jessa, but Matthew caught wind of it. I was waiting for Dallas the day she was taken. But instead of going out the back, like she usually did, I'd been watching, she walked out the front. By the time I realized she'd gone to the front, I figured I'd been spotted. I figured Alec figured it out. I took off. Figured I'd try again the next day, but she didn't show up. I figured she was sick, but she kept not showing up. I heard through the vine that she'd been taken. It wasn't by us. I'd been in contact with Ethan. He knew what was going on and was listening, too. He had guys on Jessa, but we could never get her. She had too much security for us to take on. The night you guys left your compound, we followed, but you guys were being chased by people that wasn't us. We pulled back because we didn't want a war with someone we couldn't take on. No fucking way. We saw Ace go to you guys, so we knew we couldn't get him on our side. We thought about it anyway, but there would've been no trust for anyone at that point with two of your family taken and your parents dead. We went scurrying back to Mexico with our tail between our legs per Ethan's orders."

I can't help but chuckle. "Wise fucking choice on his part."

"No kidding. We'd have been decimated," Aero continues. "I don't know what the hell happened between that night and when Matthew called us a week later. He told Ethan that he had Jessa and Dallas. He told us to give him the kid or we'd lose them. His plans would be fucked. Ethan called his bluff, but set up a drop anyway. He never intended on giving him Jaxon. What he didn't count on is Matthew outsmarting him again. We were standing on the tarmac at the airport when you guys went after him. We found out the next day when Ethan got Matthew's journal and a letter detailing everything he'd done. Including sending out numerous crews to get the kid back from us. I don't know how we thwarted him on any of the attempts. There were a lot. But the biggest thing he detailed to us was that he never planned on giving us Jessa or Dallas."

Dallas sniffles into my neck and cries quietly. I wrap my arms around her because I don't know what else to do. I don't know if something else just hit her that she didn't remember, or if the talk of what happened to her is too much.

"He did it to save us," she whispers so only I can hear her. I have no time to say anything before Aero's next words have my heart stopping cold.

"He said he knew you'd get to him before we did. He knew he wouldn't make it out alive a second time. He said he knew we weren't going to give up Jaxon, but that he'd do everything he could to help you take us down and get your son back. He said he knew you wouldn't trust him, and that if he reached out, he'd be dead before the words fully left his mouth. But he also said you'd know soon. That was a while ago. I guess you already knew a lot of this shit."

"No. No. I didn't." I run my fingers through Dallas's hair. "Fuck."

"I don't think I have any further life ruining for the day," Aero says. "That was everything I had."

I shake my head. "It's not your fault. I'm glad you came to us. I'm glad we know you and all of this shit, but I need everyone out. I don't think I need to give anyone assignments. I have a lot of phone calls to make and other meetings to get to today."

No one says anything as they get up. I know Gavin will work with Alec to make sure Aero and his daughter are somewhere safe and staying on our compound. I don't need to tell Dane and Cole to question the fucking ship's crew. Fuck the Feds and their slow investigation. I don't care how many strings my team needs to pull to get them in for an interview with them. I need answers. I know Lance and Damon will verify everything that was just said and find me their hideout with Aero's assistance.

There are two things that need my attention. The first is my crying girl. The second is my brother's and family.

And my fuck. They're in for an incredible fucking dose of unbelievable shit none of us ever thought would come to light.

Chapter Twenty

☙ Dallas ☙

(Two Weeks Later)

I yawn and jump a little when there's a knock on my door. Josh left with Alec and some of our guys, including Tyler, a little while ago. I hate more than anything that they'll be missing my graduation, but I understand fully that they need to act on things when they have information. Aero got them the location of the RW hideout in Mexico. Josh went down once last week to organize his team. Alec went with him.

They planned on going back down the morning after my graduation to plan their mission, but things changed. They think Ethan got word because he seems to be mobilizing. I completely understand they need to get going.

"Who is it?" I ask before I unlock my door. I really don't have a single reason to be afraid of anyone here. They're all incredibly protective of me and treat me like their little sister. It's just that they're all so wild and unpredictable sometimes.

"It's Bunny, deary."

I smile brightly and open the door. Bunny is like the mother of our crew. I've known her my whole life. She's the grandmother I never had or knew I needed.

I open the door wide and hug her. "Hi! I feel like I haven't seen you in forever."

Bunny laughs heartily. "Goodness, child. You saw me an hour ago."

I giggle because she's right. I did just see her an hour ago, but this is one of my favorite games. I came in to get my stuff packed up for a week with Rosie. We have a lot of stuff planned, including a major shopping spree that we both seriously need. I don't care what anyone says. Retail therapy is a special bonding time between men and women alike.

I let her go, my smile still glowing. "It's fun. I'll never stop doing it. And you're immortal. So, this will go on forever."

Bunny laughs again. "I don't know about that, my girl." She holds up a garment bag. "This was dropped off for you."

I raise an eyebrow. "What is it?"

"Well, I didn't look. It's yours. I think it's a dress fit for our princess, though."

I hesitantly take it and turn to lay it on my bed. "Who brought it?"

"A nice gentleman. And he managed to get through security, so I don't think he's the boy you were having those issues with around your prom."

I wrinkle my nose at the thought of Zack. "Eew. I hope not. Still nervous about what's in this thing, though."

"I can assure you that it isn't that boy. Now, hurry and open it. Get dressed. You don't have much time."

I narrow my eyes at her, pausing mid unzip of the bag. "Who was it, Bunny?"

"I have strict orders. Now get dressed. Hurry up." She bustles away without saying another word.

My suspicions rise, but I finish unzipping the bag anyway. What's revealed is the most beautiful evening gown I've ever seen in my life. My mouth drops, and I can't help but touch it. The fabric is so soft. Satin, and the finest kind. Black.

"Thanks for the ride, Ink," a soft voice says from my door. I look up to see Rosie.

"Yeah. She's in there." Ink points to me as he stalks to his bedroom at the end of the hall. Rosie looks after him with an expression on her face that has me curious.

After Ink slams his door, she clears her throat and walks into my bedroom. "Hi!" she says cheerfully.

"Hi!" I choose to let whatever I just saw go because I'm more curious about why she's here. I told her I'd meet her at her house after I grabbed my stuff.

"Just came to help you get ready."

"Okay, what's going on?" I turn to her with my hands on my hips.

Her eyes widen before she giggles. "It's a good surprise. Set in motion a bit ago, but I can't tell you how long. I'm not allowed." She picks up the dress with a huge smile. "It's perfect! Now, let's hurry. We don't have much time. You need to leave in twenty minutes."

I glance at the clock. It's 5:40 pm. So, I need to leave in twenty minutes to get where I'm going, and neither Bunny or Rosie will tell me more.

Rosie rushes me to my bathroom and does my hair for me. It takes nearly all of the time I have, but she makes it work. After she gets my hair up the way she wants it and curls a couple strands of hair that she's allowed to stay down and frame my face, she finishes things off with my favorite decorative comb. She places it in my hair to help hold her work together, and we both rush out to get the dress on me.

"Here. Put these on." Rosie hands me two things that look a lot like bra pads with tape.

I take them with a scrunched face. "What are these? What's happening? How do I even put these on?"

Rosie giggles. "It's a strapless bra with all of the support of a regular bra with underwire."

"But there's no hook. Where's the rest of the bra? It's just the pads."

"Read the directions. They just cup you and you tape them in. Actually. Wait until the dress is on so we know where to tape."

I furrow my brows at the pads but put the dress on anyway. It's floor length and fits me perfectly. It's light and flows with every move I make. I don't even feel like I'm wearing anything. And when I turn to look at the back in my floor-length mirror, I see why.

"Oh my God! Rosie, there's no back! I can't wear this!" I stare at how low the back dips. It's just past the middle of my back. The front is okay, but it still dips lower than I'd like and shows way too much cleavage.

Rosie holds up a shawl. "Dallas? Trust. It's going to be okay."

I turn and blink at the shawl. "Thank God."

"Now, let's get this on." She holds up the pads. I groan, but in seconds, we have it on and me adjusted perfectly.

"Wow. You really look stunning."

I put the shawl around my shoulders, but I don't have much time to admire how the dress accentuates everything it should because Rosie is pushing me out the door and slamming it behind her.

"What am I supposed to wear on my feet?" I ask with wide eyes.

"Got them! And I'll get the rest of your stuff and bring it to my house." She propels me down the stairs as quickly as she can so I don't trip over the dress.

I glare at all of the women and men grinning at me as I slip on the satin low heels. They're not as tall as the high ones. I'd never be able to walk in them. Once I have them on, Rosie opens the front door of the clubhouse. Before I can go out, everyone in the house starts filing outside, and I'm so confused, I just watch in blatant open-mouthed shock. Rosie follows them, and all I can do is stand and stare.

"What the fuck is going on?" I whisper to myself.

There's a low chuckle behind me. "Walk out there and find out."

I turn and see Ink. He's as serious as he always is, but his eyes have a little bit of a sparkle. "I'm afraid to."

He shakes his head. "Don't be." He gestures in front of him, signaling me to go.

I hesitantly do what he says, but it's only because he's behind me. He's one of my brother's most trusted friends, so I've always known I can rely on him and trust him just as much as I do Alec or Tyler.

I take a deep breath before I step around the still open door and step outside. What I see is not at all what I expected. Everyone in our chapter is standing on the lawn outside of the clubhouse looking towards the door; waiting for me. They're all smiling. A couple are even wiping a stray tear. The club girls, also known as whores in other biker crews, are also here.

I look around at them even more confused, until my eyes fall on the black stretch limo pulling into the freshly paved driveway. My heart beats rapidly. I'm certain I'm about to hyperventilate. The only reason I don't is because Alec is moving towards me. I look up at him when he's in front of me. His size alone blocks me from seeing anything in front of him, including the limo.

"You look beautiful," Alec says with a grin as Ink slips around us and joins the others. He helps me with my shawl.

"What's going on?" I whisper. "I thought you were in Mexico."

"And miss your graduation? Not a fucking chance. No, this is a special night for you."

I just look at him even more confused. "Alec?" I can feel the anxiety rising in my throat.

"And we're all here because almost everyone here watched you grow up. You're everyone's little sister. VV's princess. You ask me a lot what that really means. Well, this. This is what it means. It means when you go through milestones, we celebrate them with you because we love and respect you." He pauses. "Okay, not all milestones." He winks.

I laugh a little, though I'm still nervous. I hear a door close, but I don't dare look to see who it is. "So, what's going on? What milestone? My graduation is tomorrow."

"Well." He trails off and steps to my side.

My eyes fall to the man standing at the back of the limo dressed in a full tuxedo complete with a silver vest. On my dress, there's a little bit of silver that shimmers through the satin. Josh Lucinio matches me to a tee, and my heart is in a puddle. My knees are weak for this man, but I somehow manage to walk to him with everyone's eyes on me.

Once I reach him, he pulls out a single, dark pink Chrysanthemum, my favorite flower, from behind his back. I look up at him as I shakily take it with a soft smile. He hands it to me before taking my other hand in his. He kisses it tenderly and lovingly.

"What's going on?" I whisper. "Alec was talking about milestones. I don't know what's happening."

Josh's smile melts me, but it's his eyes that soothe my soul. "I've never had the chance to take you out on a real date. And I know you've never technically been on a date at all." His voice is soft but still holds the confidence and dominance that I need and crave from him.

"My first date," I whisper when it all dawns on me. I look back at Alec with a soft smile. He's standing next to Tyler wearing the same huge grin that everyone else is wearing.

The grin of pride.

Pride for the VV's princess, but I finally understand what Alec really meant all these years. Viper's Venom's princess isn't some delicate doll put on a shelf in a glass case that only comes out when she's needed to impress someone. Or to be traded for something more important, like my father tried to make me believe.

No.

VV's princess is me. A real human being with real feelings. Who has free will and makes choices. Someone who isn't a pawn to be used to make alliances. Someone who is truly loved and cherished. Someone who has a place, a real place, among her family. Everyone here is my family. It just took me eighteen years to let myself believe it.

Not that Alec would ever sell me off like our father would have, but it never really sunk in that everyone here believed as he did. I have more than him, Tyler, Hawk, or Ink. I have more than just those close to my brother. I'm truly just as respected here as everyone else is. I'm not disposable to all of them like I sometimes believe I am.

"I love you," I mouth to Alec.

He grins. "I love you, too, little sis," he mouths back.

I smile as Josh opens the door to the limo and helps me in the back. He climbs in beside me and closes the door. I fight myself to keep from mauling him. Barely. I'm so excited for my actual first date that all thoughts beyond that are sort of a shadow.

Except the one where I maul him.

We've been exploring each other the past couple of weeks. When he was gone, it was for a couple of days, but he kept his word and texted me when he could. The rest of those days were spent with him showing me new worlds and making me scream for him over and over and over.

Not to say he hasn't been getting any of his own. We may not have gone fully all the way, but one of my new favorite things is tasting his cake pop and licking his icing.

"You look incredible."

I blush as his arm wraps around me. He adjusts my shawl around me, making me blush a deeper shade of red. I twirl the flower he gave me between my fingers. "Thank you," I say shyly. "So do you." I look up at him with a soft smile. "We match."

He grins as he plays with the strand of hair hanging down on my left side. I don't know how Rosie did it, but she made the right side match perfectly. It takes me forever to get it just right.

"I had a feeling you'd be a little uncomfortable in this dress. I didn't expect you to wear it, honestly. I hoped you would because I knew you'd look stunning."

I lean into him. "The shawl was the perfect addition. I'm not sure I would've been brave enough to wear it without it, though I really love the way it looks."

"Do you recognize it?"

I look down at it and shake my head. "Not really. Should I?" I glance back up at him, suddenly worried.

"No. Well, maybe. I didn't expect you to. This was the dress on the rack when I took you bra shopping against my will."

I laugh but blush. "That was the best day of my life."

Josh raises an eyebrow with a teasing glimmer in his perfect, ocean-blue eyes. "Fuck. Am I really doing that bad?"

I can't help but laugh. "You're doing so well, my king."

He grins. "If that was sarcasm, I'm taking you over my knee right now."

I giggle and look up at him through my lashes. I've learned his weakness. "Please, sir."

He groans. "Stop it. We're almost to our destination." For show, or maybe not, he smirks as he squeezes his dick.

I lick my lip as I watch him. Suddenly, my throat is dry, and the only way to quench my thirst is with him. "We have time, right?"

He cups my chin and tilts my head up so I'm forced to look at him. I love his cocky grin. "As much as I love every second of you coming into yourself sexually, and you know how much I love your pretty mouth sucking my cock," he slowly turns my head so I'm looking out the window, "we're here." He turns me back to him and kisses me deeply. My head is spinning from his taste. He pulls back slowly and lets his hand fall to my neck. He doesn't squeeze. He only caresses my throat with his thumb. "And I don't want the people passing by to try seeing through the tinted out windows and get a shot of you and I pleasuring each other."

I blush before I giggle. "Okay, okay. Teenage hormones in check."

Josh laughs because it's a running joke between us. It's far from true. We've waited for each other for a long time. He's just as ravenous for me. My age has nothing to do with it.

I look up when the door opens. "Table is ready, sir."

"Thank you, Fallon."

I say nothing as Josh slides out and reaches a hand for me. I take it, but I'm fascinated by the woman who opened the door. I'm not sure if she's just a driver, or if she's a guard, but I know Josh doesn't usually hire drivers. His drivers are always guards. I've never seen a female one.

He helps me out of the car and follows his guards to the restaurant. Mastro's Steakhouse. He guides me in front of him, keeping his hand on my lower back as we enter.

"Mr. Lucinio," the host behind the host desk says. "Right this way, sir."

"Thank you, Hugo," Josh says, his voice deep and commanding, though friendly. I shiver because it's sexy. He's the boss and shows it well.

After we're seated, I can't help but notice that all eyes are on us. I tighten the shawl a little and put my head down. "Everyone is staring at us," I whisper.

Josh chuckles. "They can't keep their eyes off you."

My eyes widen a little. "Yeah. They're wondering who's with Josh Lucinio, the Mafia God."

"King."

I look up and see his teasing grin as he holds out a hand for mine. I slowly take it, keeping the shawl tight in my grip. "It's just unnerving is all," I whisper again.

He squeezes my hand gently as he narrows his eyes and glances around the room quickly. His eyes are back on me before I can say a word, and everyone else is focused back on their dinners and conversations where they belong.

He lifts my hand to his lips and kisses it. "Better, little sparrow?"

I blush at the nickname and nod. "Much. Thank you. I'm sorry that had to -"

Josh cuts me off with a firm shake of his head as he reaches into his pocket. "Don't apologize. I come here a lot. The staff is used to me. A lot of these people can't believe they're close to me. And I'm sure with the guards, it's more curiosity. Add on that I haven't been seen on a date since I was with Lyric, this is new gossip for them. Not to mention, you're pretty well recognized yourself."

I nod slowly. "Great. So, the tabloids will all have us on the cover tomorrow."

"Baby, did you see any photographers?"

"No," I say softly.

"They report what I want them to report on me. And they face consequences if they come out with some bullshit story just for views. A lot of people say that's corrupt. They're entitled to know things. I say it's protection. They're entitled to nothing. The freedom of information act covers the government. Not me. I'm nothing more than a regular, law-abiding citizen."

I giggle. "I'm not a hundred percent on that last part, but I understand what you're saying."

He laughs. He hasn't let go of my hand yet. My eyes widen to the size of saucers when I see him pull out a black box when his hand leaves his pocket. The only thing that keeps my heart from leaping out of my mouth and running around the restaurant is the fact that he's holding the wrong hand.

It still doesn't register that I'm near hyperventilation as I watch him curiously.

He flips the box open with one hand before setting it down on the table. "This," he pulls out some kind of jewel that catches the light, "belonged to my paternal grandmother. She gave one to me and one to Alex when we were born. Mom kept them for us all these years in a safe she kept hidden in my bedroom. She had money in there. Passports. Everything. I didn't know she had these for us, though." He turns my hand over and places the jewel into it before guiding my hand back to me.

I look down to study the jewel but realize it's more of a clasp. It's beautiful. It's a full moon. It's silver and so intricate that it even has the craters darkened and bordered with tiny diamonds that almost look like glitter to accentuate them. The border of the moon is encrusted with the same size diamonds. It's heavier than I thought it would be. I turn it around in my hand to study it closer. It's so beautiful that I could get lost in it.

The back of it is engraved with Josh's last name. The clip part of it looks odd to me. It looks like it's supposed to be pinned to something, like a safety pin or name tag, but it's not a safety pin at all. It's too thick to poke through clothing, but it looks like it's supposed to be worn somehow. It simply doesn't look like anything I've ever laid eyes on.

"It's really beautiful," I say softly as I look up at him and start to give it back.

Josh smiles as he stands while he takes my hand once more. I watch him curiously as he kneels. "It's a clasp for the shawl. This shawl was bought specifically with this in mind." He takes the clasp from my hand and kisses the inside of my palm before looking up at me. "May I?"

I nod. "Yes, sir," I say softly.

He shifts a little as he reaches up. He positions the shawl so two small holes that I hadn't noticed are perfectly lined up. "According to the story, these have been passed down for generations. I'm not sure how long, but they were all handcrafted. No two are alike. They've always been passed down to a daughter until they got to me and Alex. She never gave them to Matthew because she wanted to see him get married first. When my mother entered the picture, she didn't know how to feel about the fact that she'd been kidnapped, more or less, and sold to the family." He fastens the clasp and looks up at me, taking both of my hands in his. "The rule for us was that we were to save them and give them to the woman we would spend the rest of our lives with. Alex gave his on his wedding day. It's a sun. I'm giving mine to you. Because not only do I want to spend the rest of my life with you, but you're the light in my dark. You're the one who always guides me home." He keeps his eyes on me as he kisses both of my hands.

My smile is just as watery as my eyes. I can't say anything, so I just lean forward to hug him. He lets go of my hands and wraps his arms around my waist. I drape mine over his shoulders and hug him tight. I don't let tears fall because I don't want the makeup I wear to be ruined. It might not be as much as some girls, but it's a little bit, and I want this night to be perfect.

After a few moments, Josh kisses my neck and lets go gently. He gets to his feet and takes his seat once more.

"Thank you, Josh. It's truly the most special gift I've ever received. It's beautiful." I run my fingers over it lightly.

"I'm glad you like it. I wanted to give it to you a long time ago, but it just never seemed like the right time. I couldn't exactly tell you the story behind it when you were sixteen."

I blush and hide behind my menu. "You could've. It just may not have had the same effect because I know you would've left out the part where you want to spend your life with me."

"And the part where you're what guides me home."

The blush darkens, and I focus on the menu. My eyes widen in shock. "Josh!" I say barely above a whisper. "The prices are insane!" I look at him with my mouth slightly open.

He grins and shakes his head. "Baby, order what you want. Don't look at the price. It doesn't matter. What matters is the two of us having a good time and this night being as special for you as I can make it."

I hesitantly look at the menu, but don't have a single clue of what to order because not only does everything look amazing, but the prices are higher than I've ever seen at any restaurant I've ever been to in my life. It's over a hundred dollars just for a steak. When the server comes over, I'm nowhere near ready and am panicking.

"Ready to order, Mr. Lucinio?" the server asks. She's kind enough. Probably a college student.

Josh glances at me. All I can do is give him my best 'help me, I'm drowning' look and hope for the best. Josh sets down his menu and gently takes mine. "Yeah, we're ready." He reaches for my hand, and I readily take his. "We'll start with the Steak Sashimi." He gives me a reassuring smile, and I put all of my trust into him as he looks at the server. He soothingly rubs his thumb back and forth over my hand. "Please bring that out first."

"Yes, sir. Would you like our house made red wine reduction sauce or the house made soy sauce?"

"Red wine, please. I'll take the Tomahawk Chop, the thirty-two, with Asparagus and the Truffle Butter Mushrooms. Have them cut the steak in half after it's cooked. I'll take it medium rare."

"Yes, sir. And for your lovely lady?" The server smiles brightly at me, pen poised to take my order.

"She'll take the New York, eight ounce, with Garlic Mashed Potatoes," Josh says with a gentle squeeze to my hand. I shoot him a grateful smile. "Make it a medium rare like mine."

"And to drink?"

"We'll stick with the water. Thank you. When you get that in, grab orders from the guards and put everyone on my bill. As usual, I'll tip everyone out tonight."

"Yes, sir. Thank you, Mr. Lucinio." The server scurries away as Josh turns back to me.

"Tip them out?"

"Mmhmm. In most places, servers have to share their tips and don't make much. Often far below minimum wage because their tips are averaged into their salary. But they have to tip everyone that works here, so their salary is cut, and those making an hourly wage that's more fair still get some of those tips. So, whenever I come in here, or anywhere, I tip everyone. The servers tell me how much they need to tip out, and I cover it. It helps them out, and it's cash, so they can hide it easier when they do taxes." He winks at me, and I giggle.

As the night goes on, Josh and I have the best conversation and enjoy the most incredible food I've ever eaten. While I don't know what's to come, I know that this night is the greatest night of my life.

Chapter Twenty One

ॐ Josh ॐ

"Dallas, fuck!" I shout as I come in her mouth.

"Josh!" She arches as she comes, bringing her pussy closer to my mouth so I can lick her clean.

I've never had her in the sixty-nine position before, but it might have just become my favorite. Her straddling my head, giving me full access to her, while sucking my dick is something I'm never going to get enough of.

Once we've both come down, I kiss her pussy and tap her ass. "We should get going, baby. We have a couple hours to get you to that luncheon thing you're so excited about. And Rosie should be here soon."

She groans and shifts. I help her off me as I sit up. She sits on her knees next to me. "You realize I'm only excited about the luncheon because Rosie is."

That makes me laugh. "I call bullshit, little sparrow. It was half of our entire conversation at dinner last night. You wouldn't shut up." I wink teasingly.

She blushes and smiles. "Okay, maybe I'm a little excited. Just a little. I'd be more excited to just stay with you all day."

I lean over and kiss her neck. "If I didn't have so much shit to do today, I'd agree." I pull away slowly. She slumps and nods. "I have to get my stuff ready to go. We need to make sure we have all of our weapons. I have to do my brief. Make sure we have all information verified. Lance was still looking at a few things."

She nods and looks up at me. "Make sure Ethan is still there."

I reach for her and cup her cheek. She leans into my hand. "Baby, he's there. Stop feeling bad about last night, and don't feel guilty about today. He's where he belongs. If he moves, we have a lot of guys on him."

"I still worry, though. I'm really afraid something bad is going to happen."

"I'm not trying to diminish you or invalidate your feelings, sweet girl. But you know you always have feelings like this before me or Alec leave. You feel the same way as every other person here. It's okay. You know there's risks that come with what I do." I run my thumb across her lip. She melts just a little more. "You know we're careful."

She leans in and hugs me. I wrap my arms tightly around her because I know she needs all the comfort and reassurance from me as she can get. Her silky skin against mine makes it a lot harder to leave this bed, but I know good and well she really is looking forward to the luncheon. She's just very worried about me, as she is every mission I go on.

After a long hug and several kisses that I hope soothe her, I help her out of bed. The last thing I want is for either of us to put on clothes, but we need to get this day started. I take a quick shower while she picks out her outfit. Once I'm out and dried off, I wrap a towel around my hips. When I come out, she's sitting, still naked, at the foot of the bed staring at the closet.

"Hey, what's wrong, baby girl?" I quickly walk to her, kneel in front of her, and take her hands.

"I just..." She looks at me and sadly shrugs. "It's nothing."

"Baby, it's upsetting you. It's something. Come on. What's going on? What can I do to help?"

She lets out a long sigh before looking up at me. "It's just that Zack is going to be there. I don't want to be overdressed, but I want to look nice. And I don't want to show too much off because he makes me uncomfortable. But I don't want to walk in there in a hoodie because then he'll know he's gotten to me. And all of that makes me feel so dumb because he doesn't matter."

I squeeze her hands and lean in. I kiss her lovingly as I stand. "Go get ready. I'll find you an outfit." I pull her up with me.

"Really?" she whispers.

I lean down and hover right next to her lips. "Really."

She leans forward and kisses me deeply. I rumble appreciatively into the kiss and squeeze her ass. I pull away slowly when she shivers. She blushes when I tap her ass and hurries to the bathroom.

I make my way to my closet. Given it's her graduation, I also want to look nice. She only gets four tickets for her family, so she's bringing Alec, Tyler, and two others that she grew up with. Rosie also gets four, so she's bringing her dads, me, and Ink because the two of us were the only two who wouldn't have a ticket for Dallas. Not like we're not all going to be cheering for both of them, though.

I quickly get dressed in dress pants and a nice button down. There's no way anyone is getting me in a tie, I wasn't even wearing one yesterday, though I did have a vest on. Ties are too dangerous of a weapon that could be used against me. Also a weapon that has been used against me in the past. Never again.

Before the tormented darkness stirs, I focus on finding a sensible outfit for Dallas. I've bought her some dressier things lately because of how many events I have lined up to go to. Several charity events, and a few company parties I'm expected to attend simply because of the changes I'll be announcing. Usually, I have a hired escort with me. I pay her well for the entire night and send her on her way after the event. Her job is to make me look good and sound intelligent for a few hours. It's easy money for her and she doesn't need to worry about rent or food for a couple of months.

The best part is she doesn't need to give herself to me sexually in order to get that done, though I'm sure most wouldn't have an issue with it, if I'm just judging off their actions. They all want a billionaire, it seems. For me, I get to make sure that women aren't throwing themselves at me shamelessly for a few hours.

I find a sleek pair of black slacks for Dallas. The fabric is soft. They'll hug her without making her feel vulnerable. Keeping away from buttons, I find a deep red shirt with half sleeves. Like the pants, the fabric is soft. It's a half turtleneck but still a little loose. It won't show off her chest or too much of her neck while it'll also cover most of her arms without making her feel too warm and covered up. I pair it all with a pair of black panties and a deep red bra and camisole just to make sure she doesn't need to worry about anything being see-through.

I lay it on the bed. She has a pair of black flats that will match in the shoe closet downstairs. Once I'm done, I head downstairs. I'm finishing blending my morning protein shake when I hear the doorbell. I check my watch. It's close to the time Dallas is supposed to head out. I glance up the stairs and already know she's hurrying to get ready.

I swing open the door as I take a drink of my shake. "Hey, Fallon. Dallas will be down shortly."

"Okay. Do you want me to wait out here?"

"No. Come on in. She needs to meet you if you're going to be her permanent guard." I step aside so she can come in. She's small, but she's a fucking fighter and good at what she does. She trains just as well as my other guards and probably has better marks and agility than all of them.

"Yes, sir," she says as she steps inside.

"You have your attire for the evening?" I ask her.

"I do. I don't feel comfortable in dresses, so I'm doing the pants option."

"I figured you would. I didn't expect you in a dress, but I didn't know what you felt the most comfortable in."

"I appreciate the option, Mr. Lucinio. I'm still getting used to everything in my life not being dictated right down to the color of my socks. And I love that I'm treated as an equal, though I'm the only guard who is a female on both the Crane and Lucinio teams."

"Well, you're one of three. I have another stationed in Tokyo, and Ryan has one in England. But I can say you're the best." I grin. "Marks like yours are hard to come by. You could kick all the men's asses."

She laughs. "I appreciate that. Thank you."

Dallas hurries down the stairs at that moment. "I'm so sorry I'm late. I'm really trying to be on time more."

"You're not late, baby. You still have ten minutes, and you know I'll never allow you to be late."

"Oh good. I really thought I was late."

"No." I pull her close. "Dallas. This is Fallon. She's ex-military. Airforce. She's one of the best guards I have and has been guarding the family for a few years now. She lost her family to a murderer and sought our help. She's been very loyal this whole time. I'm happy to have her. So happy, in fact, that I've decided she's going to be your permanent guard. Where you go, she goes."

"Oh." Dallas holds her hand out. "It's nice to meet you, Fallon."

"Likewise." Fallon shakes Dallas's hand respectfully, and I'm pleased.

"All the top guys on both mine and Ryan's team have permanent guards assigned to their wives or girlfriends."

Dallas nods. "I understand. The more powerful you are in the ranks, the more danger comes to you and your family."

I grin. "Good girl. So, you understand the decision."

"Yes, sir." She smiles up at me.

I groan because she's learned quickly what that word does to me. "Brat," I rumble low in her ear before kissing it. She giggles. I pull away when the doorbell rings again. "Go. Have fun. Rosie should be ready by now. Pick her up on the way out. Your shoes are in the closet by the door." I open the door and let Lance and Damon in. Rosie is right behind them. "Never mind, she's here."

Lance walks right back to my office typing on his laptop. I've never understood how he can do that without crashing into anything. I always thought Damon somehow guided him, but he doesn't. Lance just fucking knows his surroundings. I've seen him looking at something on his laptop and tell me there was a threat coming from somewhere just before I actually see it. He's caught a ball the kids were throwing with one hand before I had the chance to even attempt it. He's like the Eighth Wonder of the World.

Damon follows him as Rosie and Dallas hug. Moments later, everyone I need has arrived and Dallas is on her way out the door with Rosie and Fallon. I kiss her goodbye and head directly to my office behind Gavin, my second-in-command.

"You're not gonna like the shit going down right now, bro," Gavin says to me.

"I got that from the text Damon sent when I was at dinner last night with Dallas."

"You didn't say anything to her, did you?"

"Not a chance. I want everything to be about her until we have to leave. And this shit is going to bring a lot of worry to her and only amplify what she already feels. That's why I've made the decision not to leave until the morning. Where's Alex?"

"Stuck in meetings. He said he's not sure he's going to make it. He has some fires to put out."

"It's fine. We don't really need him. I'm not letting him come with us on this one anyway. I just know he wanted to be a part of this so he knew what was going on."

"I'll fill him in later."

I follow Gavin into my office and quickly take a seat behind my desk. Gavin perches at the corner of my desk. "Let's get started. What do you got, Lance?"

"Verification of everything Aero said is complete. We have verification on the nurse who was fired being the same one on the boat. I verified the story about her being Ethan's ex. We have pictures. Morpheus was right. It didn't take long to dig those pictures up. Ethan himself is in most of them." He turns his laptop so the rest of us can see.

I wince a little. "Those are bad. Very damning. I can see why she didn't want those out."

"I also matched what Dallas said about the patches to the patches we've seen from our fake VV members. It looks like everything we had on Ruthless Warriors tracks to Matthew, but all of that ends with Gregory Franklin. I think he was alluding to Ethan being after us, but we have no real connection to Ethan with him."

"We think what happened is Matthew had his own forces and contacts. After Ethan betrayed him, we think he put his own plan into action," Cole glances at Dane before looking back at me. "I hate saying this more than fucking anything, man, but we think he was trying to fucking help you from the damn grave."

I sit back and chew the end of my pen with narrowed eyes. After a few moments, I sigh heavily. "The really fucking sad part is that I'm starting to agree. Alex hasn't even processed the other shit. I don't know how I'm going to tell him this. Nick, too."

"He definitely knew what he was doing," Damon says.

"He always has." I lean forward again, playing with the pen. "What else?"

"Well, I agree with Cole, and I think after hearing this, you will, too." Lance pauses. "We've… always thought that taking down Gregory and his brother was too easy. Same with the other fucker. Tits. It all seemed too easy."

"Yeah, I agree with that," I say.

"Well, I believe I've found the reason why. Scratch that. I know. I know I found the reason why. And it all traces back to Matthew." He takes a deep breath as I watch him curiously. "Franklin was promised to Raleigh, but Matthew knew when we showed up that night, we'd take her with us. He knew we'd never hurt her. It wasn't long after she ended up with us that we got her stuff proving that she's Damon's sister." He clicks a key, and Damon looks down. "I sent you the email that Damon got from someone I can't identify. But everything he sent, including the evidence, checks out, man."

I glance at my phone when it dings and quickly pick it up. I scan it. "Wait. This is saying he's Matthew's lawyer and executor. And that he gave permission to send the box after Matthew was killed. Why did it take so long?"

"I think it was because our parents were ashamed," Damon says looking up at me. So, they never sent it. Their executors did, who I assumed was connected to this guy. Lance verified it. He was."

"Fuck me." I drop my phone and rub my head.

"When we caught Gregory, that was the end of his line, but Matthew knew that. So did Gregory. They knew we'd catch him, so Matthew put in a fail safe. Something to keep us going."

"Don't fucking tell me Skyla is connected to all this," I say.

"She is. She was his fail safe. He had his executor send a letter to Ethan," Dane says. "According to the email." He nods to my phone. "Skyla's entire relationship is absolutely what happened. And her ex did come after her, but Ethan ordered it because of a letter saying Skyla had information he needed on a leak in his crew. It was sent anonymously."

"How the fuck did he even know about her and her involvement with us? He was dead by then."

"Yep. He was. But her ex wasn't. Matthew chose that company because of what he did. He knew Ethan needed something that could help

182

him with weapons. So, he went after the boyfriend's company and set him up with Ruthless Warriors. Ruthless Warriors recruited him because of his connections. He was with Skyla then. His executor made certain to keep up with everything going on with him so he could be sure to make sure all information was correct when he sent his letters. It was all planned long ago. He provided us phone records. Emails. Conversations. All between him and Matthew setting all of this up." Dane sighs. "Matthew was fucking pissed, man. He did all of this after Jaxon was taken and Lyric was hurt."

I run a hand down my face and glance at my phone when it starts playing *Villain* by Ryan Jesse. I see Dallas's name and pick it up, silencing the room with a finger. "Hey, baby. What's up?"

"I just needed to hear your voice is all. Zack started with me. Fallon stepped in, and he tried giving her shit."

I pinch the bridge of my nose, but refuse to show her my frustration at the situation. "Did she get you out?"

"No, but she silenced him. I didn't want to leave and let him win. We're on our way to rehearsal now, but I'm worried because he spilled a drink on me and ruined both of my shirts. They're stained so bad, Josh. The undershirt isn't as bad, but it makes me look like I'm wearing stained clothing to my graduation on purpose. I look like a mess. I don't have time to get anything from a store. Fallon doesn't have anything extra with her. It's all so fucked up."

I don't hear her swear much, but when she does, I know it's bad. "Fuck. Okay, baby. I'll finish here and meet you at the school. I'll bring something else, and I can't promise I'm not going to kill him."

"Please just don't. I just want to get through this. That's all. He'll go away after. And if he doesn't, I guess then you can take matters into your hands. I really don't think he's brave enough to fuck with me outside of school functions and school walls."

"And I still think you're underplaying. So, I'm keeping watch. One wrong move from him today, he's fucking done."

"Yes, sir. We're here. Please hurry. It takes an hour to get here. We're rehearsing for an hour before people start showing and sitting down. We start a half-hour after that, so I'll have time to change, but we have to get into our seats. We don't get more than fifteen minutes to mingle, and I have to take some out of that time to change."

"I'll get there in time, baby."

"Thank you. I love you."

"I love you, too." I hang up the phone quickly and look at the others. "Let's wrap this up. Dallas's bully is about to get a lesson taught to him he'll never forget."

Lance chuckles. "Only other thing I have is that they haven't moved. They had a party last night. Ethan was followed into town. He took a girl back to the compound, fucked her outside against the wall of the clubhouse, and sent her on her way. Didn't give her a ride back to town. He made her walk. After that, he worked on his bike for a little while. Last update I got, he was working in his garden. It's his pride and joy, after his bike."

"If he catches wind of us -"

"Our team will move in. We have him completely surrounded, and he doesn't have any allies down there," Lance finishes. "Our team and Alec's have scoured, discreetly. No one down there likes them being there. They terrorize the town on the regular, and since they've gone in, people have been going missing all over the area in a fifty mile radius."

"Explains where he's getting the people for the trafficking," Gavin says.

"Yeah. Well, hopefully we can make a dent in that shit by taking him out." I stand and grab my phone. "Get ready. Get your gear and everything packed so we can head out in the morning. I need to head to the school to help out Dallas."

While everyone packs up, I jog upstairs as I text the guards I have going with us to the graduation. I don't have a damn clue how three hours have already gone by. It didn't seem like our meeting went that fast, but unless I'm in a time warp, it must've. I don't even remember finishing my shake, but the remains of it are in an empty bottle on my desk.

I quickly find Dallas another suitable top to wear. It's a long-sleeve, deep pink t-shirt that she loves the feel of and is dressy enough to make her feel incredible. Once I have it, I head downstairs. Everyone has left. I open the closet to grab my shoes and quickly put them on before heading out the door. It's warm, but I grabbed a couple of light jackets just in case.

"Fallon checked in, sir. She said the principal assured her that Dallas's security wouldn't be an issue, and that she could stay as near as she needs to for Dallas's safety," one of the guards says as he opens the back door of one of my SUVs.

I nod. "Good. I really wasn't looking forward to arguing with a school admin today. I have more important shit to worry about." I slide in and hang the shirt on a hook in the back. "You gonna be okay with that hanging there?" I ask the driver as the guard closes the door for me.

"Yes, sir. We use mirrors just as Mr. Reddick taught us."

"Good."

Taylor Reddick is not only a cop with Chicago PD and family to us, he's also who we use for special tactics with our guards, specifically driving. All of our guards who guard the family directly go through Taylor's rigorous and downright fucked up training courses. Ryan and I went through them once and found out real quickly why our guards are the fucking best of the best.

The second we're on the road, I text Dallas to tell her we're coming. I know we'll get there in time, but I hate that she has to wait and change out of an outfit that she not only looked gorgeous in, but felt confident in. It can be replaced. I'm not worried about that, but she didn't deserve that shit today. She doesn't deserve it any day, but today is a special day for her. She was in the running for Valedictorian and only lost by one point to Rosie. She's been looking forward to this day all year long.

I know she thinks it will end, but I know better. Unless Zack's taught a lesson, he's not going to leave her alone. So, a lesson he shall be taught.

One he'll never forget…

Chapter Twenty Two

❦ Dallas ❦

"They won't let me back there, sir. They don't want the other kids feeling uncomfortable," Fallon says over the phone to Josh.

She said she was calling him because the school officials refused to allow her to the side of the stage with me. They argued that she could see me the entire time I'm not in view of everyone else. She probably can, but that's not her job. She knows Zack is right behind me and how uncomfortable he makes me. And the way he's been glaring at me since the entire debacle at the luncheon. He definitely hated that Josh got here so quickly with a change of shirt for me.

I'm realizing very quickly that Josh is right. This isn't going to end. Zack is obsessing over me, as he has been the entire school year. Obsession doesn't just stop.

"Yes, sir. They've physically restrained me three times."

"Paul Bensen," the principal says through the microphone. I sigh because I'm getting closer and closer to walking across the stage, but further into the dim light at the side of the stage. Fallon can still see me, but she has to go through kids to get to me.

"I can, but it'll take a few seconds longer to get to her. I have to go through people if she needs me. They have their own security, but no one back there."

"Brandy Camerson," the principle continues. I step forward after smiling at her. I'm now completely unseen. I feel Zack step closer. I try to step forward, but I can't.

And that's when I feel it. Zack is making his move.

He pulls me against him and slaps his hand over my mouth so I can't scream. "Don't move," he growls low in my ear. I feel something sharp against my back. My eyes widen, and I completely slacken. It's sharp. There's no way it's not a knife.

"Yes, sir," Fallon says to Josh.

Zack grabs the back of my graduation gown and starts sliding his knife down. I can feel the fabric tearing. I reach up to keep my shirt from choking me and instantly feel him slicing through that as well. The knife grazes my skin, but doesn't puncture it.

"Adam Camp," the principal says. Adam, the person standing in front of me, starts his walk across the stage completely unaware of what's going on behind him.

Zack pushes me forward. I stumble and nearly fall onto the stage but catch myself. Fallon, who must be following Josh's orders to disobey the school or something, appears like an angel in front of me. The principal is shooting her a glare, but continuing to shake Adam's hand.

"Back off!" Fallon hisses. She grabs a surprised Zack's knife, quickly disarming him like a pro. She pushes against him hard enough for him to stumble and fall on his ass as he goes through the curtain towards the back of the stage.

It all happens in seconds, but I'm already in shock and in tears, though silent. *Why? Why? Why?* I ask myself over and over again.

Zack gets up and shoots a glare at me as he tries to intimidate Fallon. "You're gonna pay for that, bitch."

Fallon glares. "I dare you." Keeping her eye on him, she moves towards me. "You're okay, honey. I promise."

"Dallas Cassidy," the principal says.

"H-he c-cut i-it!" I say in a quiet shriek. "He sl-sliced i-it!"

Fallon turns me around. "Oh my God."

I can hear Zack snickering as others, who probably weren't paying attention, gasp. "Bitch deserved it." He shrugs nonchalantly.

"Dallas Cassidy?" the Principal says again.

"What do I do? I can't go out like this!" I hiss as I wipe my eyes. I choke down more and more sobs.

Fallon touches her ear. "Stand down. I have her. Stand down."

I look at her alarmed. "What?"

"Dallas Cassidy!" the Principal says once more.

I look between her and Fallon in pure alarm. Zack is outright laughing with his arms folded over his chest.

"What did you do?" someone barks out at him.

"None of your fucking business," Zack growls.

"Oh my God." I try to take deep breaths.

"Okay. It's okay. Here's what we're going to do. I'm walking out there with you, holding your back closed. Then, we're getting you out of here. You're not sitting next to him."

"I can't walk out there with my back exposed!"

"Ms. Cassidy!" the Principal barks. Everyone is starting to murmur. I can't even imagine what Josh is doing.

"I have a safety pin," someone says from behind me.

"I said stand down!" Fallon says commandingly as she turns to the girl who spoke. "Thank you. Anyone else have a safety pin?"

"Oh come on. For fuck's sake," Zack growls.

Seconds later, Fallon has three safety pins. She makes quick work of the gown as the angry principal storms towards me.

"What is going on?" she growls.

"Dallas had a wardrobe malfunction," Zack says innocently.

"Shut up!" I hiss, finally fed up. Zack holds his hands up, cackling.

"Dallas!" the Principal warns. Respect others. One of the biggest rules in this school. Well, where's mine?

"Ma'am, I'm not in the mood to have it out with you. Go back to your podium. You don't know the facts, but you damn well will as soon as my boss and her brother confront you over your behavior," Fallon growls dangerously. Zack rolls his eyes. The Principal glares, but makes her way back out to the podium.

"This isn't how I wanted today to go," I say, teary.

"You deserve it all," Zack says.

"Ignore him," Fallon says. "Trust me."

I nod and let her finish. Once she's done, she nudges me along. I hug myself and make my way across the stage. Once I reach the Administration, I politely shake their hands. The Principal hands me my diploma, and we each smile for the camera as we hold it together. My eyes meet Josh's. He looks beyond pissed.

"Do you have any idea how embarrassing that was?" she asks me the second the picture is taken.

Fed up with everything, I turn to her. "Maybe you should refrain from passing judgment until you know the full details," I say loudly enough that the microphone picks up my voice. "Zack took a knife and sliced through my gown and shirt, leaving my back completely exposed. And that was on your watch since you're the one who wouldn't allow my guard to stay with me."

I glance at Josh, who is grinning ear to ear. The rest of the crowd is murmuring. The administration is looking at her in disbelief. Fallon meets me at the bottom of the stairs and ushers me to the back of the auditorium. We leave through the doors just as the principal continues with names, after taking several breaths to calm herself.

I let out a breath of my own. "I need to go back in there. I don't want to miss Rosie."

Fallon nods. "I know, but you can't go to the dinner after with a torn shirt, so we need to figure something out."

"There's an extra shirt in my SUV," Josh rumbles behind me as he pulls me back against him. I melt into him, instantly feeling calmer and more relaxed. "It's mine. She can wear it. We'll roll up the sleeves. Whatever needs to be done."

"Yes, sir. I'll get that done."

He leans down and presses his lips against my neck and kisses it. I close my eyes and rest my hands on his on my hips. "I called Cole and Dane. We'll have Fallon sit next to you. Everyone will move down. We already have a guard forcing the move. You'll be safe, baby."

I nod and open my eyes slowly. Saying nothing more, he leads me back to my seat. Fallon follows and sits next to a furious Zack. The rest of the ceremony goes off without any issues. After I quickly change into Josh's shirt once the ceremony is over, I follow Fallon and two other guards to the reception hall where dinner is meant to be served for us and our families.

Zack, unable to take a hint, immediately finds me and cuts me off the second we enter the hall. "Little bitch," he spits out as he shoves me. Hard.

I fall back into a hard chest. I expect it to be a guard, but I look up into a familiar set of eyes and feel instant relief. "Josh," I whisper.

"I'll take it from here," he growls. His eyes never leave Zack's, and I can see the instant fear strike him deeply.

Alec takes my hand as the two guards and Fallon step back with chuckles. Everyone in the entire room falls completely silent. Alec guides me behind him as he stands next to Josh, the same dangerous energy exuding from him. I glance up when Tyler puts his arm around my shoulders.

"Look, man. It was harmless fun. I'll leave her alone," Zack says.

"Far too late for that," Alec says. He and Josh are both big men and tower over Zack.

"This ends," Josh growls. "Today. No more games. I catch you anywhere near my girl, you'll understand why I'm called Satan himself. Got me?"

"Yes, sir. Got it." Zack backs away, but he ends up right in the arms of Lieutenant Dane Michaels.

"Zack Castle. You're under arrest for assault with a deadly weapon."

"Wait. What? I didn't assault -"

"You have the right to remain silent!" Dane says, cutting him off. "I suggest you use it. Anything you say can and will be used against you in court. You have the right to have an attorney present during questioning. Take me up on that offer. If you can't afford one, one will be appointed to you. Do you understand these rights as they've been read to you?"

"My father will never allow this!"

Cole, standing next to Dane, laughs. "Yeah? You mean Captain Castle?" He steps aside, and I can't stop myself from turning and laughing into Tyler's arm when Zack's dad steps out from behind them.

"Cuff him, Lieutenant. Lessons will be learned today," Captain Castle says.

Zack has nothing further to say as he's led out of the room in cuffs to the sound of clapping behind him.

After dinner, which was peaceful, thankfully, Josh and I arrive home. The second Josh closes the door to the house, I'm in his arms with my lips locked to his. I kiss him deeply. Wildly. His hands immediately grip my ass. He lifts me. I wrap tightly around him as he holds me and deepens the kiss.

"I can't take the teasing touches anymore," I whisper against him as I kiss down to his neck. "I feel so out of control, but I want you. I want more. I want it all." I tighten my legs around him and kiss across his throat to the other side of his neck.

"Fuck, Dallas."

With one hand and me holding on to him, he reaches back and removes my shoes. His lips meet my neck, and he kisses it before nipping lightly then sucking hard. I gasp and moan. He reaches back with his other hand and takes the other shoe off. I don't know what he does with them, but I don't care. As long as his arms are back around me where they belong.

Locking his lips with mine again, he tries to slow things down, but I don't want that. He starts carrying me off somewhere, but he passes the couch.

"I can't make it to the bedroom," I say against his lips before diving back into him.

"You can, and you will." He nips my lip as he starts climbing. "Because I'm not fucking you for the first time on a damn couch."

"The floor," I nearly beg

"No." He slaps my ass as he kicks his bedroom door closed.

"Josh, please." I am begging now. I don't even care how desperate it sounds or makes me look. I want him. I want all of him. "I'm ready. I -"

He tosses me on the bed and cages me in before I can even bounce. He leans down so his lips are just brushing mine. "I'll give you everything you want, but I'm not hurrying it."

I shake my head with wide eyes. "You're not! I just -"

"Dallas," he rumbles dominantly. My heart races at the tone. My pussy clenches on its own. My stomach quivers. "I'm not fucking around. This is important. I know how you feel. I feel the same way. I want you, but I don't want to hurt you." He puts a finger to my lips to stop me from speaking. "Trust me."

The love in his eyes mixed with his tone manages to calm me instantly. There's no one I trust more than him. I let my body relax into the mattress as I look into his eyes. "I do."

"Good girl. Now, close your eyes. Breathe. Calm your racing heart for me."

I do as he says. I let my eyes fall closed and take one slow, deep breath after another. While I'm focusing on my breathing, I feel Josh get up, but I keep my eyes closed and my focus where he wants it because I really do trust him.

A few moments later, I feel his hands slowly moving up my legs. I let out a long, slow breath because his touch drives me crazy.

Once he reaches the button on my pants, he undoes it like he's done so many times before. His fingertips slide gently across my tummy, making me shiver, before hooking into the sides of the waistband. He pulls the pants down, running his knuckles down my skin all the way down until he's pulling them off my feet.

He straddles me, and I feel his arms on either side of my head. "Open your eyes." His voice is raspy, gravelly. It's all I can do to not snap them open and drink every command he gives me. I open my eyes slowly and blink once.

Josh's lips meet mine, and fireworks explode all around and inside me. His lips leave a passion-filled trail to my neck and across my collarbone as he unbuttons my shirt, well, his shirt that I'm wearing. There's something so erotic about the way that he does it. Something so sensual. I arch into him, begging for him to take all he wants from me.

It's then I realize he's taken off all of his clothes and is completely naked. "Josh," I rasp out shakily. I feel him smile against my skin, and it creates another combustion deep within.

Once he's finished with the buttons, he sits up, still straddling me. He takes both of my hands as my eyes wander his body. He makes everything sexy. His muscles. His tattoos make my mouth water. There's a skull with a crown over his left pec, and a cross with dead branches cascading down it on his chest and stomach. It ends just below his waistband. It's that one that my eyes are focused on because it points right to his length, which isn't at all small. I haven't found the courage to ask how big it is, but he's long and thick.

I inhale sharply. I'm suddenly not at all sure he'll fit inside me. My eyes snap to his when he pulls me up. My throat is suddenly dry. I watch him as he slides the shirt down my arms. He leans in and kisses me again, but this time, it's different. It still holds the same passion that makes my head spin, but he pours so much love into it that my heart skips a beat. Several.

He tosses the shirt and glides his hands up my arms. He lightly caresses my skin until he reaches the clasp on my bra. With very little effort, he flicks the hooks. Using the same care as he had with the shirt, my bra slips off and is tossed. All that's left is my panties.

"Move yourself up to the pillows. Get comfortable."

"O-okay," I stammer. I look behind me and move to the pillows quickly. Once I'm there, I lie back and focus on him once more. I can't help that my eyes fall to what's between his legs. I'm getting more and more nervous that he won't fit.

"Relax, little sparrow," he says as he leans down. His hands grip my thighs. He pushes them apart so they're spread wide for him.

"Josh," I manage to whisper.

"Relax, baby." His tongue lashes my pussy.

I let my head fall back on a moan. I grip the cover beneath me. With each slow lick, I feel myself unclench and give in to him. He sucks my clit into his mouth. I moan again when his tongue flicks it back and forth. I arch into him, thrusting my hips to the pace he sets.

"Josh," I breathe. I open my eyes and look down at him. His tongue slides deep into me. It makes me jerk and clench.

He pulls it out and goes back to lavishing my bud, but he doesn't leave me wanting anything. I feel his middle finger sink into me as he groans against my clit. I let my head fall back again as I moan. My eyes roll back in my head. My pussy clenches again around him. I feel myself get wetter as he thrusts.

He pushes a second finger inside me, and I relax more. All tension leaves my body. I thrust my hips into him more and more as his pace quickens. My pussy pulses around his fingers.

"I'm so close," I pant. "Oh, Josh. So, so close." I feel my body about to erupt and tense, ready for the orgasm about to hit me, but Josh pulls back. He pulls his fingers out of me. I look at him wide-eyed. He's never stopped like that before. "D-did I do something wrong?" I ask. I'm already embarrassed for whatever it was.

Josh chuckles low and deep as he shakes his head. "No." He puts his fingers into his mouth and sucks on them. It takes me a second to realize it's me he's sucking off his fingers. I blush furiously and look away. "Oh, no you don't."

I look up at him as he leans down, holding himself over me. He smiles and kisses the corner of my mouth before covering my lips with his. I blush an even deeper shade of red when I taste my own sweet and tangy taste on his tongue.

He reaches between us and grips his length. A moment later, his tip is against my sensitive clit. He leisurely moves it from my clit to my pussy. With each moment, he brings me higher and higher, never letting me take the fall.

But I trust him. I always trust him.

"Ready?" he asks, his eyes meeting mine.

Suddenly, the nerves come crashing back over me in waves. "I... I'm..." I bite my lip. Josh leans down and licks it with a low growl of warning. I immediately stop biting it because I know he takes that as a form of me hurting myself. He's slowly sliding his dick towards my pussy. "Will it fit?" I ask in a whisper, genuinely concerned.

"It'll fit." He stops right at my entrance. "I promise."

His voice portrays his confidence, but also the gentleness I need from him right now. I tremble a little as I grip his arms. "Okay," I whisper.

His tip penetrates me, and I gasp in fascination, pleasure, and just a little pain. He thrusts a little bit and pushes in a little deeper each time.

"Fuck," he moans against my neck. "You're so tight, baby."

I wrap my arms more around him and nod so he doesn't see me cry. I want him to keep going, but I'm getting more and more nervous about how much it will hurt. The pain is outweighing the pleasure.

He pulls out slowly and thrusts just as slowly back in, but doesn't go further than how deep he's already gone. It's like he knows without me telling him that I'm getting more and more tense. Like he can feel it. He starts massaging my hip and ass while he continues the gentle ministrations.

"Just relax, my girl. If it hurts too much, I'll stop, okay?"

I nod and bury my face in his chest. He's managed to relax me once more, and with each stroke of his dick, I get wetter. He slides in easier and easier, though he doesn't go any deeper.

Before long, I start moving with him, letting my body do what feels natural. Josh kisses my cheek and leaves a searing trail to my lips. He quickens the pace a little, but still doesn't slide deeper, I'm not sure I could take him any further anyway.

"Good girl," Josh rumbles against my lips. "You're almost taking all of me."

I look down and watch myself taking him. He's in a lot further than I thought, and I feel slightly foolish for thinking I wasn't taking nearly as much of him as I am. The feeling doesn't last long because I watch with pure lust as he thrusts into me over and over again. Each thrust brings him deeper and deeper until I can feel with absolute certainty that I'm taking all of him. I don't need to see it, but I keep watching anyway because it makes me feel more sexy.

"Oh, Josh." I meet his thrusts and submit completely to him.

He groans. "Dallas, holy fuck, baby."

Once he breaks through what feels like a barrier to me, I start to take him a lot easier and faster. He's so thick. So big. "More," I whisper. "More, please."

"Say 'sir'. Ask me the right way."

Every cell of my being wants to obey his every wish, so without a second thought, I do just that. "Please, sir. Please. I need more, please?"

His eyes darken. His mouth crashes to mine, and he starts thrusting harder. I know he's still holding back for my sake. I know I can't handle more than what he's giving me. I'm so grateful to him that he knows that because I know instinctively there's so much more to this.

I sink into his kiss and start to tremble. I wrap my legs around his waist, and he groans when he sinks even deeper. His thrusts never become erratic, but Josh is still in complete control just like he is with everything, and it comforts me more and more. My trust in him only grows.

"Josh... I..." I hug him tighter. My whole body feels like it's about to explode more powerfully than it did when I had my first orgasm ever with him. "Josh!" My pussy clamps around him like a vice and pulses erratically.

He moans against my throat as his dick thickens. "Come for me. Now, little sparrow."

I throw my head back and shout, "Josh!" My hips jerk into him uncontrollably as I come so hard, I almost shoot up from the bed and hit the ceiling.

"Good girl," he rumbles. "All mine. All for me." In the first show I've ever seen of Josh losing any semblance of control, his stomach tightens against me. "Dallas!" he roars. His head drops to my shoulder, and he comes. His dick jerks inside me as he fills me with everything he has. I moan loudly as we both hit our peaks and slowly float down afterwards.

He slowly pulls out after we both catch our breath. He flops on his back, and I snuggle into him. I'm so content and beautifully exhausted that I don't feel when he gets up. I barely pay attention to him cleaning me. When he crawls back into bed and pulls the blankets over us, I simply melt into him and fall asleep wrapped in the arms of the man I'm going to spend all of eternity with.

Chapter Twenty Three

☙ Josh ☙

I look up at the belt swinging down at me and instantly freeze. If I cry or move, he lashes me more.

"Why do you have to be such a disobedient fucker?" my father asks me. The lashes sting, but I barely jump. "Why can't you be more like Alex, huh?"

Alex. Alex. Alex. Who the fuck cares about Alex? He left me to go to fucking college. Not me. I didn't get that opportunity. I'm not the fucking golden child.

When I feel the familiar jealousy creeping in, I choke it down. Jealousy is an emotion. Emotions can get me fucking killed. I won't show emotion any more than I'll let myself feel pain.

So, I take the lashes. I count them and tune out his words. I won't let him get to me. I'll be out of here soon enough anyway. And when I am, I'm taking my mother and his precious mafia with me when I burn his ass to the ground.

He stops after six and tosses the belt. "Do it."

That has me glancing up at him. He sneers at me just as his guards take over.

They want a fight?

It's on.

"Josh? It's okay, baby," a soft voice calls to me. I feel her in my heart. I feel her envelop me. Her scent fills me. I feel her heartbeat.

For me.

I don't feel the kicks. The punches. I don't hear the screams. All I hear is her beautiful, soothing voice.

"It's okay, baby. I got you."

Tighter. I feel her pulling me into her.

Closer.

"I'm here. I'm always here," she whispers just as everything goes dark.

"I won't let go, Josh. I'm always here. Right here."

Dallas.

"Mmm…," I groan. I can feel myself sweating. I'm trembling.

"I won't let go. I promise. I love you. I love you so much."

It takes me time to fully come out of the sleep haze I find myself in, but when I do, Dallas is hugging me as tightly as she can, and I don't know what happened. As soon as I remember a small fraction of the dream, though, I jerk away from her.

"Fuck, did I hurt you?" I sit up and grab her gently. I reach for the desk lamp and turn it on. Both of us wince at the sudden light, but I don't let it stop me from looking her over. "Did I do anything?"

"Josh," she says softly.

"Did I hit you?" I pull the covers down. "Did I kick?"

"Josh." She presses both of her palms against my face and forces me to look at her.

My heart is going to beat out of my fucking chest. "Please tell me I didn't hurt you." It's a whisper. I don't trust my voice to not betray how vulnerable I feel.

She shakes her head slowly with a loving smile on her face. "No. You didn't hurt me. You jerked in your sleep. I wrapped around you then and just held you. You thrashed, and I started talking. That's all."

I study her for a long while until I'm sure she's telling me the truth. But the war raging inside me forces me to pull back and sit on the edge of the bed with my hands on my face. I expect her to stay right where she is. I don't expect to feel her crawling across my Alaskan king-sized bed towards me. I don't expect her small hand on back. I don't expect to feel instantly soothed.

But mostly, I don't expect the words that escape from my mouth to come. "It was a beating. It was just after Alex went to college. He took the belt to me because I mouthed off to him. I told him I wanted to go to college, too. He told me no. That I didn't need to waste my time. I'd never be anything anyway. I told him Alex didn't need it either. He didn't even want anything to do with the family business. That was all it took. He just didn't stop with the belt. He got the guards involved."

"Oh, my king," she whispers in my ear. She wraps her arms around me, and I can't help but turn and hug her back. Only tighter because I can't believe she's real and really here. That she really loves me enough to stay.

Interrupting my moment, though, my phone starts vibrating. I sigh into Dallas's hair and contemplate not answering it.

Until I realize it's four in the morning. "Nothing good comes from a phone call this early." I pull away from her slowly. She doesn't move, though. She keeps close and rubs my back. She'll never know how grateful I am to her for just that simple gesture. "What?" I say into my receiver when I see a guard's name.

"Sir, we have a problem down here," he says, his voice a little shaky.

"What?" I growl.

"Ethan had to have made us. We saw him and his crew all getting ready to take off. Everyone. We went in after him, per orders, but he had a lot of firepower. Sir, we lost a significant amount of people. So did he, but not as much as us. We have people following him, but he took off through a fucking desert or something. Our SUVs couldn't get through the terrain. He's fucking gone."

"Trackers. Tell me you got fucking trackers on the bikes."

"Yes, sir. We did."

I breathe out in relief. "Fuck. Thank fuck. Where is he?"

"It looks like he was heading for the border."

I kiss Dallas and get up quickly. I stride to my dresser and start to get dressed but pause. "Wait. What the fuck did you just say? You didn't just say 'was heading for the border' to me."

"Uh. Yeah. I did, sir. He had to have found the trackers. They stopped about a mile from the border. We notified Border Patrol and Blade in Texas. We notified our teams in Texas. We lost them when they stopped. One by one. We were already mobilized and after them. By the time we reached the point we lost them, they were gone. We checked in with our contacts. No one saw them. They fucking vanished, sir."

"Jesus Christ." I glance at my caller ID when my phone beeps in my ear signaling another call. Dallas is looking at me with wide eyes. "Baby, get dressed, please." She jumps into action with no hesitation. "I'll call you back. I have another call." I switch to the other call. "Cole? What -"

"Josh, I'm in fucking trouble."

"What? What the hell is happening?" I quickly start getting dressed once more. Dallas hands me a pair of jeans from my closet.

"They just arrested me, man. I didn't do a damn thing. I was on my way home from serving a warrant with Dane. Next thing I know, I'm being pulled over by six fucking squads at gunpoint."

"Fuck, Cole. That raises more questions than it gives answers."

"Hurry it up, Westwood," someone says in the background as I'm putting jeans on.

"Josh, get me a lawyer. Dane is trying to figure out what the hell they're charging me with. I'm in a fucking interview room at Headquarters."

"Time's up, Westwood."

"Give me a damn minute, Peterson!" Cole growls. "Josh, man, I'm not fucking kidding. I don't know what the hell is going on, and no one is telling Dane shit."

"I'm coming. I'll be there. Don't say a damn word to them."

"I won't." The line goes dead, and I throw my phone on the bed. "Josh?"

I pull Dallas into my arms. "I don't know. Ethan got away. There was a gun fight. We lost some people."

"Oh my God," she whispers into my chest as she hugs me. "What do we do?"

"Well, I planned on going down there, but then Cole called. They arrested him. He doesn't know why."

She looks up at me in horror. "What?"

"Yeah. I need to go down there, baby. Dane isn't getting anywhere."

She nods. "Let me just grab my phone. I can go to Rosie's."

"Good girl." I lean down and kiss her, glaring on my phone when it rings again. "What now?"

"You better answer it. Should I call Alec?"

"Yeah, baby. Thank you." I pick up my phone. "Zeke. What's going on?"

"Josh, I have you and Ryan on the line. I need to make this quick. I don't know what the fuck is going on, but we have a crowd of over a hundred people walking up the street. It's peaceful, so far, but they're chanting 'Killer Cop'."

"What the fuck?" Ryan asks, a little groggy.

"Oh no. Fuck no." I rub my head.

"What? What am I missing?" Ryan asks again, sounding a little more awake. "Shit. Taylor! He was executing an arrest warrant!"

"Taylor is home, sir," Zeke says. "He got in over an hour ago. Dane and Cole are still out."

"Ryan, we need to mobilize everyone we have to Headquarters. I'm on my way there. I got a call from Cole. They arrested him. He doesn't know why."

"Baby?" I hear Ariana say sleepily.

"Ryan, they're getting more rowdy. They're still two blocks away, but the closer they get, the more angry they seem to be getting."

"Lockdown," I say.

"Agreed," Ryan rumbles.

"Wait. I have to get Alex and Dallas over to Lyric's. Matt and DJ were with Dane and Cole going through their training. The transfers came though. If you put us in lockdown, she'll panic, and so will Dallas."

"I'll wait for your signal, man, but you need to hurry." Zeke hangs up. I hang up and immediately dial Alex as I take Dallas's hand. She's still talking to Alec, but she follows me with no hesitation. I run down the stairs.

"Yeah?"

"Alex, get up. Get Raleigh. Run to Lyric's. I'll meet you there. We're going into lockdown."

"Oh fuck. Okay. We're moving."

I put my phone in the back pocket of my jeans and pull Dallas to the closet. I give her shoes and put my own on quickly. She slips hers on and runs with me out the door. I grab my keys on the way and slam the door behind me. The second I see Alex leave his house with Raleigh running behind him, I call Zeke back.

"Yeah," he answers.

"Do it. I'll bypass it with my code. Get everyone going. I can hear the chants."

"They're at the edge of our property now and slamming bats and other things against the fence. Get underground, Josh."

"On the way."

I keep running down the street dragging Dallas with me. She's not as fast as I am. Her legs aren't as long, but she's doing a fuck of a job keeping up. When we reach the guest house, where Lyric is staying, it's already gone into full lockdown. Dallas is out of breath.

"Alec," she pants. "He's coming... for you... to help."

"Good. I'll need it."

"The fuck is going on, bro?" Alex asks when he catches up as I'm entering my bypass code. I can already hear Jaxon screaming and Lyric crying. I'm sure Mariah and Luca are attempting to console them, but they don't know what's going on. Lyric has been trained on the system, but she's never had to use it.

"Riot. They arrested Cole. Remember that cop that killed that unarmed guy?"

"The guy everyone is up in arms about because he was Black?"

"Yeah. I didn't understand that. He's a fucking man who was unarmed and cooperating. I think Cole is going down for it."

"What?" Raleigh squeaks.

The chants get louder and louder. "Yeah." My bypass goes through after Nick sees it's me through the cameras.

The second we're inside, the front door automatically locks down again. The only person who can open it now is whoever holds the control, and that's Nick.

"Lyric!" I call.

"In here!" Mariah yells. "By the escape door!"

I tug Dallas after me. Alex follows. I yank the door open and see Lyric curled over Jaxon protectively. Both are crying. Mariah looks terrified, and Luca looks like he might pass out.

"Daddy!" Jaxon cries.

"I'm right here, buddy." I pick him up and pull Lyric up. Jaxon clings to me. Lyric's hand trembles in mine. I look at her with the most dominant look I can muster. Her eyes are darting all over the place, and I know she's already in a full panic attack. "Lyric. Look at me." Her eyes snap to mine. "Alex is going to get you to the safe room. Okay? You need to follow his directions. Do what he says."

"Yes, s-sir. Yes, sir."

I hug Jaxon and squeeze Lyric's hand before moving aside so she can see Alex and Raleigh. I give Jaxon to Alex. "Uncle Alex will protect you. Okay? Can you be a big boy and help him for me?" Jaxon wipes his eyes as he nods and grips Alex. I turn to Dallas and hug her tight. "I'm sorry, baby."

"Don't. Don't be. You need to help Cole. He's our family." She hugs me tight.

"You have no fucking idea how happy I am that you understand."

"Just come home, Josh."

"I'm always coming home, little sparrow." I kiss her again before letting Alex lead her away from me. He ushers them all behind the secure door. The second it closes, I have my phone to my ear.

"Letting you out now. Are they on the way down?" Nick says when he answers.

"Yeah. Alex will fill you in. Ryan will be with me."

"Got it."

"Keep everyone safe, Nick. This is going to get bad."

"Don't worry about us. Worry about you and coming home safe. Door's open."

I quickly open it and run outside. "I'm out. Ryan and Alec are here. We're taking off now."

"Be safe." Nick hangs up at the same time as me as the house goes back into lockdown.

"We're going out VV's gate," Ryan says when I jump into his SUV. "He has Tyler. The rest of his team will follow us."

"What about ours?"

"They're already heading out. Gavin took the lead, so some are gone. Some will follow behind us in a third wave. A fourth and fifth are coming behind them. Might be overkill, but I think this is about to get fucked up quick."

I nod and look out the window as we cross into VV's compound. I've never been more fucking thankful for them deciding to ally with us and move their compound with ours. It makes escape in this situation a lot easier.

Chapter Twenty Four

❦ Dallas ❦

I hug myself as I watch the big screen TV mounted on the wall in the massive underground safehouse. I'm perched on the arm of one of the couches. The kids are playing quietly as all of the adults are glued to the events going down.

Except Lyric.

Lyric is burrowed into Alex. If Jaxon hadn't wanted to play with the others, she'd still be rocking him. Luca is close to her and holding her hand, but I don't think she even feels him. I'm not sure he even knows he's holding her hand. Mariah was called out, along with Nick, and Taylor. A second riot broke out at Headquarters.

Chase is hugging Breetana and Nicole. Jason is swaying with Jessa and Dani. Raleigh and Harleigh are snuggled together with Damon. Lance is holding a crying Rosie. Luke is helping Ariana, but I feel like that's what I should be doing.

I can't.

I can't focus on anything other than the TV because Josh and our family are out there. Alec is out there. Ryan. Matt and DJ. And the riot seems to be growing by the second. The National Guard has been called, but it takes them time to mobilize, I guess, because they haven't arrived.

"Evelyn Andrews, reporting live for CNN. I'm on the ground here in Chicago where a riot has broken out in front of Chicago Police Department's Headquarters building. Michael, we've seen a lot more officers guarding the building where several higher up officers are barricaded. We have very little information on what's happening, but we do know that the Sergeant accused of gunning down an unarmed Black man during a routine traffic stop last week may be inside this building."

I watch the bubbly blond-haired reporter talking into a microphone with her hand up to her ear like she's trying to hear some voice talking to her. My alarm is growing more and more because no one on any news station has really given a lot of information, but they certainly showed up to the scene quickly.

"Evelyn, can you tell us what's being chanted in the background? Do you have any information you can give us to catch our audience up?"

The reporter nods a few times. There's a delay before she looks over her shoulder. "Michael, they're chanting 'Killer Cop' over and over again, but they've been switching to 'Kill the Killer Cop' as well. I have very little information, but to catch up our audience, last week, a Chicago police detective, who we've now identified as Sergeant Cole Westwood, was filmed by an anonymous passerby. The stop seemed cordial enough until the man was pulled from his vehicle and thrown to the ground. The video shows the man being very cooperative and following Westwood's commands. Westwood then shot the man in the back of the head while he was lying on the ground. He can be heard on the video calling for backup. The man was later identified as Miles Evers. Evers's family has been asking the department for updates and justice, but the department has not given any comment besides they are investigating. Westwood has not been suspended."

"Do we know why Sergeant Westwood wasn't suspended during this time?"

"We know, according to the department, that Westwood was put on desk duty until the department has more information, but there are reports coming in that the department was lax with his orders, and he has been allowed to resume his duties fully."

I sniffle but can't turn away. I can't walk away. I can't do anything but watch the entire shitshow go down.

"We have video of the alleged incident," the news anchor, I guess his name is Michael, says. "If you have children in the room, please tell them to leave now. We warn you. This video is graphic."

I roll my eyes because it's the same video they've shown a hundred times already. It shows a man that I can't personally identify as Cole, and I see him almost every day, stepping out of a black Crown Victoria. It's obviously an undercover squad, but there are several huge problems with the first few seconds.

Firstly, the camera is already filming when the vehicle pulls over and the squad comes into play. It seems weird to me that they keep saying things like some passerby caught the ordeal when it seems like the passerby was filming right from the beginning.

Secondly, Cole doesn't drive a Crown Victoria. His squad is actually his truck, like Taylor's, Nick's, and Dane's. It was something they worked out with the department long ago. The only time Cole drives a Crown Victoria is literally never. He simply doesn't do it. He's not even assigned one. If they have to go anywhere undercover, they take cars from their impound lot.

Thirdly, he doesn't do traffic stops. Cole once told me that he hasn't done a traffic stop in five years, ever since he transferred to Chicago and joined Dane's team. I asked because I was curious how one works and asked if I could go on a ride along with him. Since he's not patrol, he couldn't take me, but I learned a lot about what he does that day.

The video continues with the man stepping out in uniform. Cole hasn't worn a uniform since he went to a funeral for an officer who was killed in the line of duty. And that was his dress blues, as he called them. He makes his way to the car and has what seems like polite conversation, until he starts yelling about getting out of the car.

I shake my head and sigh. There's no voice coming from the person filming. Nothing at all. No gasp. No screaming to stop. It doesn't even look like it's moving. Not even when the shot goes off. It's like the camera is…

"Secured to something…" I mumble, tilting my head.

"You see it, too?" Robby rumbles next to me.

I look up at him and nod. He's not looking at me. He's standing with his arms folded across his chest and his feet shoulder width apart staring at the TV. "Yeah," I whisper. "So much is wrong with all of this."

"I know. I've been feeling the same way. I'm going to hack CNN's servers and pull this video. I really want to know what tipped the scales for Cole to actually be arrested."

I shake my head. "Nothing makes sense. And all of this is completely out of control."

"Seems set up, huh?"

"Yeah. Yeah. Absolutely, one-hundred percent a set up. From start to finish. And I can't help but think it has something to do with Ethan's disappearance."

"All I know is we've been watching this for hours, and they're all reporting the same thing. We're coming up on night. We haven't heard anything from anyone. We still have rioters outside our gates." Robby glares at the TV. "Something is all wrong."

"I think we need to call in everyone we can. I just wish I knew how."

"Call Josh," Ariana says after handing out drinks to everyone and small sandwiches for the kids. Luke puts down a meat and cheese tray with vegetables. "Luke and I were just discussing that. He's going to call Ryan right now. Gavin isn't here. He's with Josh, so I think you, as Josh's girlfriend, need to call him. You're right. We need more people."

I nod and take out my phone as I walk to an empty room down the hall. I call Josh, hoping he'll answer. I haven't wanted to call or text him to check in because I can see everything that's going on. He needs to focus on that.

"Hey, baby," Josh answers. He's tired. I can tell.

"Hi. Is… Cole okay?"

"The arrest warrant was issued by the Sheriff's Department. The Sheriff himself is here and says he never saw it, nor does he know who the deputy who issued it is. He doesn't work for him at all."

"The news is reporting that Cole did it. They're showing video and everything, but it's not him."

"We know, baby. We're seeing it. Everything about this is screaming red flags."

"The crowd is getting bigger, Josh. And there are still rioters outside the gates. I'm afraid our guards are going to get overwhelmed. I was talking to Ariana, and we both agree that it would be a good idea to get more guards here and to help with the riot. They're saying you all are barricaded in there."

"We are. We can't get out without hitting the crowd and we don't want to take resources away from keeping everything contained to here."

"Is there anything we can do? Can we call in allies?"

"Is Lance near you?"

"I went into one of the bedrooms. I can get him."

"No, honey. You don't need to. Tell him that I said call in our forces. Everyone he can. Ariana and Luke are being told the same thing."

"Okay."

"As soon as the National Guard gets here, we'll be able to get out. We have the State Patrol and Sheriff's department here already."

"Can they call in other cities near us? That's a thing, right?" I start walking out of the room and back to the room everyone is gathered in, making a beeline for Luke.

"Already done, baby. Get Robby and Lance on that video once they call in our forces. We're working to get Cole free, but they have no choice but to do an internal investigation right now. And since he's been arrested, the DA is involved. She doesn't like this at all because the judge who signed the arrest warrant is dead."

"How does it just get worse?"

"Fuck, I wish I knew. There's so much unanswered shit right now, I don't even know what to say. Start with getting our forces here. Then, get them on that video. Tell them everything I just told you. They'll know where to go with it."

"Okay."

"I love you, little sparrow. We'll be home soon. I promise."

"I love you, my king." We hang up with those words, and I put my phone in my pocket as I clear my throat, attempting to quietly get Luke's attention.

He looks down at me with a soft smile. "Yeah. I got it. I'll take care of it."

"Was that Ryan?" I ask him quietly.

"Yeah, he was giving me an update. What's up?"

"I'm not sure what he said, but -" I cut myself off and blink when I spot Lyric pawing at the wall. "What is Lyric doing?"

Luke looks over at her and sighs. "She's been trying to get out. She wants to help DJ and Matt. She keeps finding different places to try even though she knows she's not getting out of here without me letting her."

"I've seen her struggle against Alex a few times, but I didn't know she was doing that... Is she going to be okay?"

"She'll be okay. She's been going between catatonic and wanting her husbands. Wanting to help them, I mean. But she'll be okay."

I watch her for a few minutes and notice that Alex is also keeping his eyes on her. I feel better knowing that he's watching. I look back up at Luke. "Josh said to call in more forces. Everyone we have. I hoped you'd help me. He also said that he wants Robby and Lance on the video CNN keeps showing. Also, he told me that the person who issued the arrest warrant was a deputy with the Sheriff's Department who doesn't work there. And I guess the judge who signed is dead. That seems unbelievably sloppy to me." I jump when Lyric screams at the wall and punches it repeatedly. "Oh my God."

"Alex has her."

I watch Alex jump up and go to her. He wraps around her from behind and pulls her back from the wall with him. "Poor girl," I whisper.

"She hasn't heard from DJ and Matt. They're with Nick, Mariah, and Taylor outside the building, so she's not holding up too well knowing they're in danger."

I watch as Alex sits down with her. Her teenage boys sit next to them and hug her. Luca's eyes are still glued to the TV. I let out a breath. "Anyway. I guess I don't know how to go about all of this. I mean, I can tell them everything, but I feel like since you're Ryan's second-in-command, it should come from you?"

"It can, but, Dallas, you have just as much power as he does. If he's asking you to step up, it means he knows you can in his and Gavin's absence. Damon is his third-in-command, so he can also give commands in their absence."

I nod but look up at him. "I don't really know how," I whisper. "Do I just... go up and start telling Lance what to do? That seems weird."

"No. Just sit next to him and tell him what Josh said. He'll know what to do. I'll handle Robby and getting our forces together. How's that? We'll work together."

I nod again. "Okay."

He smiles and guides me towards Lance. "You'll be fine."

I take a deep breath and sit down next to him. "Hi," I whisper, keeping complete focus on my hands.

He puts an arm around my shoulder and hugs me to him. "Hi. How are you holding up?"

"Not well. But at least I got to talk to Josh. That's more than I can say for Dani or Lyric or Nikki."

"Well, we can see they're okay. The situation is under control. They're holding everyone back."

"Yeah, but for how long?" I look up at him. "Robby and I were talking a little, and he convinced me I should call Josh. I didn't want to because I didn't want him to get distracted or hurt by a phone call."

"Josh hasn't come out, honey. We know that because no one has come out. And Josh won't leave without Cole. Even if they go out the back, the news would see. They're covering everything."

"I know. Deep in my heart, I guess. Josh also confirmed they're still there. That whole area just has so many people. That building is surrounded."

"What else did he say? Anything about Cole?"

"Yeah. The video. It looks as fake as it feels to me. He wants you and Robby to look at it. The arrest warrant. He said it was signed by a dead judge and created by someone who doesn't even work for the Sheriff's Department, even though it came from the Sheriff's Department. It just seems so sloppy. And then the DA is pissed. Josh said they have to do an internal investigation. I can see why they have no choice. They have to do something. I feel like the reason they hadn't done more than put him on desk duty was because that video is so obviously faked, but I don't even think he was on desk duty. I feel like nothing had happened at all to him because he was very confused talking to Josh. I could hear little pieces of it. Nothing makes sense."

"I agree. Robby and I have already been talking about pulling the video. I texted Dane. He's getting a copy of the arrest warrant for me."

"Good, because Josh wants you to look into it. And he also agrees with me in that we need more forces. The riot is split. The bigger one is downtown, but there's still people here. We need more people. We have to call in our allies. We're helping the police to gain control and spreading ourselves thin. Not only that, it seems weird this is all going down after Ethan escapes. It's too coincidental, and one of Josh's biggest beliefs is that nothing is coincidence. I don't want us spread thin. If we're focused on this riot, then it means our attention is split and not as much on Ethan. When it comes down to it, I really think that he is the source of all of this. It's intentional. His plan."

"I agree there, too. It's something Matthew would do," Damon chips in. "It has him written all over it."

"That's why I think priority should be calling everyone we can in. All hands on deck. There are thousands of people out there. They keep saying tens of thousands." I let out a breath after getting all of that out.

Lance squeezes me to him. "You're extremely intelligent. Nothing you said didn't make sense. You're right about everything. We all feel just as you do. Trust me." He reaches for his laptop on the table in front of him. "I'll send the S.O.S. now. Then, we'll move to the video and warrant."

"Thank you, Lance." I turn and hug him before settling with my knees tucked into my chest as I hug them to me.

"Breaking news, Michael," the blond reporter cuts in. "We're just getting word that there's a second riot in the city, and it's at the Crane and Lucinio compound. You heard that right, everyone. Rioters are currently taking over the mafia's compound. We're sending a second team to cover this."

"Thank you, Evelyn. For those of you just tuning in, there are now two riots in Chicago. We've just learned that rioters are overtaking Crane and Lucinio compound. The stakes have gotten higher with the mafia now involved."

I can't help but start laughing hysterically. "The stakes are higher? No shit!" I yell at the TV before laughing even harder.

Before I know it, I've broken. I don't know who wraps their arms around me, but they sway me back and forth while I cry a tearless cry.

The stakes are higher? Yeah. My family is under attack.

Chapter Twenty Five

❦ Josh ❦

I lean against the wall and look down at the crowd still gathered outside the Headquarters building. Several squad cars have been destroyed. One is on fire. I've watched some of these assholes spit in both my men's and the cop's face. The crowd multiplied from hundreds to thousands, quickly overpowering the police. When mine and Ryan's men entered, the crowd only grew.

"National Guard should be here within the hour," Ryan rumbles. He's standing across from me doing the same thing I am. Looking down at the crowd.

"Good thing we've had extra forces arriving throughout the night," I say. The sun is just starting to rise. None of us have slept. The building has been shot at. Molotov cocktails have been thrown at the windows. People, cops and civilians alike, have been hurt. Some have been arrested.

"I really just want to end this."

"I know, Josh, but some things can't be solved with overpowering. We have to be diplomatic for Cole's sake. If we overpower with the force we're capable of, it can fuck up Cole's life very quickly."

I sigh when another wave of people attempt to overpower the barricade made up of my men, Ryan's men, Alec's men, and the police. They want to get into the building to take down Cole. At least according to every single news outlet who has done an interview with anyone down there.

Our men and women, brave as they are, are getting fucking tired. Some of our family is down there.

"Do we know where Mariah is?" Alec asks, appearing at my side. It's only the hundredth time he's asked. "Do we know where anyone is?"

"No. No. We have no idea," I respond. "All we know is they haven't been injured. They'd be in here if they had been."

"How the fuck do we end this?" he asks.

"We're going to have to start escalations," the Chief says from behind his desk. "We can't do what the city wants anymore."

"Tear gas. Pepper spray," Dane chips in. "We can ask the fire department to hose them down before we resort to the rest of the stuff. I'm tired of doing what the city wants. We have people, good people, being hurt out there. I don't know how no one got hurt when the shots popped off towards the building."

Cole, with his head in his hands, sighs. "Maybe it's best if we just give me up. I'd sacrifice myself for all of them."

I shake my head and look at him. "Not an option, Cole. Knock it off."

He looks up at me. His eyes are just as bloodshot as the rest of ours. "Why? I'm the one they want."

"Yeah? And what happens when they get you?" I growl.

He glares. "It stops. Simple."

"No. It doesn't stop with you. They win if they get you. Then, they go after all the other cops in the city because all of you are bad cops. All of you. Cops getting shot in their squads. The city runs amok because the department is too afraid to stand up to them. Just give them what they want. I fucking know you, Cole. I know you'd sacrifice yourself if it meant saving anyone else, but you know as well as I do that never works. They'll just want more. A person is decent. People are fucking rabid animals."

"It would -"

"Enough," the DA says, cutting Cole off. She's watching the TV. "It looks like the rioters at Crane and Lucinio compound are dispersing.

Your men came in and overpowered them. That's the answer here. We don't use the level of power the mafia is capable of, but we get enough people to overpower and use nonlethal measures, as they did, to get this under control. That's how we stay diplomatic about this. This has been going on for twenty-four hours. Longer than that."

Ryan and I look up at the TV. As she said, the riot has all but ended at our home. They never got past the gate, thankfully, but it didn't matter, because they also threw a lot of their own cocktails at our guards and onto the property. And they were all there because they knew that's where Cole lives. Everyone knows who resides in that compound. It's not something that's easy to hide in this day and age. It's why we have a higher security clearance then the fucking government.

"She's right," the Chief agrees. "Andrea is right. The Mayor is cozy in his own home. City officials aren't here. There are injured cops and others stuck in this building." He looks at me, Ryan, and Alec. "Give the order. We can't wait anymore."

I nod. "Finally," I rumble as I grab a radio. All of our guards are on the same frequency as the police. "Phoenix One to all," I say over the radio with my own call sign. "Escalation stage one. Now."

"Copy," someone says. "Fucking finally. This is out of hand."

We all gather at the window. Police and guards work as one. They reposition and start pushing people back with shields raised. I don't know if we have enough people, but we can't stay trapped here. We all need to get home to our families. All of us.

The feat isn't easy. While we've managed to push everyone back from the building, at least, the crowd still fights. I tune out the TV talking about us making a move. How we're moving the crowd with force and violence.

"Do we have the fire department here? Can we have them surround our guys with trucks?" Alec asks.

"We can." The Chief makes a call as Cole moves to stand next to me, making sure he's not seen out the window. We don't want him to incite the crowd even more.

"Looks like we can get Cole out," Dane says.

The crowd pushes back, and I panic when our line moves the wrong direction. "Fuck," I rumble.

"Viper One, we have Mariah!" someone yells into the radio.

Alec closes his eyes and swallows. "Thank fuck," he whispers. "Keep her close," he commands into the radio. I make a point to ask him about that later. He's beyond worried about her. I've never seen him act like that for anyone other than Dallas.

Just then, we all watch fire trucks roll in behind our line, providing an extra line of defense. While they do what they need to do, I don't like seeing our line get pushed further back.

"I want to be out there," I say.

"We all do. But Cole is the priority here," Ryan says to me. "So is our family."

I look at him and glare. "We have family down there."

"I know. My brother is down there, Josh. They have coverage. If we go down there, everything changes, and not in a good way. The focus shifts. The focus down there needs to be on what's happening so everyone goes home alive."

I put my hands over my face and groan. "Okay. Okay. I know."

He puts his hand on my shoulder. "We can't allow our hearts to get in the way of our heads. This is the time our trust has to lie with our team. We can't do everything on our own. That's why we have them."

I nod and let my hands fall. "I know. It's fucking hard."

"It's time," the Chief says. "Let's hit them with the water and get Cole out of here. Use the water as a barricade."

"I'm not leaving Mariah, Taylor, Matt, Nick, or DJ out there," Alec says.

"We're not going to," Ryan says. "All of us combined have enough power to take over for the cops. All of them. The National Guard is close. We get the cops on the ground out of there when we drop the tear gas." He puts the radio to his lips. "Freedom One to fire. Open the hoses."

We watch as the water starts spraying from the hose. I can tell it's not full force, but it's effective. We're able to push back even further.

"Freedom One to all law enforcement. Our team is replacing all of you. When we drop the tear gas, get out. Back to Headquarters. It'll be a seamless transfer with lots of disorientation. You'll be getting help and direction. Probably pushes in the direction you need to go. Buddy up. When it drops, try to cover your mouth and nose so you can see enough to run. Acknowledge."

A chorus of voices acknowledge the plan, but it doesn't ease my fears. "Do they all have earpieces?"

"No," Alec says. "Some have radios."

"That was heard by some, Josh. But it's not going to matter at all. Trust me. Are your teams ready?" Ryan asks.

I take a deep breath. "Phoenix one to Lucinio Mafia. All teams in position."

"All teams in position," one of my guards say. Ryan and Alec follow. Once we have confirmation that everyone is where they need to be, we start putting on vests, making sure Cole is the one who has the most protection.

"Let's move." Dane says. "We need to be ready to get the fuck out of here the second they hit with the gas."

"Andrea, let's go. You don't need to be here." I hold my hand out for her. She takes it, and I guide her out of the office and to the staircase behind everyone. Ryan is in front. Dane is behind him with Cole. Alec is in front of me.

"We can't go out there with Cole with just the three of you," Andrea says.

"We won't be. I have guards guarding the doors. They'll be replaced just as everyone else is and get us out of here."

"When we leave the building," Ryan begins, "Cole, head down. Andrea, you'll be in the center with Cole. We're running, so keep up. If you can't, you're going to be dragged with us. I can't begin to tell you how I wish you weren't wearing heels."

"I'll break the heel," she says. "As long as we can get out and he's safe."

We make our way down the rest of the stairs in silence. The second we reach the bottom floor, Ryan is through it with his gun drawn. Dane is right behind him. I stay back with Alec because if, for any reason, the bottom floor has been compromised, we need to be prepared.

"We're clear! Move!" Dane yells. I'm annoyed as fuck that we didn't have enough earpieces for ourselves. After we got here, we handed them out to everyone on the ground. It was fine while we were able to use radios, but now that we're leaving, I don't like having to key a mic, even if it is clipped to me.

Alec goes first. Cole follows. Andrea follows him. Once we get to the door, I've never been so fucking happy to see cement.

"Ma'am, please put this on," a guard tells Andrea, handing her a hat. "Tuck your hair in. We don't need them thinking we paid off the DA to get Cole out."

I'm grateful we have such a good team to have our backs. Andrea takes the hat and tucks her hair into it. He hands her a black handkerchief that she ties around her face. Once that's done, I make sure she's secured in her vest.

"How attached are you to these pants?" I ask.

She looks at me flabbergasted. "Wh-what?"

I kneel next to her and look up as I take out my knife. "You came in wearing these and high heels. You can't go out wearing it. You'll get recognized by the news crew."

"Um...uh... I... not... not attached."

"Good." I cut from the middle of her calf and down. I remove the cut pant leg and do the same to the other side. "Use me to steady yourself. Give me your foot." She does as I tell her. I take the shoe and snap the heel. I put it back on her foot and do the same to the other. I leave the pant legs and heels on the floor. "What about the shirt? Can I cut the sleeves?" She nods and I make quick work of them, dropping them in the same pile I've already left.

"Time to move," Ryan says. "No more time. They're pushing back. Everyone out there is fucking tired."

"Let's go," I say.

"Viper One to officers. Take out your pepper spray. Relief teams. Deploy the gas. Get the officers out. Our cops out there, find a guard and move your ass." He looks up at the sky, trying to spy the choppers hovering.

"We have two blocks to run," I say to Cole.

"I can handle it," he responds.

"Don't grab Andrea's hand. I know you're going to want to help her. It's instinct. But everyone is watching. They'll want to know who the fuck she is, and if they figure it out, this is going to get even worse. Especially if they think you're romantically involved."

"Got it."

As soon as we see the tear gas deployed and our guys moving in, we run out of the building. Several other guards are waiting to enter to relieve the ones leading us out. The crowd is in the street on both sides of the building, so our timing has to be perfect. If we're spotted, the entire plan could be fucked.

Once we're out, we're surrounded like Cole is the president. He may as well be. He keeps his head down and is wearing a hat just like Andrea. While we're sprinting down the sidewalk, we're joined by a few others. The tear gas is starting to sting my eyes, but judging by the gagging from those who have joined us, I'd say they've gotten the worst of it. Thankfully, they're being helped by some of the guards we're with as the switch happens around us.

"Fuck," I rumble, thankful that our family was led to us so we can get them out.

Mariah, the only one who had been missing when everyone initially joined us, is pushed into me by another of our guards with a gas mask before he takes off back to the line. She stumbles and gags as she furiously tries to keep up while rubbing her eyes. I grab her arm and pull her next to me.

"Fuck me, it's bad. It stings. I was right near one," she coughs.

"Run, Mariah."

Hearing her name, Alec glances back. Relief washes over his face, and he takes her hand. He pulls her to him, leading her. I cough, the gas stinging my throat, but I don't stop. We're almost to the SUVs.

Once we get there, Ryan pushes Cole into the backseat. "Josh! Take Andrea in the second SUV!"

I don't question him. I open the door and push her in the back. "Get on the floor."

She quickly does what I say. Matt climbs in the back with her. DJ jumps in the front as I run to the driver's side. Alec nearly throws Mariah into his vehicle as Tyler jumps in the front. Alec runs to the driver's seat as Nick gets in next to Mariah.

I glance to make sure everyone is in vehicles before following Ryan at a breakneck speed as he flies down the sidewalk, where there are no people. It's not until we're safely moving with traffic again that my heartbeat returns to normal.

The moment the cement wall in front of us parts and everyone sees us, we're all bombarded with hugs, kisses, and questions. We manage to get inside the room before Luke shuts the wall behind us. The guards, having gotten the mob to disperse by overpowering them completely, lifted the lockdown. Luke made the decision to keep everyone down here until we got here. I can't blame him.

"Where's Lyric?" Matt rasps, his throat hoarse from being in the middle of the tear gas attack.

Alex smiles tiredly. "I finally got her to go to the bathroom, at least. I'm sure she'll be running out when she hears the commotion."

DJ and Matt both shake his hand as they hug Layne and Beckett. As promised, Lyric flies out of the bathroom. When she sees them, tears burst from her eyes. She runs into the arms of her family, and they all embrace her, surrounding her with their love as they whisper reassurances.

Dani carefully hugs Nick. Breetana, Chase, and Nikki all group hug Taylor. Everyone is locked in the embrace of someone except the younger kids. I'd be curious where they are, but I'm sure they're all sleeping. The commotion will wake them up, and that makes me happy. I want to see my son just as much as my girl. I catch Mariah disappearing into a room wiping her eyes just as I catch Dallas's eye. Alec, not missing a damn thing, sees it, too, and takes off after her. I can't help but notice Luca is nowhere in sight.

I make my way to Dallas. When I reach her, I take her in my arms and feel her breakdown. She cries silently as she hugs me tightly. "I was so scared," she whispers.

"I know, baby. I know."

"When we saw you running out, the news instantly knew it was you and Cole with Ryan. They saw the other cops leave the crowd and retreat to the building. I don't know what's going to happen."

"Shh…," I soothe as I keep her locked tightly in my arms. "No one knows what's going to happen, little sparrow. All we can do is take a day at a time and deal with it all as it comes."

"What's going to happen to Cole?" she asks with a sniffle.

It takes me a moment to answer because I'm trying to decide what to say. "I don't know, baby. I don't know."

The kids pick that moment to run out of the room they were in. Tait runs directly to Taylor. Chris hobbles to Ryan. Jackson, Nathaniel, as he now wants to be called, walks to Ryan as well. I'm sure it's because he sensed him being gone and didn't like that his uncle wasn't here. He stopped wanting to be called Jackson when he met Jaxon. Because it might have started to get confusing to the kids, we've all started calling him Nate. Nathaniel is his middle name. He responds to it quicker than he ever did with his first name and seems to like it a lot more.

Jaxon stands at the edge of the room. I've noticed a few things about him over the time we've had him back. The first is that he's really smart. The second is that he's very curious. The third is a concern to Lyric, but I'm not sure how I feel about it. Jaxon doesn't show very much emotion. He observes. He internalizes. No one can blame him after what he's been through, but Lyric is concerned because she doesn't want him to feel like he can't express feelings. I don't think it's that he feels like he can't. I think it's that he doesn't know how. I didn't either for a very long time, but I'm confident he'll learn. He has a very strong support system.

Keeping Dallas close, I kneel and hold out my arms with a half smile. Jaxon walks to me. His lip quivers, but he doesn't cry. Once he reaches me, he holds out his arms and steps into me. I wrap my arms around him and lift him as I stand.

"You 'kay, daddy?" he whispers to me.

I put my arm around Dallas and pull her tight into us both so we can hug him. "I'm okay, buddy."

"Papas?"

I smile. He calls Matt and DJ papas and me daddy. He hasn't decided what to call Dallas yet. He just calls her Liss. "They're safe. They're here."

He keeps hugging me as my phone rings. I let go of Dallas and reach for my phone. "Safe."

"Safe, my boy." I furrow my brows and glance at Dallas when I see Xavier's name. "Hey, what's up?" I ask when I answer.

"Josh, you need to get to Dylan. Something bad is going down. She's fucking scared. She called me saying someone was after her. Something about a riot and someone chasing her."

"Whoa, whoa. Dude, hold up." I turn to Lyric and give her Jaxon, knowing he'll want to see Matt and DJ. I kiss his head before taking Dallas's hand and leading her to a different, more quiet, room. "Okay. What's going on?" I put my phone on speaker.

"Fuck, I know you guys had some kind of a riot. Something about a cop killing someone. I saw it on the news. Dylan is up there. She left a couple days ago, and she's scared. She's at the university. Kingston."

"The riot is under control, man. She has no -"

"She's not scared about the riot. She said that she just got to campus. There was a riot going on. She was staying in a hotel downtown until they could get her into her dorm. Which was today. She's moving all her stuff in today. She said she felt like she was being followed around. She's hiding in the office right now. The admissions one. I told her to stay there."

Dallas looks at me, alarmed. "Someone is following her? From the riot?"

Suddenly, things start making sense. "Oh fuck. Fuck! Tell her to stay there. Give her my number. Tell her to call me!" I hang up my phone as I sprint out of the room. "Alec!" I bark, searching for him. "Alec!"

"Josh, what's going on?" Dallas asks me, panicking.

"Ethan. He's after Dylan. Alec!"

"What? What?" Alec sprints around the corner.

"With me! Right now! I'll explain on the way!" I run to our living room. "Nick! Get everyone back home after making certain it's safe! Let me out right now! Alec and Tyler! With me!" I look for Gavin. "Gavin! On me now! Lance! Damon! Let's move!"

"The fuck is going on?" Ryan barks. He waves Luke over. Both are ready to follow me.

"Ethan is after Dylan! We need to get to Kingston University!"

Nick lets us out. I know he'll control everything else involved with getting our families home safe while we head out on our second rescue mission in only twenty-four hours.

Only this time, I might get the fucking prick making my life and the lives of my family fucking miserable...

The End

Concluding The Lucinio Family Series

The devilishly dark and alluring Lucinio Family Series concludes with ***Defending Her Honor***.

My position as a Sergeant with Chicago Police Department's Major Crimes Unit comes with a lot of perks and is a dream come true. One of the many things I love the most is that I don't have to patrol. I haven't done a traffic stop in over five years.

Ironic when I'm busted for gunning down an innocent man on a stop I was never a part of wearing a uniform I haven't worn in years.

The city of Chicago, my girlfriend included, doesn't seem to care about that, though. They want my head on a shiny platter made of gold and diamonds.

As if my life imploding isn't enough, the Lucinio Mafia, the only family I have, is facing its own problems. A rival who thinks he stands a chance against us.

The cherry on my messed up sundae comes in the form of a beautiful, very young, brunette with sultry eyes and curves that make me weak. Dylan Remington. Our rivals are after her, and I'm tasked with being her protection.

She hates me, but that's fine. She's a brat who loves getting on my last nerve and sending me straight to the bottle. There's nothing in my orders that says I have to be nice to her, and I have no intention of catering to her ego anyway.

But damn… Why does she have to be my ultimate temptation?

I don't have time to play games with her. Not only is her life on the line, but so is mine. I can't afford to let the pretty distraction come between me saving us all.

~ Defending Her Honor is a steamy, dark mafia, forced proximity, enemies to lovers, age gap, cop romance with dark themes and violent content that may not be suitable for all readers. ~

Order your copy of *Defending Her Honor* today!

The Lucinio Family Series

Available Now

Rising From The Ashes
The Player's Rebel
Encrypting My Heart
Fighting My Fate

Other Books By Melony Ann
The Beautiful Dream Series

Available Now

Loving You
My Love, My Heart
Softening Lyric
Undercover Temptations
Captain Charming
Breaking Boundaries
Crashing Into You
Tactical Inferno
Ravishing Our Queen
Cherished By The Texan
Unveiling Our Passions

Box Sets Available

The Beautiful Dream Series: Box Set: Part 1
The Beautiful Dream Series: Box Set: Part 2

The Crane Family Series

Available Now

The Reluctant Mafia King
Sweet Lies
Billion Dollar Love Story
Be Mine
Protecting Her
Dangerously Forbidden Love
His Heart
Love In The Dark

Box Sets Available

The Crane Family Series

The Deimos Trilogy

Available Now

Connor's Legacy
Aryan's Alpha
Kade's Redemption

Box Sets Available

The Deimos Trilogy

The Forbidden Temptation Series

Available Now

The Detective's Forbidden Temptation
The Running Back's Forbidden Temptation

Multi Author Series
Piper Falls: Firehouse 49

Available Now

Ignite My Fire by Melony Ann
Regain My Fire by Kindra White
Playing With My Fire by D.L. Howe
Fight My Fire by Darley Collins
Against My Fire by Anneke Boshoff
Relight My Fire by Louise Murchie
Harness My Fire by Ayana Lisbet
Quench My Fire by Havana Wilder

Let's Be Friends

Follow me on

Bookbub

Facebook

Goodreads

Instagram

Tik Tok

Visit my website
www.melonyannauthor.com

Subscribe to my newsletter and get a FREE never-seen-before NOVELLA
just for subscribers!
https://www.melonyannauthor.com/exclusive-content

Join my Facebook Reader Group!
Melony Ann's Sizzling Book Nook

The official Lucinio Family Series Playlist on YouTube
https://youtube.com/playlist?list=PLGEiD5wbQmDdjFYhMKrFsomQOTr
RK7x9Y

Dedication

To all the ones who we beg not to go, who we beg on our knees to stay, who make us look crazy, but it's okay because we're crazy in love with them.

Acknowledgements

Brad - It's the way that you understand what I don't.

Laura - It's the way you make me crazy in love with you.

Jay - It's the beat that my heart skips whenever you're near.

Anneke - It's the way you make me believe.

Jason - It's the way you do what no one else can.

Kayla - It's the way you push me.

To the Bookstagram Community.

To my family.

To all of those who believe in me and support me.

To all of those who don't.

Cover by: Carter Cover Designs

Edited by: Alyssa Skaggs

About Melony Ann

Melony Ann began writing short stories and poetry as a child. She continued honing her craft over the years until she took the plunge and began publishing her work, despite having severe anxiety.

Melony writes contemporary romance stories that are full of suspense and a lot of steam.

When she isn't writing, she is loving her family and working to make her life something she deserves.

Melony believes that if her writing can inspire just one person, then all of her hard work is worth it.

Her hope is that her writing allows each and every one of her readers to escape for a little while. To dive into a different world one book at a time.

www.ingramcontent.com/pod-product-compliance
Lightning Source LLC
Chambersburg PA
CBHW070445260626
47161CB00004B/1213